watch
you don't
fall
a novel

watch you don't fall

a novel

Bettina von Kampen

GREAT PLAINS
PUBLICATIONS

Great Plains Publications
420 – 70 Arthur Street
Winnipeg, MB R3B 1G7
www.greatplains.mb.ca

Great Plains Publications gratefully acknowledges the financial sup-
port provided for its publishing program by the Government of
Canada through the Book Publishing Industry Development Program
(BPIDP); the Canada Council for the Arts; as well as the Manitoba
Department of Culture, Heritage and Tourism; and the Manitoba Arts
Council.

Design & Typography by Relish Design Studio Inc.

Printed in Canada by Friesens

CANADIAN CATALOGUING IN PUBLICATION DATA

Main entry under title:

Von Kampen, Bettina, 1964-
  Watch you don't fall / Bettina von Kampen.

  ISBN 1-894283-51-1

  1. Title.

PS8593.O556W43 2004   C813'.6   C2004-904014-6

For my dear friend Andrea,
for the good company and sound advice

For their faith in my literary endeavours, my heartfelt thanks to: All the Great Plains staff — Gregg Shilliday, Cheryl Miki, Jewls Dengl, Ingeborg Boyens; Penny Fowler, Anne McDermid, Gwen Morrow, Kevin Patterson and Shauna Klem; Ellen Reid, Andrea Smits; Helen and Garrett Smits, Caley Strachan, Ricki, Ed, Lindsey, Matt and Lexi Valcourt; Erika von Kampen.

Chapter One

Inside the Wiltshire Hotel, Carmen struggled to untangle a ball of lights. They were spilled out onto the bar. She regretted not putting them away more neatly last year. Every year after Christmas she balled them up and stuffed them back into the same crinkled bag and then every year she hauled them out again and spent an afternoon trying to straighten them. From his table near the kitchen, Walter watched. The television was on, but muted, and the radio tuned to Classic Rock Q108, the only station that didn't accost them with lame Christmas carols all day long.

The hotel had deteriorated in the last three years since the rumours of its being sold started. Every year was potentially the last and Carmen didn't want to waste her time making a neat package out of the decorations if they weren't going to make it to Christmas again. But so far, the end hadn't come and for three years now there had been a snarled ball of lights to deal with at this time of year. There were fewer and fewer customers and more and more repairs ignored and undone. Half the windows were broken and boarded up. The last they heard from Mr. Bradley, the hotel's owner, was that the place would be sold in the spring. They had heard it all before and had vowed to stop worrying until there was a wrecking ball dangling from a crane out back. At this point Mr. Bradley was just a voice –

five martinis talking from a pool deck somewhere in the Bahamas.

"Well Walter," Carmen said. "How many Christmases have we had here?"

There was a long silence from where Walter sat. "Did you order my hamper?"

"Yes, I ordered your hamper. It'll be delivered before Christmas sometime. That's why it's called a Christmas hamper."

"When?"

"What's the rush? I won't let you starve. It'll be here in the next few days." She took the ball of lights and gave a vigorous shake. "Ah, shit, I can't be bothered with these lights. We'll look at the ones across the street."

Carmen balled up the clump of lights and stuffed them back into the green garbage bag. Her cigarette had gone out. She mashed it into the ashtray and lit a new one. It was gloomy outside. Clouds behind the fabric outlet store across the street threatened snow. A brisk wind blew down from the north and the few people who scuttled past had their hand at their throats, holding tight their jackets to prevent the arctic air from fighting its way in. Most Winnipeggers didn't bother with scarves – that would be like admitting winter had arrived.

The room, except for Walter, was empty. There were twelve tables and five stools at the bar, but Carmen never had to work a full room. Perry came in to refill his coffee cup. He sat down at the bar, facing Carmen. "What's in the bag?"

"Christmas lights. I'm not bothering this year. Half of them don't work."

"Fine with me." Perry said, half-listening to her and half-listening for his phone. He helped himself to a drag of Carmen's cigarette. "You mind if we don't decorate this year, Walter?"

Walter never answered Perry or looked him in the eye. Every hotel manager he had encountered in his life had ripped him off somehow and he had no reason to believe Perry was any different. In his hunter's cap, flaps up and a couple of layers of sweater, Walter sat and watched out the window. His eyes widened. "Cops," he chirped when he saw a cruiser pass.

Perry jumped and his head swivelled around. The car was out of sight.

"Why do you always do that? You like to see me jump outta my skin?" Perry picked up his coffee and Carmen's cigarette and rose to go back to his office. "Crazy old fart."

"He loves messing with you. Gets you every time, doesn't he?" Carmen felt the top of her head with her hand. She wore her hair short and spiked up with an intense hair gel. She could put an eye out with her hair. "Got any plans for the weekend?"

"I always have plans for the weekend, Carmen. I just never know who they're with until it happens." Perry blew smoke rings into the air. "I'll let you know on Monday."

"What happened to Rachel?" Carmen lit a new cigarette.

"Rachel? Was that her name?" Perry rubbed his chin. "I'll go back to Montana's again tonight and see if I can find her and double check. I hope I can remember. I wouldn't want to sleep with the same woman two weekends in a row. She might want to get serious."

"Yeah, you mentioned that before. Why do you think I'm always after you to marry me?" Carmen winced at the thought. "You're a woman's worst nightmare."

Perry didn't go for waitresses. Those women he respected. He didn't even flirt with them. It was the women who hung out at bars all weekend, hungry for a decent lay. And there were lots of them, in their tight, low-cut tops and pointy-toed shoes. Lots of pink lipstick and stuff in their hair, their eyes roaming the room for men to claim and cozy up with. Those were the ones he went for. There was something in their desperation that fired him up. And they fell for him every time. All he had to do was wander over with a drink in his hand and ask where the washroom was. Then, ask her to watch his drink while he went and found the washroom. When he came back, they had always finished theirs and all he had to do was buy them one to thank them and that was it. It worked every time. Rare was the Friday night he spent alone. It helped that women found him attractive. He had the kind of dark brooding features and stylishly long hair that made most women waver. Pure ego drove him to use these attributes for his own pleasure, guilt- and conscience-free.

There was smoke all around them now and Walter pretended to choke in the corner, flapping his hands in front of his face to clear the air. Donald came in, bringing a gust of wind with him. He was bundled so tight that only his eyes were showing.

"Close the door, you moron," Walter yelled. "We're cold enough as it is in here."

At this Donald merely sniffed and took his time turning around to shut the door. "A person can't very well get inside without opening the door, Walter. Unless that person happens to be a relatively astute magician. Besides, you can hardly be that cold in here with seventy layers of sweater on your person."

"Yes, hello Donald," Perry drawled in a bad English accent. "Jolly good to see you again and how many sweaters are you wearing today?"

Donald made a derisive noise at the back of his throat and made his way to his table along the wall.

"I'll be in my office," Perry said and sidled out with his coffee cup. He tugged at the front of his t-shirt and got a whiff of his own B.O.. "God, I reek."

Donald's table was closer to the window, but close enough to Walter's to put Walter on edge. Donald unwound his piano key scarf and revealed a tattered burgundy toque. This too, he removed and with the palm of his hand he swept his hair way over the top of his head towards his right ear. Underneath his black galoshes he wore a pair of grey leather slippers, shiny and worn through the bottom of the left one. As he did every day, Donald wore a suit and tie. It had something to do with his eastern European roots. From a distance he managed to look distinguished, in a brown corduroy jacket and tan pants, a cream shirt and gold flecked tie. But, up close, the clothes smelled like hot dogs from a convenience store and the collars and cuffs were frayed with age and grime.

He carried with him a briefcase in which he transported his work. Donald was an artist or so he thought of himself. In his mind there was little distinction between being an artist and believing you were one. As long as he sat at his table each day and glued bits of magazine pictures onto a piece of paper, he felt productive. There was no cohesiveness to his creations, nor any common theme. Just whatever caught his fancy, he snipped out with his scissors and arranged on an eight by ten sheet of white paper and glued it all down pat. There was a thick file folder full of these things, brimming with images of diapered babies' bottoms, car bumpers, women's hairdos, lawn mowers, porcelain figurines and kittens. A hodgepodge of the worst in magazine advertising all committed to paper and saved in the name of high art.

"What are you making us today, Picasso?" Walter asked.

"I will take that as a compliment, even though I know you don't intend it as such. And, as usual, you will have to wait until I am finished before you get to see what I am working on."

"You're making garbage out of garbage. Everyone knows that."

"Well all you do is shit your pants," Donald said without even looking up.

Walter giggled. Mission accomplished. Donald was getting red in the face. Walter sniffed the air. "Hey, I do smell shit. Where's that coming from?"

The point was not to get an answer and before Donald could say anything Walter took out his harmonica and blew a few discordant notes meant to sound like a pen of bleating hogs being led to slaughter. Following this brief exchange, both of them fell silent.

The back door flew open and Tibor and Harv clomped through in their big basketball shoes with the laces untied, their parkas open and flapping. They stopped at the bar and helped themselves to coffee and proceeded to the office door.

"Hey guys. Help yourselves. You can leave my tip on your way out." Carmen said from across the room where she fiddled with the television.

"Yeah, sure."

"The coffee's not free you know. I'm running a tab on you guys. It's getting up there. And don't expect me to make you burgers again unless you're going to pay for them."

The door swung shut behind them as they made their way to Perry's office. "Idiots," Carmen muttered.

* * * * *

Perry sat at his desk and crumbled a generous amount of pot onto a Zig Zag paper. He took his time rolling it up, careful to tuck in the edges and to smooth out the wrinkles. There was nothing finer in the world than a well rolled joint. For a moment, he held the cigarette in his hand and admired his work. Down the hallway he heard the clomp, clomp of Tibor and Harv. Perry threw the joint into the top drawer and shut it fast. He didn't feel like sharing with them right now. He was trying to cut down anyway, but it was hard when the safe was always full of the stuff.

The door opened and Tibor and Harv traipsed in and fell into their chairs and plunked their coffee cups onto the desk.

"Morning, gents," Perry said.

"Morning." The two of them simultaneously reached deep into their jacket pockets and pulled out wads of cash and tossed it onto the desk.

"How much do you want?"

"It's the holidays. Give me two ounces, I guess." Tibor said. "My lawyer friend is giving all his friends joints for Christmas."

"I'll take two, too." Harv pulled off his toque and scratched his head.

"Two, too," Tibor aped.

"Shut up." Harv gave him a jab in the shoulder.

Perry got up and went over to the wall safe. It was behind a framed movie poster from *The Godfather*. Each time he made the trip to the safe to dispense of his goods, *The Godfather* approved. The safe itself was broken and swung open at the flick of a finger. Perry set the poster on the floor and pretended to twirl the dial. He reached inside and pulled out two Ziplock baggies and brought them over to his desk. From the top drawer, he pulled a scale and started tossing buds onto it. Once two ounces were measured out, he dumped the buds into a new baggie and shoved it across the table.

"You want to smoke some?" Tibor asked.

"Always," Perry replied. He handed Tibor the pack of papers. "Here, use this."

"You want to smoke mine?"

"Yeah, I threw in an extra bud anyway. For Christmas."

"Gee, a Christmas bonus," Harv said. "Swell."

The three of them sat in a cloud of sweet smoke and listened to an old Pink Floyd song on the radio. Nobody spoke, nobody in a hurry to get anywhere. The heaters hissed and clanged. Perry counted the money they had deposited on the desk. In under two minutes he had made nearly nine hundred dollars. He rose from the desk and put the money in the safe and made a show of locking it again. He replaced the poster. The Godfather. Now, there was a business man, Perry thought. Respected, feared and surrounded only by loyal people. And filthy rich. He looked over at Tibor and Harv, sporting greasy pony tails and paint spattered parkas and was reminded of how far he had yet to go. He scratched his head, itchy and in need of a good scrub.

Carmen opened the door and leaned in. "Hey, I'm going a bit early today. I've got some shopping to finish up."

The pot didn't bother her. It made Perry easier to deal with. Without it he became edgy and short. With it, there was only a small degree of paranoia and the munchies to deal with, but generally a mellower human being. Today, Carmen hoped to get out before they decided they wanted chili dogs. All three looked at her, Harv grinning for no reason and Tibor staring at her chest. Perry waved a cigarette at her and said she could go. She slipped out before they changed their minds.

Back in the bar, Donald was asleep in his chair and Walter hummed tunelessly in his. "Walter, I'm heading out. I'll take your clothes with me to wash over Christmas, okay?"

"Did you find out about my hamper?" His eyes darted over to where she stood.

"It'll probably come tomorrow."

Carmen went back into the kitchen to change for the outdoors. The buses ran erratically and she never knew how long she would have to wait. The afternoon light was waning and the street lights were on at three-thirty. This time of year they were joined by Christmas lights so if they were all on by three-thirty, nobody minded too much.

* * * * *

Perry spent the afternoon in a bar with Harv and Tibor where they drank beer and watched women on television perform strangely erotic fitness routines in skimpy spandex outfits for some kind of national fitness award. This kind of programming normally held Perry's interest, but today it left him feeling hollow. His attention was focused on Tibor and Harv who behaved as their usual lewd and obnoxious selves. Harv drummed his index fingers on the table. Sometimes he carried his drumsticks in his back pocket and drummed those on whatever table he was at.

Both Tibor and Harv wore Led Zepplin t-shirts and sweat pants. Perry had no idea when they washed their clothes or if they did. His own clothes weren't in great shape either but he was convinced that Harv and Tibor smelled worse than he did. He wondered if they owned anything other than those big stupid shoes or ever wore a shirt with buttons and a collar. These were the guys he hung out with most and he didn't want whatever affliction had gotten hold of them to get a hold of him too.

The two of them had a rock band that they played in all summer. They played Steppenwolf covers and a few Black Sabbath tunes. Tibor played lead guitar and Harv played drums and they had a couple of other guys to fill in the rest. Last summer they invited Perry out to a party in some hay field where they set up a stage and different people drifted on and off all afternoon playing god-awful Jimi Hendrix riffs and smoking way too much reefer, so the guitar solos went on and on. They were just like the guys in *Spinal Tap* except for real. Perry didn't ask them about it much because he didn't want to spend another afternoon out in some remote farmer's field, with no way to get home.

Hanging out with the two of them bummed him out. There was something in their company that made Perry feel as though he was being dragged down to a place he didn't belong. Sitting there watching his two best friends, dressed in those loser clothes and flirting stupidly with an exceptionally patient waitress created in Perry such an agitated state he felt an uncontrollable urge to reach over and grab each of them by the side of the head and wham! Crack their skulls together.

Perry decided that the two of them were somehow responsible for holding him back. From what, he couldn't say. He had known them both a long time and he trusted them, but he didn't lump himself. A cut above was what he considered himself. A player, a mover, a wise guy even. Like the Godfather, he lived and worked on the other side of the law, he had his people, he even had a half-decent car, a sleek black Monte Carlo. Every weekend he brought home a different woman, every one of them willing and eager to please. And yet he was sitting in a sports bar, watching bimbos compete for some meaningless prize. The beer came in big, scratched plastic pitchers, there were bowls of bright yellow popcorn. Much of the popcorn was on the floor. The waitress serving them did so with disdain rather than respect. It was all wrong.

Something hit his cheek. Then something stuck to his hair. He reached up and brushed a piece of popcorn onto the table. Harv and Tibor were snickering. When he looked over they pelted his face with a few more pieces. The popcorn landed on the table. The snickering stuttered and stopped. Harv flicked another piece at Perry which he smashed onto the table with his fist.

"What's wrong with you, pouty Sue?" Harv laughed.

"Yeah, lighten up. It's Christmas, man."

They both teetered in their chairs waiting for Perry to crack a smile. Instead, he scraped his chair along the floor and stood. "Get a life."

He grabbed his jacket and turned to go.

"What? You're telling us to get a life? We could tell you the same thing, since we pretty much all have the same lives here." Tibor said, reaching behind his head and smoothing his ponytail between his fingers. Perry turned and walked towards the door.

"Well, Merry Christmas to you too," Harv said with a sneer. He flicked a last piece of popcorn at Perry's retreating back.

* * * * *

Perry sunk into the car seat and fished around in the ashtray for a roach. That was the last thing he wanted to hear from those guys. That they were all alike. It had never occurred to him that they viewed him as one of them. That they all were on equal footing. Good God! How could they think that? Clearly, he was the boss. How could they possibly think otherwise? Thank God the hotel was closed over the holidays. Carmen was making some arrangement for Walter to fend for himself and the rest of them could go someplace else or stay home. He needed the break to regroup and think. The bar could wait a night. On the way home he picked up a movie; Goodfellas, one of his favourites. The answer was out there. A jangling restlessness settled behind his knees as he drove, pushing him onward, demanding action.

* * * * *

On Christmas Eve, Carmen phoned about Walter's hamper. She was leaving at three and nothing had been delivered and Walter was in a state of great agitation. He glared over at Donald and waited for him to break. Walter was sure Donald had taken it. This morning Donald had pulled a fresh row of Arrowroot cookies from his briefcase and made a fuss over getting them open so that everyone noticed by the persistent rustling of the package. Never did he have food in that bag. Not once in all the days Walter and Donald sat eyeing each other, did Walter ever see Donald pull anything other than weak art from that bag. And Arrowroot biscuits were a staple in the hampers every year.

Walter didn't say anything. No words were needed. Walter saw what Donald wanted him to see and now it was a matter of whether Walter's suspicions were correct or if the whole act was one of Donald's psych-outs.

"Walter, they said it went out with yesterday's hampers. They're very busy getting all the hampers delivered on time and they don't know what happened to yours since it was marked delivered on the sheet." Carmen replaced the receiver. She had used the phone behind the bar so that Walter would hear every word and not count her in with Donald and think they had somehow stolen his hamper. She had no idea what happened to it. Donald, on the other hand, did.

It came after Carmen had left. Donald saw the white van pull up outside and pulled his toque on. He greeted the delivery man on the sidewalk. "Walter Beach?"

"Yup, that's me." He rubbed his hands together and his legs tingled with a rush of adrenaline. The delivery man handed the box over and placed a check mark beside Walter's name on his clipboard.

"Merry Christmas, Mr. Beach."

Donald was quick to reply. "And Merry Christmas to you too."

Donald stashed the box inside the front door and stole back inside for his boots and coat. Walter hadn't noticed a thing. The van had pulled up out of view. He had no idea and Donald, suppressing the giggles that rose like bubbles to the back of his throat, snuck off down Main Street with a box of Christmas cheer.

Now, Donald stood and walked over to Walter's table, extending the package of cookies. "I'm tired of you staring at me. Here, have the cookies, if you want them so much."

"Where'd you get them?" Walter barked.

"I got them at the cookie store. Where do you think I got them?"

"I think you got them out of my Christmas hamper."

"Well, that might be a possibility, Sherlock, but you didn't get a hamper this year for me to steal cookies out of it. Besides, I would have taken the tinned ham if I had the choice."

Donald left the cookies on Walter's table and returned to his own. For the rest of the afternoon Walter threw cookies over at Donald. Crumbs littered the floor since the distance was a bit far for Walter's withered arms. Donald pretended not to notice since none of them reached his table and he only glanced over at Walter when Carmen came in with a broom and took the cookies away from Walter and threw them in the garbage.

"Maybe it's just as well they forgot your hamper, if this is the way you treat a gift."

Donald grinned from ear to ear. Victorious, he left the room and wished them all a heartfelt Merry Christmas.

* * * * *

Perry spent Christmas morning playing game after game of solitaire on his computer. It was nearing noon and he sat in his underwear from the night before and stroked the stubble on his chin. Half a cup of black coffee sat on the desk beside him. There was no cream in the fridge and so now Perry was deciding where he could get breakfast on Christmas morning without people staring at him.

Watch you don't fall

He had been up since six-fifteen when the first yelps
and shrieks were heard from the kids downstairs. There
had been about an hour of noise and chaos as they ripped
into their Christmas presents and all was now quiet. Perry
had watched from behind the curtain as they packed up
their car and drove off, hopefully somewhere far away for
the rest of the day. Dave and Darlene, each of them with
equally long hair and flowing Mexican style ponchos and
their three kids decked out in polar fleece.

Perry checked the fridge again. Half a loaf of old bread,
three slices of anchovy and olive pizza, three cans of
Heinecken, an unopened jar of Dijon mustard bought some
time ago when he'd had a craving for those skinny German
sausages. The pizza had a slimy feel to it when Perry
peeled back the plastic wrap. He shoved it back into the
fridge and went to get changed. The casinos were open and
there he could have a meal and a beer and join all the other
non-believers for a day of gambling.

He drove down St. Mary's Avenue. All the billboards
were up for vacations in Cuba or Jamaica. People hiding
out from the sun under huge umbrellas or wide brimmed
hats, as if it was the sun they were escaping and not the
paralyzing cold. The casino was decorated with palm trees
and yellow and green stuffed cockatoos. The bars were set
up like bamboo thatched cabanas and if you ordered a
cocktail it came with an umbrella in it. The idea seized
Perry as he sat at one of these bars and drank a Heineken.
He didn't bother with the slots at first but mulled over his
idea and worked on some of the details. In a place like
Winnipeg, where half the year the climate was no different
from the North Pole, an idea like this would surely catch
on. It was so brilliant he didn't know why nobody had tried
it before. He already knew where he would do it. There was
an old car dealership right at the intersection of three
major thoroughfares in the centre of town. None of the
businesses there ever lasted. It was a high end arcade for

awhile, a paint ball arena, a roller skating rink, a drop in centre for teens. Nothing ever lasted there. But the problem with most ideas was that they targeted a small portion of the population. How many people out of a hundred are going to want to play paint ball? Maybe twenty. And how many of those on a regular basis? Maybe five. The math just didn't make sense.

Perry snickered to himself. He knew he was onto something when he focused in on every person who came within three feet of him and imagined that person at his establishment. And they all fit. Everybody would want to come. He would have what everybody in the winter craved and in his mind he was already adding up the admission fee and the total capacity and his annual salary. He would be a millionaire in under a year. Giddy with the satisfaction of coming up with a sure fire way to make some money, he slid onto a stool in front of a slot machine and began throwing tokens in. The woman next to him kept a wary eye on his progress. When the light on top of Perry's machine started flashing and the horn wailed, she got up and left. Once a machine paid out big it took awhile to make it pay again. Perry walked out of the casino with seven hundred dollars in his pocket.

He picked up a bucket of chicken and a side of gravy on his way home. He watched an old Columbo movie on television and tapped a pen on a pad of paper beside him, ready if any other brainstorms came his way. He felt very much like a man at the top of his game. A James Bond movie came on and he felt doubly blessed. Half way through the movie, his pen tapping stopped and he stared at the screen. Another revelation hit him square in the head. Suits. All those men he considered successful and respected and feared. James Bond, all those gangster types, Columbo even. They all dressed in suits. You never saw any of them in anything other than a finely tailored suit. And they got what they wanted all the time. That was it. He had his business, he had his new proposition for the first person he encountered that might be able to help him out and now he had to dig through his closet to see if he had a suit. It he did, then he would quickly consider this the best Christmas ever.

The chicken bones and leftover gravy congealed in their containers beside him. He stretched his arms up over his head. He had an urge to pick up the phone and call someone to tell them what his next scheme was, but thought better of it. Not until he had some of the details worked out and some money to invest would anyone hear of this. In the mean time he determined to step up his image and get Tibor and Harv hustling a little more to get the cash together.

Chapter Two

Theresa was glad the holidays were almost over. Tonight was New Year's Eve and she and Paulie were going to a nice German restaurant for dinner. The holidays had started badly with Paulie losing his job on Christmas Eve. His employers made him work overtime and then they handed him a pink slip. When he showed it to her, it really was pink. She hadn't expected that. It was just temporary, he assured her. Something that the company did when business was slow. They would all be hired back in the summer. It hadn't happened before and Paulie being out of work made Theresa uneasy and more tense than she usually was over the holidays.

On Christmas Day, Anton had gotten drunk and dressed up like Santa Claus and scared Dustin half to death. The poor kid screamed so much he threw up Fruit Loops all over Theresa's Christmas sweater. This put Theresa in a foul mood for the day, since Dustin had already had the wits scared out of him at the mall when Theresa took him there to get his picture taken with a real Santa and now Theresa was afraid Dustin would be forever scarred or delayed in some way.

Rosa and Antonina had prepared an elaborate Christmas meal. They had put Theresa to work setting the table and ironing napkins.

"Gee," Theresa had said when they finally all sat down and the table was spread before them, "This is like everything you know how to cook and we're having it all at once."

The food was over-cooked and over-salted but everyone had eaten like guests at a Tsar's wedding and then sprawled throughout the living room and moaned and loosened their pants to make room for Turtles.

Now, for New Year's Eve, Theresa was looking forward to dressing up and getting Paulie to dress up for a change too. Her hair was rolled up in a pink towel. She sat on the bed cradled in a pillow with arm rests wearing her yellow sweat suit. A glass of 7Up stood on the night table beside her and a bowl of salt and vinegar potato chips nestled between her legs. The television was on top of the dresser. It was New Year's Eve on *The Young and The Restless* too. Theresa rarely missed an episode. She licked salt from her fingers and reached for her glass. She didn't want to spoil her supper, but then she didn't want to get ravenous either. Theresa hadn't yet lost the extra weight she had put on while pregnant. Paulie didn't seem to mind but then his whole family had a healthy respect for food.

They still had an hour or so before they had to go. Outside, it was dark and cold. The frost was half way up the window and cold air could clearly be felt six inches away from the wall. The walls were insulated with sawdust and balled up newspapers dating back to 1928. Not much of a barrier to the arctic air beyond them.

The law firm where Theresa worked had closed for the days between Christmas and New Year's and that made for a long stretch of time to be cooped up inside the house with everyone else. The news of Paulie's job loss had rattled her and she felt like all these days off were setting them even farther behind in their plan to move out into their own house.

Paulie's suit lay on the bed. All through the holidays he managed to avoid wearing it and had hung around the house in his t-shirts and jeans, joining Anton on the couch most days to watch hockey and drink beer. Normally, he would have worked through the holidays but now he found himself with a generous vacation that might last until late spring. Theresa worried he would grow to like sitting on the couch with his father, who had sat on that same couch for nearly two years now with an incurable back injury, collecting compensation. Anton had put on at least fifty pounds since then.

Theresa's mother had kicked her father out of the house for the exact same thing, sitting endlessly on the couch, drinking beer and watching hockey. Theresa did not want Paulie to end up in a corset on the couch for a year. He played hockey twice a week for the North End Benders, a stupid name for a bunch of guys who took their hockey way too seriously and were mostly lazy about anything else. Theresa sometimes took Dustin to watch just to get out of the house for awhile. When she and Paulie first got together the hockey playoffs were on and Paulie passed up a lot of games to take Theresa out. Now it seemed she owed him a lifetime of hockey to make up for all the games he missed.

Paulie came upstairs and saw the suit on the bed. "You laying out my clothes for me now?"

"I want you to wear your suit at least once in the holidays. It's New Year's and I hear that restaurant is pretty nice."

"I doubt if it still fits." He patted the paunch his belly had become and let his stomach hang out as much as it could.

"It better fit. It's the only one you've got." She reached over and poked his stomach. "You're doing that on purpose. Suck it in."

Watch you don't fall

Outside the wind howled and a tree branch tapped uncertainly at the windowpane. The whole business of being laid off seemed to put Paulie on edge. Theresa didn't want him to wait to be hired back. She wanted him to find a new job right after the holidays. She hated that he worked installing insulation and wore coveralls to work. She thought this was the chance he needed to find some other kind of work. If she had her way, he would be wearing a suit every day and then this question of whether of not his suit still fit would never come up. It was going to be hard trying to convince her to let him loaf around for the winter. He had to come up with some productive, or financially advantageous project. Something to invest his time in that would benefit her in the end. Or else she would be lining up interviews for him.

"I'll take a shower and then try it on," he said.

"Okay." Theresa licked the salt off her fingers one last time and stood to return the dishes to the kitchen.

Dustin sat in his high chair. He banged a plastic spoon against the plastic tray. On the counter across from him a plate of mashed potatoes, gravy and sausages cooled. Every so often Antonina puffed out her cheeks and blew on it. Dustin knew that was his supper and he watched the old woman in great anticipation.

Theresa appeared in the doorway, her hair still wrapped in a towel. "Oh good, he hasn't eaten. I'll feed him his supper, Avò."

Antonina waved her hand over Dustin's bowl. "It's too hot. A few more minutes."

"Well, you sit down. I'll take care of that." Theresa plunked her empty chip bowl on the counter and sat down beside Dustin. She tickled his stomach. "Mama's going to feed you supper."

Dustin ate with his usual gusto. He was developing a strong set of teeth and gave the spoon a good jawing each time it reached his mouth. When he was finished, Theresa struggled to get him out of the high chair and carried him on her hip to the living room.

The lights from the tree blinked on and off and cast a faint light across the room where Anton sat on the couch and stared at the television. The strings of his corset were loose and he sunk into the couch cushions. Rosa beamed when she saw Dustin. "Bring him here a minute," she said. Theresa held him out towards her. "His mouth is dirty."

Rosa spit on her thumb and wiped at the corners of Dustin's mouth. He began to fuss and push her hands away. Theresa pulled him back. "Don't do that. He hates that. Now he's all upset."

"Sure, but he's clean. And he's a good boy." Rosa reached out to pinch his cheek. She was a sturdy woman, with facial hair and teeth that overlapped. Her dark brown hair was rolled into a bun that did not budge all day long. She wore pink terry slippers on her feet and a smock over her dress. Both she and Antonina had thick muscular forearms and gnarled but mighty hands. "Tomorrow we take the tree down," Rosa said as she stroked Dustin's cheek.

There was nothing under the tree anymore except for needles and curled bits of ribbon. In the middle of the coffee table stood a nativity scene. The donkey lay on its side and Joseph had his back to Mary. Theresa sat Dustin on Anton's lap and flopped in the armchair beside the couch.

"Fine, maybe next year Paulie and I will have our own tree and you can come and visit."

"We'll see," said Rosa, both doubtful and hopeful. "We'll see."

"You looking forward to tonight?" Anton asked as he pulled Dustin's foot out of his crotch and settled the boy down on his lap.

"Yeah, it'll be nice. Paulie'll get to see his old buddies from work. I'll just be one of the working wives, I guess."

Theresa leaned forward and re-arranged the figurines. "I better get upstairs and change. Thanks for putting Dustin to bed for us."

"No problem. He and I are going to watch Dick Clark."

Rosa clucked and shook her head.

Upstairs Paulie, with wet hair dripping down his back, sucked in his gut and did up his pants. He was barely able to fasten them. It was the one pair of dress pants he had. The idea of spending the night in too-tight pants, when they had pre-paid for a six course dinner, did not please him much. He rifled through the hangers in the closet with the hope that there was a forgotten pair of pants in there. When he found none, he went across the hall to his parent's room and pulled a pair of Anton's grey cords from a hanger. They were roomy. He felt much better about the evening now that he had on comfortable pants.

"Jesus! Where did you get those pants? Where's your suit?"

Theresa stared from the hallway. Paulie hitched up his pants. "They're Dad's. My suit is way too small."

"What? How can that be? Put it on and let me see." She strode towards the bed and picked up the pants and held them up to Paulie's waist. "They do seem small. When's the last time you wore these?"

"I dunno. Last Christmas I guess." He stood by sheepishly with his hands in his pockets. "Come on, these are fine. None of the other guys will be in suits."

"How do you know that?" Theresa demanded. "All I want is for us to dress up once in the holidays and have a nice night out." They stood on either side of the bed. The suit lay between them. Paulie rocked back and forth on his feet, not sure if it was his turn to speak.

"Look," Paulie said, his voice softer. He wanted to tell her he was dressed up. More than most times. "I'll make sure I fit into it for my first job interview, okay? I may be wearing that suit a lot more in the new year."

That was all it took. "Do you mean it?"

"Of course I mean it," he said and pulled her towards him. Theresa gave Paulie a mighty hug that set his glasses askew.

* * * * *

At the restaurant, the mood was festive, with a Christmas tree lit up in the corner and carols coming from the speakers. Winter coats were crammed into the coatroom and boots stood in puddles where they had been exchanged for shoes. Waiters hustled with drinks and food. The hostess was dressed in a Dirndl dress and guided Theresa and Paulie to a table. They sat with the other laid off workers and their wives. The men drank and joked and toasted their lost jobs. They went back and forth to the buffet table and ate mountains of free company food. The woman next to Theresa told her all about the house she and her husband just bought and the fabric she was choosing for her furniture. They gave away some prizes and Theresa won a day at the spa. "After tonight I'll be needing this," she said to the woman beside her, though she didn't know what she meant by it. It was just something to say.

At the end of the night, Paulie had eaten and drunk so much he had to undo his father's pants. Theresa helped him to the car, praying that the pants wouldn't fall down in the parking lot. She drove them both home, then put her husband to bed where he moaned and groaned for a long time before he finally fell asleep.

Dustin was still sleeping soundly in his crib up against the wall. Theresa sat up in bed awhile and listened to both Paulie and Dustin snore. Across the hall Rosa and Anton were in bed for the night and, in a room downstairs,

Antonina slept. For three years Theresa had been going to bed surrounded by all these bodies. Crammed into the tiny rooms like too many dolls in a doll's house.

Theresa had almost four thousand dollars saved in the bank. It was her portion of their house fund. If Paulie had matched her like he said he would then they would be ready to buy their own house later this year. Theresa sighed. His money went in all directions except his savings account. And now he had no job. Some days it seemed as though she had been dropped into this life by complete chance. And on nights like these she wondered if she had to wait for complete chance to fish her out again.

Chapter Three

Perry stood in his boxers in front of the mirror. On the bed behind him lay his grey suit, still in the bag from the dry cleaner. The last time he wore it was two years ago for his cousin Gerald's wedding, who now was already divorced from his wife. Time warped that way. For what must have been an eternity to the two newlyweds as they struggled through the first and last years of their marriage, Perry had not even had another opportunity to wear his expensive new suit. Until now. Until it had dawned on him that he needed to make some adjustments to his image if he expected his life to change.

The kids in the rental downstairs were already outside in the yard. The swing squeaked with irritating regularity and the screen door slammed every thirty seconds. Maybe this morning, once he was in his suit, Perry would go down there and bang on the door and ask the parents to do something about the noise.

Dave and Darlene, Perry's downstairs neighbours, home-schooled their kids, which meant the kids played outside while the parents smoked pot and listened to The Beatles with the stereo cranked to top volume. At the moment, "Maxwell's Silver Hammer" and the smell of grass wafted up through the heat vents. Over and over, that stupid polka rhythm and those insipid lyrics: Bang bang Maxwell's silver hammer came down on his head.

Watch you don't fall

Bang bang Maxwell's silver hammer was sure he was dead, like some demented children's song. Perry tossed down his razor and marched to the living room. His stereo speakers stood three feet tall and he took each one and placed them side by side, face down over the air vents. He then stomped over to the stereo and twirled the volume knob to ten and pressed play. The opening riffs of "Highway to Hell" ripped through the floorboards. Perry could feel the vibrations up the front of his shins. He stood in his underwear, satisfied at the noise. "Freaking hippies," he muttered and returned to the bathroom to finish shaving.

He stroked his hand over the stubble, careful to shave around his moustache. Then, after not even a nanosecond of thought, he took the moustache off as well. Why not make the transformation complete. His naked face stared back at him. Looks good, he thought.

With his new plan, the morning routine took awhile longer, since he was doing more than splashing water onto his face and pulling on jeans and a sweatshirt. But, a well-groomed man is a successful man and Perry was excited and determined to make things change for himself. If the rumours about the hotel turned out to be true, at least he had a business proposition for the first person that would listen. And, if that person happened to appear on the scene today, then Perry would be ready.

Perry turned off the stereo and righted the speakers. A gentler, quieter version of "Octopuses' Garden" now could be heard from downstairs as Perry made his way to the car. Something caught his eye in the front window. The four year old was standing in the window stark naked, staring at Perry. He held his penis and pointed it at him.

"Jesus Christ," Perry muttered when the image fully focused. He looked away and got into his car. There was a layer of frost which had to be melted away by the car's heater and by the time the windshield cleared the child was gone.

Perry eased his black Monte Carlo onto the road. The giant elms which created a massive archway all the way to the corner in the summer, were bare, their skeletal arms reaching for the sun. There were thick ruts of ice on the street.

It was hard to get used to doing something as automatic as driving in a completely new set of clothes. The thin fabric of his suit pants did little to insulate him from the cold vinyl seats. An open can of Coke sat in the cup holder. The ashtray was open and full of cigarette butts. Perry closed the ashtray and tossed the can out the window as he passed a back lane.

On St. Mary's Avenue, Perry merged with the rest of the morning traffic. The city was emerging from its post holiday hangover that would develop into a severe depression by mid-January, manifest in a spike in petty crimes and angry horn-honking down Portage Avenue. That Indian summer everyone prayed for every year was a distant memory as people chipped away at ice that froze their garage door shut. But, for a man re-inventing himself, there was no time to pay attention to the weather.

* * * * *

When the temperature soars to thirty-eight degrees Celsius in August on the prairies, nobody wants to complain too much because the winters are so much worse. Nobody remembers a summer heat wave in the middle of January when their teeth chatter violently as they wait for the car to heat up.

Winnipeg was four weeks into a deep freeze, where the day-time high didn't rise above minus twenty-eight and the wind screamed day and night and froze anything in less than two minutes. You could walk across drifts of snow eight feet high, solid as icebergs and listen to the snow creak and groan underfoot with a metallic ring. Prairie people defined themselves by these fierce winters. There was nothing hearty about sweating out a heat wave. There was air conditioning and beer for that. But take half an hour to get layered into winter clothes and then strap on snowshoes in the middle of a two-day blizzard and hike to the 7-11 on the corner for baby food, now that was something. There is not that same hint of pride in everyone's voice when they complain about the heat as there is when they complain about the cold. Heat makes people crazy whereas the cold makes people tough.

At nine in the morning, the light finally spread over the horizon to reveal thick plumes of smoke and exhaust which spiralled high over the city. The faint light cast a peach glow over crystals of frost. Carmen felt her thighs prickle as the heat on the bus made her sweat. All the windows dripped with condensation which people kept swiping at with their mittens. Beside her sat the green garbage bag full of Walter's clothes, freshly laundered and folded. A faint smell of urine still seeped through, even though she had doubled up the bag and ran the clothes through the washer two times with Javex. That smell was there to stay.

She wore a down jacket that made her puff up like a moonwalker, a striped hand-made scarf, army issue arctic tested boots with two pairs of socks, long underwear, sweater, etc. No wonder she sat there bathed in perspiration. She pulled her toque off and her hair bristled with static. Most of the office girls on the bus with her had carefully styled hair to make them look older and wore earmuffs to preserve the look. Many of them were young. Carmen rode with these women everyday. Their office jobs provided them with the sort of stimulation their brand new marriages did not. And to watch their bland, unmoving faces as they rode the bus, Carmen thought you would have to be pretty under-stimulated at home to get a charge out of sitting in a cubicle and waiting to see what the next elevator ding would deliver.

To let some air flow through her wet armpits she undid the zipper to her jacket and held her arms away from her body. Carmen had given up on trying to smell good or stay perspiration free on the overheated bus every day. It was a losing battle that required more energy than she had.

She shifted her butt and tugged her thermal underwear away from her skin. To hell with dignity. Her ass would be soaked by the time she got to work. The plastic bag leaned up against her leg and generated its own amount of heat. It was worse than riding the bus in the summer. The bus hissed and groaned in and out of traffic along Main Street. The same people got on and off all week. Nobody spoke. Everybody rode the bus alone, captivated by their own physical sensations and last night's conversations.

Carmen pulled the cord for the bell at the Wiltshire Hotel and wrestled the garbage bag off the seat. The office girls parted and let her through. Darren, a city-bred Ojibwa, was sitting in the bus shelter.

"Hey, Darren," she called. "Give me a hand, eh." She handed him the bag and together they walked around to the back of the building. The heavy back door had a metal grid over the window and a reinforced steel sheet housing two deadbolt locks. Scuff marks all along the side marked the most recent attempts to kick the door in. Inside she flipped on the switch for the ceiling fan. Fly paper hung in the middle of the kitchen ceiling, still stuck with flies from the summer. Darren wore the same thing he wore all summer and all winter: cowboy boots, jeans, black t-shirt and a denim jacket.

"How do those clothes keep you cool all summer and warm all winter?"

"They don't," he said, without the slightest hint of humour.

"Right. I'm going to put the coffee on and come out and have a smoke with you."

Darren headed through the swinging door to the bar. Carmen peeled off her layers of clothing. Her Calvin and Hobbes t-shirt was clammy with heat. She ducked into the bathroom to take off her long underwear and put her jeans back on. She found her running shoes under the stainless steel sinks where she had kicked them the night before. She carried them out to the bar with her and started the coffee before she sat down to put them on.

Soon Perry would arrive to sit and smoke with them. There was not much work at the hotel anymore. At ten o'clock Carmen would open the front door and the bar would be open for business. A few people would trickle in. Staying long enough to warm up and then leaving again to do whatever it was they did when they were not sitting in bars and coffee shops.

* * * * *

Perry pulled in behind the hotel. A fine dusting of sand grated under his feet as he trotted up the steps. Carmen had the back door propped open and he removed the broom and let the door slam shut behind him. Darren and Carmen stared at him.

"Good morning all," he said, puffing up to fill his suit.

"Gee," said Carmen. "Who died?"

Darren snickered and smoke came out his nose.

"No one you know," Perry said. The faster he got to his office, the better. He could try a grander entrance later. His back was aching and his feet were killing him. All he wanted was his swivel chair.

"Hey, stay awhile. Have a smoke with us." Carmen waved her cigarette at him.

"I don't want to wreck my suit."

"You've got to be kidding. What are you wearing that for? Seriously." Carmen couldn't believe her eyes. His moustache was gone and his hair was combed in a different direction. It looked like his mother had dressed him up for picture day. Hair slicked down, and flat grey shoes with the wafer thin heels and pointy toes. He reminded Carmen of the guy who took her to grad.

"Yeah, where's your corsage?"

Darren? Perry blinked. Darren never said anything and even he was cracking up. Perry wished he had a gun to flash at them, or a big ring. Anything to shut them up right now.

"What's so weird about a business man in a suit?"

"Nothing," said Carmen. "But it is weird seeing you in a suit. And hearing you call yourself a businessman for that matter."

"Well, what do you suggest I call myself then?" Perry grazed past them and slapped across the floor to get a coffee.

"I don't care." She scratched at a bit of dried food on the table with the corner of her du Maurier pack. "Call yourself Vito if you want to."

"I want to see you in my office in ten minutes." Perry said. "And bring me a coffee when you come. I have a busy morning ahead of me."

At that Carmen raised her eyebrows even more. "I'm here right now and you already have a coffee," she said pointing at the cup he was holding. "What's in ten minutes?"

"In ten minutes you have a meeting with me. That's what's in ten minutes." He spun on his heel and marched down the hall.

Carmen grinned at Darren. "I wonder what spooked him?"

Darren didn't answer but stretched out in his chair and gazed out the window. For him it was enough to be inside. It didn't matter much what other people did.

* * * * *

The desk in Perry's office was littered with a week's worth of the *Winnipeg Sun* and a stack of crinkled movie magazines from the video store. In the corner stood a Zenith colour television which Perry had moved from one of the rooms upstairs, with an old VCR sitting on top of it. Right beside the desk was a bar fridge filled with pop and Extra Old Stock beer. The heavy glass ashtray spilled over with butts. Beer cans left behind by Tibor and Harv rolled on the floor. Perry picked them up in disgust and put them on the table. He had to get this place cleaned up. It was his first day back since the new year began and here he was, dressed to the nines, and his office looked like a frat house.

The room had high ceilings and huge windows and silver steam heaters that scalded if you got too close. The walls were painted an industrial green. The view from the window was of the brick wall of the next building, but at least it let in some light and Perry didn't mind that outside traffic couldn't see what was going on inside. Through the other window, if he stood to the extreme right of it, he could glimpse the street and the people who milled about all day. There was no air conditioning in the building but its construction was such that it stayed cool in the summer and retained the heat nicely in the winter. The walls were brick and must have been two feet thick.

The desk was a massive piece of furniture that took up most of the south wall. It was about the size of a barroom pool table. Behind it was an upholstered oak swivel chair, which Perry swivelled in quite a lot. The paint on the walls was peeled and cracked in many places and brown water marks stained the pale paint. Last year's calendar from the Ellice Meat Market hung on one wall.

The floor was a dark green tile, cracked in many places and missing in some. Maybe he could get someone in to take a look. The only problem was the money. He wasn't about to put any of his own money into this dump and it was not likely that old Bradley was about to put any more money into his tax shelter than was necessary. Perry figured he could call him and claim there had been some catastrophe and the place needed a new floor and paint job. He could pocket the extra money by getting Harv and Tibor to do the work.

Bradley kept saying he wanted to sell the place but so far nothing ever happened. In fact Perry was convinced the guy was senile. Why else would he hang onto a place like this and pay his staff to do nothing? The main extent of Perry's tasks was getting the liquor order filled each week. He had to pay the utility bills, for which he had set up automatic bank withdrawals so all he really had to do was make sure they weren't getting ripped off, and even if they were, it wasn't his money. The food in the kitchen was ordered by Carmen since she cooked for the few people who ate there. Once in awhile the health and safety inspector dropped by. Carmen kept things in good shape in the kitchen, so really his job took up about thirty minutes of each day. Not a bad deal, he thought. Plenty of time to think great thoughts and come up with ideas that one day would make him rich.

From his desk drawer he pulled a deck of cards and shuffled them from one hand into the other. It was something he wanted to get good at. With his right hand he splayed the deck across the tables and flipped the last one over. Cards flew off in every direction and scattered on the desk and floor among the garbage already littered there. For a moment he ignored them and then much to his surprise, Carmen walked in with a coffee. Maybe things were going to change around here.

"Is everything okay with you?" she asked. "I mean, nobody did die, right?"

"Carmen, what do you think of the name Stork?" He stooped to pick up the cards on the floor and flicked them onto the desk.

"For what? A bird?"

"No, for me." The coffee steamed on his desk and he admired the effect. Methodically, he gathered up the cards and tapped them into place and began shuffling again.

"You want me to call you Stork?"

"I think it sounds cool. I want people to take me seriously." He sat up and took a sip of his coffee. "Perry is not a serious name."

"And Stork is?" Carmen had come in ten minutes just like he asked.

"For the business I'm running, I think it's a great name."

What was up with him this morning, Carmen thought. What business? Perry was a drug dealer who used his job at the hotel as a front and now he was developing some Godfather complex.

"So, what? You want to change your name so that Tibor and Harv will take you seriously? Those two idiots?"

"Those two are my best men, but they need to respect me more. I am taking my life in a new direction and I want them to know it."

"I don't see how they could miss it." She gave her head a shake. They were his only men. Tibor and Harv were two losers who rifled through their mother's purses for five dollar bills and sold joints to twelve-year-olds at recess. Now they were his best men and Perry wanted their respect.

Perry swung his feet onto the desk and loosened his tie. This small gesture was one of the things that had been missing from his life. Loosening his tie, but tightening his grip.

"Well, Stork, I'm going to get to work now." She paused at the door. "How long have I known you, Perry?"

"Stork."

"How long have I known you?"

"Ever since I got here. Three years or so."

"I don't know if I can start calling you something else now. After all this time." She tugged at her hoop earring. It sounded too weird calling him Stork. It sounded like something she would call him behind his back.

"Well, everybody else is going to be calling me that and it's the only thing I'm going to answer to."

"Whatever," she said and turned to go. "Call me if you need anything."

"I need some help cleaning this place up."

"I'll bring you a bucket and a mop. You can get your two goons to do it for you. I've got to get Walter. It's almost noon."

Carmen closed the door behind her and sighed. It was a classic mid-life crisis, even though he was only thirty years old. Soon he'd be driving a red car and trying to impress nineteen-year-old women with his business savvy. She couldn't imagine what direction Perry was talking about. She had never known him to care much about direction.

* * * * *

Whenever Perry asked Carmen how long she had been working at the hotel she always said the same thing. "Seems like forever." After awhile Perry stopped asking since it was starting to feel like forever to him too.

With a shiver, Perry suddenly thought of Walter, who sat day after day in the same spot, drinking coffee and waiting for Carmen to bring him a plate of eggs. He had been there longer than any of them. What did he think of when he thought about his life? The crummy room he lived in for three hundred dollars a month? Did he consider that his home? All he did was get off the freight train one day when it stopped in Winnipeg because that was the end of the line and he would have frozen to death if he didn't get off. He could have ended up anywhere. It didn't matter to him. There were two types of people in this world, Perry mused. Those who believe they can never go home again and those who believe they can. Or maybe there were more. There were those people who never left their homes at all. What was the matter with them? Some people wanted to get as far away as possible and others couldn't bear the thought of being more than five minutes from where they were born. Those people were paralysed by even the thought of a vacation. Like some kind of danger lurked in the Caribbean that did not lurk in their own back lane. Bad shit can happen anywhere. Now that he thought about it, maybe Walter was one of those people that never went anywhere. He was totally paranoid about anything going on outside. If Carmen didn't go and get him every day and bring him downstairs, he would stay in his room and talk to the shadows.

When people say, you never can go home again, they must mean people like Walter. The physical space which most people conjure up when they think of home did not exist anymore for him. It existed only in his mind as a vague memory. Maybe, he missed it the way a person misses the Acropolis after a trip to Greece. A distant memory of some tourist attraction that they experienced once and have no need to visit again. No real nostalgia or warm memories. Just a place he once knew that popped into his head from time to time.

How did someone end up like that? Walter had been there even before Carmen. It was fascinating to Perry. He tried, while he sat at his desk, to deconstruct the lives of Walter and Ruby and that other big man, the one with the piano key scarf, Donald, to figure out what to do to so he wouldn't end up like them. Something made them bail on life somewhere along the way and now they hung out on the streets, in boarding houses and in his hotel. He would rather die than end up in a place like this day after day. He reclined in his swivel chair, touched the fabric of his suit and stroked his face where his moustache used to be. He felt he was at least on the right track. This re-invention was long overdue. Those people in the hotel bar, more of an inspiration to him than they would ever know. They were the ones to spur him on to do better. Become a more vital person.

Later, Perry decided, he was going to buy a couple of cigars and see what difference those would make to his new-found self. And he would dig through his top drawer for his grad ring. Some flashy jewellery would be nice. His mind then drifted to thoughts of women. Maybe now with a new image, he could find a new kind of woman. Rich, gorgeous, buxom women who would be impressed by a man in a suit. He would have his pick. Oh, the tricks he would have them perform... they would be falling over each other to get to him.

* * * * *

Carmen made her way up the dimly lit stairs, chuckling to herself. She couldn't wait to see if Perry actually did convince Tibor and Harv to mop his floor.

The stairwell was dark and each step uneven and worn. Some were coming apart and wobbled loosely underfoot. The small windows at each landing were caked with thick dirt and didn't allow much daylight through. Naked bulbs dangled from the ceiling at each landing and cast a dim pool of light downward day and night. There was an old lift which ground to a standstill years ago and was never fixed. The lift was a testimony to the hotel's grand past, when a hotel with a lift was the ultimate in pampered luxury.

Carmen used the railing and felt each step with her foot. Gold striped wallpaper, old, yellowed and peeling, hung on the walls. There were many hotels like the

Watch you don't fall

Wiltshire along Main Street: the Occidental, the Savoy, the Leland, the McLaren. There had been a need for all of them at one time, when Main Street meant something more than desperation and decay. One by one the hotels were condemned and torn down and the strip was starting to resemble rotting teeth with more and more gaps every year.

Walter lived in room 323. Carmen knocked at the door and after some rustling and shuffling inside, Walter barked, "You're late."

The door opened a crack and Walter's beady eyes shot out from beneath his craggy eyebrows. He studied Carmen's face for a long moment, as though he had never seen her before in his life.

"Need some help this morning, Walter?"

"Walter who?"

"Walter Cronkite. Come on. Open the door. The coffee's ready."

"You're late," he said again.

"What do you mean late? You don't have a clock in there." He didn't have anything in there. Not even a calendar on the wall.

"I can tell by the light on the wall."

"Oh yeah? You know what the problem is? You don't get enough stimulation, Walter, when all you do all day is watch the light move across the wall. Why don't you get a radio or something in here? Or a picture on the wall. I'm sure Donald would make you one."

"Ha, very funny. Help me with my boots."

His room was dank and stifling hot. The old steam radiator hissed and clanked and generated enough heat to roast a chicken. The window only opened a crack and stayed that way summer and winter. It was swollen in that position and could not be budged up or down. Not that Walter would ever let Carmen open it. She would have to convince him first that there were no evil humours swirling around outside.

A sagging twin bed with faded blue and green striped sheets was shoved against one wall with a rumpled old purple blanket and a sweat stained pillow with no pillowcase. This was where Walter now sat in his waffle long underwear, with the buttons undone to his belly and the fly gaping and yellowed.

There was a puddle under the bed, about a foot from a Miracle Whip jar.

"You missed the jar by a mile, Walter."

"There's a jar?" Walter chirped.

Carmen grabbed some rags she kept there for these very instances and got down to mop up the mess. The skin on Walter's feet was dry as parchment and his toenails, thick and cracked. His feet ached all the time and he only wore slippers, a pair of genuine Cree moccasins with rabbit fur around the edge and flowers done in traditional beadwork. Ruby was impressed the first time she saw them. She said they were nicer than any moccasins she ever had, and she was a real Indian.

"There was some guy trying to break the door down last night."

"Your door?" Carmen asked, more interested in cleaning up the pee on the floor than Walter's nutty stories.

"No, some other door. He didn't have a gun though and gave up."

"Well, good thing." Carmen stood up and tossed the rag into the corner. "You could at least try to aim. Weren't you ever a gentleman?"

Walter sat in his ragged underwear and watched Carmen. His stomach wrinkled over on itself when he sat hunched with his arms on his thighs. The arthritis had spread everywhere and he couldn't use his hands anymore. His fingers flopped uselessly and Carmen had to do up his buttons and the fly of his pants. No wonder he missed the jar. He had no grip and not a lot to hang onto. His ribs jutted out from under his skin. A sprinkling of brittle grey hair covered his chest. Covered in layers of clothes gave the illusion that there was some substance to him, but sitting the way he was now, on his bed waiting for Carmen to pick his pants up off the floor, he looked terribly frail. Those bones had no more strength than breakfast cereal. The slightest jolt could make them crumble.

"I washed all your clothes, so you can put on clean pants and socks."

"I need to wear my boots."

"What for? You going someplace?"

"Maybe. Just get my boots."

He stared at the wall while Carmen rummaged through the garbage bag for his thick wool socks. The dreary, pale light in his room, the empty walls and the infinite silence gave him too much time to think. He heard every creak and moan of the building and conjured up wild stories. Carmen was sure he sat there all night, bolt upright and ears perked, hearing things that weren't there and watching shadows on the wall which turned into villains in the tunnels of his mind.

The boots stood by the door, the leather stiff and cracked from years of wear through rain and bog and muck. The laces were stiff and unmoveable. Carmen lifted them up. They weighed a ton and reeked of urine.

"Are you sure you can walk in these?"

"Sure I can walk in those. Don't they look like they been walked in before?"

"That they do."

He sat on the side of the bed while Carmen smoothed the wrinkles out of his socks and pushed the boots onto his frail feet. Once he was properly shod, he stood up and shuffled to the sink.

"All right, get yourself washed up. I'll see you downstairs, okay? This room is impossibly hot."

"I like it this way." He sounded like a chimpanzee, chirping and squawking. It was from the arthritis. His voice got higher and squeakier all the time.

Carmen knew she didn't have to do it – look after Walter like the hotel was some kind of nursing home. She didn't have to do anything. Perry wanted her at the hotel as security in case he had a deal going down in the office and didn't want to be interrupted. That's why he hired her. The place only needed a waitress on the off chance someone came in who actually had money in their pocket and wanted to spend it there. The simple fact was she liked crazy old Walter and since nobody else seemed to give a damn about him, she decided that she would.

Back in the bar she poured herself a cup of coffee and lit a cigarette. Darren hadn't moved and was the only one in there. "How's the coffee?"

Darren replied with raised eyebrows. He was more likely to talk if he was outside. The door swung open and Ruby came in with a collection of plastic shopping bags flapping around her legs. Her wet boots squeaked on the floor as she made her way to a table. Starting with the men's belt that kept her coat shut, she peeled off layers of clothing until she was down to two sweaters , jeans and her orange Edmonton Oilers toque.

"You keeping warm, Ruby?"

"Sure, I'm always warm. My wardrobe never changes." She piled her clothes on the chair next to her and sat down. "How about a coffee, sweetie? I'll roll you a smoke, free of charge."

Ruby reached into her bag and pulled out a coffee tin from which she emptied a pile of cigarette butts onto the table. On a good day, she could get ten whole cigarettes out of a haul. Depended how much of a cigarette people smoked. They didn't always smoke the whole thing.

"Aw Ruby, do you have to do that in here?"

"What do you mean? I always do this in here. This is my office."

With the pile of pre-smoked butts to her left and a Ziplock baggie on her right, Ruby picked open each butt and shook the remaining tobacco into the baggie.

"Put the garbage in there," Carmen said and tapped Ruby's coffee tin on the table. The cigarettes stunk and the thought of all those wet lips on the filters which now littered the table made Carmen nauseous. Some of them had bright pink lipstick wrapped right around the filter.

"That mess is enough to make me want to puke," Carmen said.

"Well, you'll be the one cleaning it up." Ruby cackled. "Just wait, I'll roll you a good one."

Carmen stood at the table and watched Ruby's hands. Her fingers, swift and precise, worked the tobacco from the rolled paper and let it fall into the baggie. One continuous motion of plucking a cigarette out of the pile, releasing the tobacco and dropping the filter into the empty tin with a dull ping. She didn't rest until all the old filters were in the bottom of the tin. The tips of her fingers were black and her weathered face smudged with ash.

"Are there any up there?" Ruby pointed to the bar. Sometimes Carmen left extra long ends of her cigarettes in those ashtrays for Ruby.

"Just one." Carmen dumped her old butt into the tin with the others.

"What about him?" Ruby nodded towards the hall and Perry's office. She didn't like to deal with Perry directly. She thought he was shifty, never looking her in the eye. And when he blew smoke rings he blew them straight up into the air and asked her to guess what he was saying.

"I'll go check. Where did you get all of those?"

"Eatons." Ruby said. "Eatons is good. Ever since they went no smoking and put the ashtrays by the doors. Those big ones full of sand. I have to dig around a little but I got this spoon, see?" She held it up for Carmen to see. It looked just like the spoons from the kitchen.

"So all I do is dig around with it and the butts float up to the top. Works good. I go to every door. Two ashtrays each, eight sets of doors, twenty butts in each, fifty cents a butt, that's sixteen bucks, that's about fifty cents a day for a month, that's one cigarette a day, if I was buying. Ha. I got it figured."

Chapter Four

Perry sat, much as Carmen had left him, feet up and staring vacantly at the high ceiling. The television was silent, odd for this time of the day. He was still tugging at his tie, unable to get used to it either way, tight or loose. On the pad of paper in front of him he had jotted down a few things: rent, liquor licence, advertising, payroll. Then the list tailed off and the rest of the page was filled with spirals and tornadoes and tiny sketches of beaches and palm trees. If it weren't for his drug dealing, there would be nothing for him to do all day. His list quickly became oppressive and his project seemed impossible at the moment. Perry was a man of great ambition but was not in possession of a great deal of drive. So far in his life he had not needed a lot of drive.

He thought about old Bradley down there in the Bahamas, living in some palatial house with servants bringing him eggs Benedict and champagne. A guy who spent his days sucking papayas and fanning himself with hundred dollar bills. What a life. Who wouldn't want that for themselves? Perry would trade places with the guy in a second.

The Wiltshire was one of several properties Bradley owned. But he still hadn't sold this dump. For some reason he continued to pay staff to run an establishment frequented only by a handful of people who couldn't afford to go anywhere else. It was a matter of speculation when Bradley last set foot in his hotel and whether or not he would recognise it today. None of them had ever met the man, not even Walter.

"Don't get up and rumple your suit," Carmen said. "Got any butts in here for Ruby?"

Perry banged on the desk and wagged his pencil at Carmen. "Tell Ruby not to peddle her second-hand smokes in my hotel. I'm going to turn this place around. It needs a little class."

"Yeah, sure. I'll tell her, Perry," she said.

"Stork! Goddammit."

"What's your problem these days anyway?" There had to be some explanation for his weird behaviour. "You ever think of getting a hobby? You've got way too much time on your hands."

"For your information, I am working on something right now." Perry continued waving his pencil in the air. "I am brainstorming and now you have interrupted my train of thought."

Carmen got a quick look at his list and doodles. "Must be a pretty short train. What are you working on?"

"I can't discuss it yet. It's too soon."

"Hey, are you still going to bring that fish tank in here? I think Walter would like it."

"Yeah, I might." Perry had inherited a tank full of guppies from his grandmother when she died and it was growing thick with algae and he always forgot to feed them. Carmen wanted it for Walter to give him something stimulating to stare at. Besides, it needed cleaning and Carmen would probably do it for him. She had a soft spot for living things.

* * * * *

Perry got up and closed the door behind her. The frosted glass rattled in the frame. Manager, was spelled out in gold stencilled letters across the glass. A whole lot of good that did him. What was he managing? Nothing. The place ran itself. The truth was he needed this place more than it needed him. Carmen at least had a job description. Waitress. That had clearly defined tasks. What the hell was he supposed to be doing?

He swivelled once, twirled the radio dial to the classic rock station, remembered his mission and found some jazz instead and tried to enjoy the cacophony that was "Love Supreme". He waited for Tibor and Harv. He was tired of this shit. All of it. The same thing day in and out. Watching over his shoulder constantly. He no longer kept anything at home. Everything was in the broken safe. He didn't dare keep anything at home. If those new age neighbours ever found out, they would be up his ass so fast for free weed. A drug dealer never really knows who his friends are.

There was a dead plant in the corner of the office, a gift from Carmen when he first started and never watered since. The floor around it was littered with brittle leaves which he swept aside with his foot. He picked the plant up and tossed it in the garbage can. Potato bugs scurried to parts unknown. At this point, unless something changed soon, he wouldn't be surprised if he ended up like that, wilted and dead, with bugs trembling underneath him.

Did they give people like him electroshock treatment? That's what he felt he needed. His body felt lifeless as a dead sturgeon. The jazz station DJ was on some non-sensical Sunday afternoon acid trip. He spun himself around four times in a row without using his feet and when he spun to a stop, there were Tibor and Harv standing in stunned silence.

"You going to a funeral, man?"

"Yeah, man, who died?"

"Ha, ha. You guys are a scream. Like Cheech and fucking Chong."

They sat down, slumped into the chairs where the slightest tilt would slide them out like freshly shucked oysters. They stared at Perry and waited for him to say something to explain his clothes. He decided the best thing to do was to start right away with his new image and pretend like he had been behaving this way all along and they had simply failed to notice.

"How are sales?"

"What? What do you mean?" Tibor asked, chewing on his thumbnail and working something over between his teeth.

"I mean how are sales? You guys are salesmen, right?"

"Are you talking about weed or something else? What's he talking about?" Harv looked at Tibor for help.

"Yeah, he's talking about weed," Tibor said. "It's fucking Christmas. All the schools have been closed, but I'm sure it will pick up soon. I forgot my bar graph. Jesus, what is this man? I mean, seriously. Is this your idea of getting a life?"

Perry reached down and opened the fridge door. "Let's have a beer, okay?" He didn't want to scare them off. He still needed them or he would be ruined. All he wanted was for them to know there was a difference between him and them.

"Sounds good to me," said Harv, whose leg swung back and forth and kicked Tibor's foot each time.

Perry sat back down and took a sip of beer. He didn't want to explain everything. All he wanted was for things to change without a whole lot of talking. He should have known when he left them at the bar the other day that this would rattle them.

"Are you wearing that suit to let us know you're the boss? So that we know you're in charge?" Tibor asked. He took a swig of beer and unabashedly belched. "That's about all I have to say about that, if that's the case."

"Nothing's changed, okay? It's all the same except I thought I would try to dress better. That's all. I was tired of the same old thing everyday." Perry was ready for them to leave. He wanted to be left alone with his thoughts. Fantasy works better in isolation.

"Well, it feels different in here with you in a suit," Tibor said. He drained half his beer in one go. "I feel like I'm in the principal's office."

At this Perry felt a slight glimmer of satisfaction. They did notice a difference and it wasn't completely ridiculous that he was wearing a suit.

"Can we just get the weed? I gotta get home and help my mom throw the Christmas tree out." Harv said. He reached into his pocket and threw a roll of cash on the table. "I need about three."

They each scooped up their share as Perry weighed it and swept it off the desk into baggies. They stood to go, and Perry stood with them. He walked over and held the door open for them.

"Hey, what do you guys think of the name Stork?"

"Like the baby delivery bird?" Tibor asked. "Isn't that your last name?"

"Kind of."

"It's an all right name."

"Rhymes with dork," Harv said and snickered.

They shuffled through the door and down the hallway, leaving their money in a heap on the desk and the smell of stale unwashed clothes behind them. Perry pulled his wallet from his inside breast pocket and neatly tapped half of the bills in place. There was quite a bulge to it now. The other half went into the safe.

* * * * *

One of Walter's boots came tumbling down the stairs and landed at Carmen's feet.

"My boot. My boot."

"I can see your boot, Walter. Do you want me to come up there and put it back on or are you coming down here?" Carmen stood, hands on her hips at the foot of the stairs.

"Come and put it on. I can't get down these damn stairs without my boot."

"Well, you've done it often enough before. Why can't you today?"

"Bring me my boot."

"All right, already." Carmen picked up his boot and climbed the stairs to where Walter waited. He held up his double-socked foot and let her slip it on. "Do you feel like Cinderella?"

"What?"

"Never mind. Come on, I'll help you down the stairs."

Walter hung onto the railing and onto Carmen and with each step a puppy grunt came from his throat.

Walter made his way to his table. His boots clomped on the floor, heels first since they had no laces. On his way past Ruby's table he said, "White man coming. Hide your land," which caused Ruby once again to laugh out loud and bare her only teeth: a trio in the middle of her bottom gum.

"Crazy white man," she said. "I can hear you coming a mile away. You'd make a terrible Indian."

"What about him," Walter said pointing at Darren. "He's wearing cowboy boots."

"I never know when he's around. He's good."

When Ruby told Carmen that Darren was her son, Carmen could not believe it. They sat in there day after day at different tables, staring in different directions and never said a word to each other.

"You gotta be kidding me." Carmen said. "He's your boy?"

"Sure," Ruby said, "can't you see the resemblance?" She cackled, but Carmen didn't know at what.

Again, this morning, the two of them glanced at each other but didn't speak. Carmen brought Darren another coffee and then disappeared into the kitchen to fry an egg for Walter and one for herself.

The sunlight cast a dusty, pale beam of light onto the floor through the front window. A bus hissed to a stop outside. The side doors opened but nobody got off. It pulled away, exposing the other side of the street where, at the Chinese 'eat-in or take-out', someone was sweeping salty, snowy dirt out the front door. A similar assortment of people would soon be gathered in there, idling, lingering, taking up a space at the counter or a booth for as long as they could before being asked to move on. The days broken up into cups of coffee and stacks of creamers, leafing through sections of the newspaper, reading flyers advertising barbecues and patio furniture and sets of plastic dishes, thinking if they had the money that would be the last thing they would spend it on.

Chapter Five

T heresa tossed her briefcase in the back door and went outside to watch Dustin. The first stars were visible in the evening sky and the kitchen light shone into the back yard. She sat on the back stoop while Dustin drove his truck around the edge of the sandbox. The wheels were clogged with snow and grated when he tried to make the truck move. He banged it on the side of the box, the way he had seen Paulie do and tried again. He dug down past the snow and found the sand underneath and filled up the back of the truck with it. When he drove the truck, the sand spilled out over the sides of the sandbox. Theresa smiled as she watched her son. He seemed so focused, so serious. Clearly, he got that from her side. As she watched the boy play, she knew that her plan to make something of their lives would be good for Dustin. Her son would grow up with all the advantages she never had.

Theresa leaned back and contemplated the waning light. The days were supposed to be getting longer. But at five o'clock, with almost no trace of the day's light, it was hard to tell.

Paulie was in the garage, working on his car. The hood was up and there was an array of greased parts on the workbench behind him. There had been nothing in the newspaper classifieds worth following up and so he had spent the afternoon in the garage taking stock of the work that remained to get the car finished.

Theresa still wore the tan pantsuit she had worn to work and her thighs were burning with the cold. She debated whether to get Paulie away from the garage and ask him to come and watch Dustin. But, as long as she was outside she would not be asked to help with dinner. Her waistband dug into her stomach and she could feel the red ring forming there. The kitchen window was open and through it Theresa smelled supper cooking. It was hard to tell what they were cooking since it always smelled of fat and onion. She heaved herself up off the stoop and shook out her legs. Dustin never seemed to get cold, his cheeks red as crab-apples and snot running into his scarf. It didn't bother him one bit.

She opened the garage door. A bolt slipped out of Paulie's hand and clanked across the floor. "Shit, you scared me."

Theresa attempted a smile. "Was there anything in the paper today, honey?"

He slid his glasses up on his nose and turned the bolt around between his fingers. "Not unless I want to be the drive-through guy at Burger King."

"So, you didn't make any calls or anything?"

"There was no place to call. I'm telling you, Terri, this is just for a couple of months. They're hiring us all back in the summer. I'll collect pogie for now and finish up the car. Do you know how much I can get for this thing if it's all fixed up?"

Her legs ached and she was tired from her day at the office. It made her extra tired knowing Paulie had all day to do whatever he wanted. She raised her eyebrows, waiting to be impressed. To her it was just a car that never ran and had sat in the garage as long as she had known him. To him it was his baby. A 1977 lemon yellow

Barracuda. Paulie was convinced this car would turn out to be the best investment of his life. He got it off his friend Kevin when he couldn't come up with some money he owed Paulie. Now, with a bit of cash from unemployment and the winter off, he could finally finish it and sell it if only Theresa didn't lean on him too much.

"Guess how much," he said again.

"I have no idea," she said. "Guess how much you would have made if you went to work today?"

"Aw, never mind," he muttered and turned his back to her and wiggled a wire under the hood.

Just then Rosa's voice pierced the air. "Theresa, don't let him spill all the sand. It will kill the grass." Rosa's face peered from the kitchen window. The skin on the back of Theresa's neck prickled when she heard it. Dustin had stopped scooping and was now flinging sand up high in the air and watching it catch the wind and scatter across the snow.

"Well, it's pretty impossible to keep it in," Theresa shouted back. "How's he supposed to play in a sandbox without spilling any? Besides, it's the dead of winter for Pete's sake. The grass has been dead for months." She shut the garage door and marched over to the sandbox.

"Come on Dustin. Want to get on the swing? I'll give you a big push."

Dustin dropped the truck and toddled over to Theresa. "Wing, wing." He punched his mittened hand at the swing set. Theresa leaned down to pick him up. What did those women feed him all day? He weighed a ton. The swing creaked when she sat him in it. His bare belly peeked out from under his jacket and she tugged it down to cover it up. "You're starting to look like your grandad," she said.

"Theresa," Rosa shouted again. "When are you coming in? The men will be hungry soon. Someone has to set the table."

"Yeah, in a minute. I just put Dustin on the swing."

The men, the men. Their world revolved around those two. Theresa pushed Dustin and felt the blood pound at her temples. There was no point in arguing with Rosa and Antonina about this. They were a united force when it came to the housework, adamant that it was women's work and quick to shoo the men out of the kitchen as soon as the meal was finished. At the same time, they were just as quick to rope Theresa into helping them, determined to make a good wife out of her.

Paulie, to prove a point, one day rose from the supper table and began to clear the table. This was met with a strained silence since they all knew it had something to do with Theresa and Paulie and the state of their marriage. But, when he ran the water and looked as though he was going to wash the dishes too, Antonina could not hold back and scraped her chair back against the floor. She rose and forcibly turned off the taps, grabbed the tea towel he had put over his shoulder and slung it over her own. She ushered Paulie out of the kitchen and muttered something in Portuguese that Theresa couldn't understand. Rosa's eyes followed Paulie out of the room and then landed on Theresa.

"Why you want his help? If you don't work so much all day you have time for the dishes."

"But, it makes no sense," Theresa wailed, her face red with frustration. "Why can't they help?"

"Because we don't want their help," Rosa stated emphatically and Antonina clucked her approval. What Rosa meant was, she had to stay on Antonina's good side if she wanted to meet with her approval. It also meant that Theresa, who was in a similar position, being married to Paulie, better do the same. Antonina was the grand matriarch. Everybody knew and kept their place. Theresa knew as long as she and Paulie lived under this roof, things would be the way Antonina said they would be.

Theresa wondered sometimes why the family had left Portugal at all. They may have been happier if they had stayed. Paulie could have married some nice Portuguese peasant girl who wouldn't dare help herself to more potatoes without offering him some first. The three women could have sat around the kitchen all day peeling potatoes and boiling fish heads. They lived as though they still were in the countryside of their native land, with chickens scratching in the dirt outside and a cow resting its head on the kitchen windowsill.

They set about their life in Winnipeg as though they had never left Portugal, as though nothing had to change all the way across the world. The radio dial was tuned to a local Portuguese station. Dated Lisbon newspapers littered the kitchen. The church they attended on Sunday was Portuguese. Rosa and Antonina took two buses to shop at a Portuguese bakery across town rather than the Safeway at the end of the block. And the buns they brought home, which Antonina gummed for hours in the evening after her teeth had settled in their glass for the night, had the consistency of charcoal briquettes.

Antonina, a good thirty years after arriving in Canada, still barely spoke English and she and Rosa carried on in Portuguese all day long. Theresa never knew what they were talking about. When the whole family got going Theresa thought they sounded like a bunch of wild turkeys. Any small reminder that they were now on Canadian soil, like when Theresa poured Creamy Cucumber salad dressing on her salad, got Antonina's tongues clucking.

"What now?" She would ask, incredulous. "It's salad dressing. I'm not trying to insult you. I am enhancing the flavour of my salad. You put salt on everything. It's no different. Sheesh."

* * * * *

In the back yard, sheets hung out on the clothesline. Dustin tried to kick them with his feet with each push on the swing. Even in the middle of January, Rosa hung the laundry out and then took it in, frozen solid. Many of the women's habits, Theresa did not understand. Like the millions of jars of zucchini relish they made every year from the harvest of watermelon-sized zucchinis which lay scattered in the garden all summer like undetonated bombs. One day Theresa came home to find dozens of jars of relish on the counter which would be added to the unopened jars from the last five years in the pantry. She admired the women's industry and thrift but had to wonder at their estimation of how much relish a family could consume.

"God almighty," she had finally exclaimed last year. "I could understand if this was real food. But you two are sweating over a stockpile of relish. You could ship all of this to Africa and those people would still die of starvation."

Rosa and Antonina simply stared at her like she was some naïf and went back to their task.

* * * * *

"Theresa," Rosa called again. "Come inside now. He's getting cold."

Inside, Rosa stood by the sink, scrubbing potatoes. Antonina took them off the counter and peeled them and then let them drop into a pot of water on the floor beside her. When she was finished, Antonina hoisted the pot from the floor to the stove.

Antonina watched out the window into the back yard where Theresa sat with Dustin.

"She didn't answer," said Rosa.

"Call again. She heard you the first time. Give her a push." The women exchanged glances and sighed. Paulie had married Theresa. What could they do? Now, she was one of the family.

"Theresa, the table's not set. It's five o'clock."

"Geez, don't you ever give up?" Theresa yelled at the back window from the yard. "I just got home from work. I'm spending some time with Dustin if you don't mind."

"You want to spend time? You stay home and you have lots of time. All day."

"Sure, and then we'd never get out of here. How will we ever buy our own house if I don't work?"

Antonina closed the window to keep the cold out. They had heard it all before. All the talk about moving out.

Theresa put Dustin up on the slide. She glanced towards the garage and wondered if Paulie could hear everything. He wouldn't come out until it was quiet and Theresa had Dustin inside. He would appear precisely at the point when his pork chop landed on his plate.

Dustin slid down the slide and fell into the snow. He turned and ran to climb up the steps again and hit his chin on the third rung. After a two second pause, a loud and mournful wail erupted and he ran to Theresa with fat tears clinging to his cheeks.

"All right. We'll go inside." Theresa looked towards the window but Antonina's face had disappeared.

Theresa plucked Dustin off the ground and swung him onto her hip. With her free arm she yanked open the screen door and swung it out hard so that it was still swinging when she put Dustin in his playpen, where he lay down with tiny fists in his teary eyes, while she went to get out of her work clothes. Half way up the stairs she changed her mind and stomped back down. Both women turned to stare pointedly at her when she came back into the kitchen to give Dustin a Ritz cracker for each hand to calm him down. She was used to them staring. It had been going on for almost three years.

"There you go Dusty, eat some crackers while Mommy gets ready for dinner. Daddy will come in soon to play with you."

"How is he ever going to grow if all he eats is crackers?" Antonina said to Rosa in Portuguese. All Theresa understood was 'crackers'.

"At least he'll be quiet. A couple of crackers won't kill him. I think I'll have some too." Theresa grabbed a handful and went back upstairs. Rosa smiled at Theresa and helped herself to a cracker as well. "See. They're good aren't they? Everybody likes Ritz."

Dustin licked the salt off the crackers and they slowly turned to mash in his hands. Antonina and Rosa chuckled.

"She's stubborn, like a child," one of them said.

"Or a mule," said the other.

* * * * *

Theresa lay on the bed in her sweat pants, allowing her stomach some relief after a long day. Like a defiant teenager, she would stay upstairs until they yelled for her to come for dinner. She couldn't help it. That's how they made her feel in that house. Did they really expect her to get up everyday and put on a polka dot, sleeveless house-dress and wash the floor with an ancient scrub brush until her hands were pink and raw as a cured ham? Well, probably yes. That was exactly what they wanted, which was why Theresa spent so much time up in the bedroom. She had given up on fulfilling their expectations and did what she could to keep her life out of their way.

Until the call for dinner came, she lost herself in *The Young and the Restless*. Everybody seemed to live with their parents on that show, but somehow they all loved it. Maybe it helped that the houses were palaces decorated with fancy furniture and plush fabrics and maids and servants took care of the mundane details of living. That would help. People could focus on the drama of their lives that way rather than the boring, predictable elements that made up this household. Heaven forbid anyone have a crisis that threatened to delay dinner. Theresa allowed herself a brief fantasy. At five-thirty there would be a clatter from the kitchen and a shout up the stairs and Theresa would trudge back down those stairs, trying her hardest to imagine the banister was mahogany. When she got downstairs, the dining room would be aglow with candles and flowers and Paulie would be sitting there in a suit, smiling romantically at her and they would eat something exotic, like lobster and drink wine and water out of different glasses and dab their lips with linen napkins.

As soon as she opened the bedroom door, the smell of pork chops and cream of mushroom soup wafted upstairs. She cast one last longing glance at the television, where John and Jill Abbott were dining in a private restaurant booth. Then she shrugged and went down to her dinner.

Paulie had Dustin up on his knee and was trying to drink a bottle of beer while Dustin pried the glasses from his face. His weary eyes met Theresa's. The shadow of his beard darkened his face. She kissed the top of his head and took her place between him and Dustin. Antonina placed a bowl of potatoes on the table and also kissed the top of Paulie's head.

"He's been out working all afternoon," she said.

"Well, whoop-di-do," Theresa said and took her seat. Paulie just grinned as he played peek-a-boo with Dustin.

They all sat at the table, each in their usual place while Antonina loaded everybody's plate with food. Paulie was in his undershirt, Anton in his corset, undone for eating, Antonina and Rosa in their house-dresses and Theresa in her pale yellow Daniel Hechter sweatsuit. This scene played out night after night. They were like poor immigrant families in the movies, everybody bickering and banging fists onto tables. It wasn't as charming when it was your life for real.

"Nice girdle," Theresa said to Anton.

"I wore it for you."

"It wouldn't kill you to put a shirt over. A person could lose their appetite."

"If I put a shirt on you might eat us out of house and home. There's nothing the matter with your appetite that I can see." Anton leaned back and loosened the ties some more and then heaped more food onto his plate.

When Paulie's plate was empty, Antonina leapt to her feet and loaded some more food onto it while keeping an eye on Theresa.

"What are you looking at me for? He can take care of himself." Everyone was content to be serving or be served. And Paulie's uninterest in their financial situation irked Theresa. Their plan to buy a house and get out on their own was bogged down and going nowhere. She couldn't do it on her own and he didn't seem to care one way or another as long as someone made him dinner.

In ten minutes all their plates were empty. Only Dustin still played with his food. The women were on their feet, clearing the table and scraping all the leftovers into a pot, to be cooked up into soup for tomorrow. Dustin smacked at his potatoes with his spoon and bits of potato stuck to the floor all around his chair. Anton pushed his chair away from the table and belched. In response to this Rosa smacked the back of his head. "You take the garbage outside."

"My back is killing me," he moaned, sliding down in his chair.

"So is mine killing me. Now go." She looked to Theresa when she said this, eyebrows arched. Theresa gave her the thumbs up sign. Once in awhile they were on the same side.

Anton had been off work for two years now after he slipped in a puddle of blood and guts on the kill floor at the plant and wrenched his back. Now he wore a corset all the time. It didn't fit him anymore. He had put on so much weight from sitting around the house complaining about the pain he was in. He wore it over his undershirt and his boobs hung over the top and his gut bulged out the bottom. He fiddled with the strings all the time, loosening them when he sat in front of the television and tightening it up for church on Sunday. He went for rehabilitation three days a week, but whatever they were doing there for him didn't seem to be helping. He was getting fatter and fatter and complained about his back all the time.

Every time Dustin slopped potatoes onto the tray of his high chair, Antonina was there to scrape them back into his plate, interfering with Theresa's efforts of trying to get him to eat with a spoon and not his hands. There were too many mothers around. Dustin spit milk down his already saturated bib and Antonina smacked his hand.

"Don't hit him." Theresa stood up from the table, scraping her chair on the floor and stomped upstairs without any explanation. Everyone paused to hear the door slam and then carried on. Paulie followed her up the stairs and he peeked inside the door.

"Terri? Is everything all right?" He knew it wasn't all right. And he knew he had a lot to do with that.

"You know damn well everything is crap. I can't believe we are still living here like this. And now you don't have a job and we'll never get out of here. Look at this room." She waved her hand at everything. "How are we supposed to live in here? It's terrible. I hate it." Her eyes teared up and she couldn't stop it.

Paulie sat beside her on the bed and held her hand. When it came to a crying woman, he only had a vague idea of what to do. His mother and grandmother rarely cried and when they did they sent him out of the room. Now he was supposed to comfort Theresa somehow and he had no idea what to do other than give her a pile of money to roll around in and that was the one thing he did not have. He lay down beside her and stroked her hair. "It'll be all right," he murmured into her head. "There, there. We'll get out soon."

She sat bolt upright and smacked his arm. "When Paulie? When? Can't you see I'm going crazy here? I don't know how you can stand it. They treat you like a child. How do you like that? They treat you and Dustin exactly the same. You are a man, Paulie. Show them you are a man. Show me. This is making me nuts! Get a job and get me out of here."

She fell back onto the bed, exhausted. Her shirt half open and her hair flayed about. Tears streaked her face, flush with emotion. Theresa blew her nose. A small pile of tissue grew on the corner of the bed.

"There might be some sales positions opening up at work. I'll call tomorrow and find out about it. Okay? Maybe I can work in sales and that would be all year." Paulie didn't know if this was true or not, but he had to say something to ease her mind. When she got upset like this he became very afraid that she would leave him and he did not want that at all. To try to keep her happy was the one duty as a husband he understood. He lay beside her, their heads sharing a pillow. He held her hand, not sure what else to do. Outside the tree swayed and tapped against the frosted window. The frost had crept up the window about two inches and stayed that way all winter. One of the sure signs of spring was when that half moon of frost disappeared and left the faint shadow of residue behind.

"I'll believe it when I see it."

They lay quietly awhile. Theresa sniffed and dabbed her nose with a tissue. Paulie stroked her hair.

"I want to go home," she sobbed, startling Paulie who thought she had calmed down.

"You are home."

"No, home to my mother. I think I'll go this weekend. I need a break from this. I'll take Dusty. Just a couple of days, okay? I'll be back Sunday night."

He kissed her damp cheek. "That sounds like a good idea. Hey, why don't you get Dusty dressed and come to my game tonight? It'll get you out of the house and Dusty likes the arena."

All Theresa wanted to do was continue sniffling and have a bath. The number of baths and showers Theresa took was one of many bewildering habits, which to Antonina and Rosa, defied all reason. They couldn't understand how a person needed a shower every single morning and often a bath at night.

Theresa thought a minute and decided Paulie was right. She didn't want to be in the house tonight. And she could have a bath when they got home.

"Okay, I'll get Dustin."

Paulie gave her a hug, happy he had been able to offer a solution. He left her drying her tears and went to the basement to get his hockey bag.

* * * * *

The arena was cold. Theresa clutched a hot coffee. The game was tied at three. Dustin's mouth was covered in chocolate. The box of Smarties had lasted nearly three periods. There were a few other girlfriends and wives there but after the initial hellos they sat apart and spoke only if a goal was scored. It had been awhile since she watched Paulie play. He played defence and was good at killing penalties. He had taught Theresa enough of the rules so Theresa knew that right now Paulie should be on the ice. They had one player in the penalty box for high sticking and the coach always put Paulie in when there was a penalty to kill. "Hey, why isn't Paulie in there?" one of the other girls asked Theresa.

She turned and said, "I don't know. Paulie should be in there." She shook her head, pleased that someone else noticed that Paulie was missing. When the other team celebrated their power play goal, with a minute left in the game, she joined the other women in booing.

On their way home she asked Paulie. "How come you weren't on the ice for that last goal? I thought he always played you for the penalties."

"I don't know. Trying something different I guess. He won't do it again, that's for sure." He reached over and squeezed Theresa's thigh. "Thanks for coming."

"Yeah, it was good." She stroked his hair, damp from the shower. Dustin snored in the back seat. "Listen to him. He sounds like you."

They held hands the rest of the way home.

* * * * *

Everyone was still up when they got in. Paulie put Dustin to bed while Theresa went to have a bath, explaining she was cold from the arena. She stepped gingerly into the bubbles. The door was locked. No one could bother her now. The bath was the only sanctuary available to her under that roof. The family wondered why she spent so much time in here and she wondered why, given the number of bodies crammed into this tiny house, they didn't spend more time in here. Her body relaxed in the water and she lay still until nothing moved. She lost all sense of where her body ended and the water began. Her mind carried her out the window and she peered into the house the way God, or some almighty being might see them there. All of them attached by coarse strings which didn't give when one of them moved but jerked and jolted so that an independent action by one was immediately followed by an involuntary and clumsy response by all the others. The tension was inescapable and ever present. Theresa could feel it pulling her out of the tub and back to the kitchen. It was not easy to resist.

For almost three years this had been going on. They should have moved out right at the start. There were plenty of cheap apartments in the city, but Theresa and Paulie had a plan that would see them buying a house after six months. That was how long it was supposed to be. Six months and then they would move out. But Theresa became pregnant and the family put the thumbscrews to them and convinced them it was no time to move out with a baby on the way. Dustin would be three years old in June and they were no closer to moving away than before.

Chapter Six

"What the hell is that fool up to out there?" Anton stood by the kitchen window and glared at the sight of the neighbour flinging snow over the fence into his back yard, "That son of a bitch. What does he think? I don't notice an extra five feet of snow in my yard?"

"It's just snow," Rosa said. "It's good for the garden."

"Well, we got enough snow of our own. I don't need any of his. When he's done I'm going out there and I'm going to throw it all back. Paulie can help me."

The bright morning sun streamed through the window but outside the air was frigid. In the yard the birds fluttered around the bird feeder, defying the cold. The newspaper lay spread out in front of Paulie and he scanned the employment column before focusing his attention on the car parts and accessories. He circled a few of the jobs to make it seem as though he paid some attention to what was there. Toast crumbs littered the page. Paulie turned to Anton.

"I need to pick up a decent halogen light for the garage. It's a bit dark in there to do a lot of the engine work."

"It warm enough in there?" Anton asked. The thump, thump of the dryer could be heard from the basement.

"Yeah, it's good. As long as I'm doing something." Paulie picked up the paper and shook the crumbs into the sink. "I'm going to head to Canadian Tire. Want to come?"

"Paulie, I have an idea," said Anton. He listened briefly for any sound of Theresa, who was upstairs packing for the weekend. He dabbed toast crumbs from his plate with his thumb. "How would you like to build a nice place for you and Terri and Dusty in the basement? I took some measurements yesterday and there is enough room down there for two small bedrooms. We can make the bathroom bigger and add a shower. Dusty's getting bigger and needs his own room. We can have it finished before you get called back to work and it will get Terri off your back about finding a job. It will do us both some good to have a project for the winter. What do you say? We'll get started this weekend and you can surprise Terri when she comes home."

Paulie wasn't sure what to say. Anton slid a sketch of his plan across the table. If Theresa came home and found out they were moving into the basement she would kill him. She would become completely unhinged. On the other hand, their bedroom upstairs was so small and it was right across from his parent's room. It was impossible to have sex or a fight in that house without wondering what everybody else heard. The basement at least would be sound proof.

"What do you think?" Anton dug for something in his ear, eyebrows arched expectantly. Paulie bit his lip. Disaster pinched at the pit of his stomach.

"Okay, but don't say anything until she's gone. Let's surprise her." Paulie chewed hard on his pencil. His stomach fluttered. Theresa wasn't going to like it but he didn't know what else to do. To him it sounded like a fine idea. Maybe if they had things well underway by the time Theresa got home, he could convince her. It only had to be an in-between step. Nothing permanent. He could stress that. And if he could get her to go along with it he could forget about pretending to look for work.

Paulie peered over the rim of his glass of orange juice when Theresa appeared in the doorway with an overnight bag of clothing and another bag full of diapers and toys. Instantly, he felt a flush of guilt. He wasn't one to deceive his wife. She had a hard enough time with the truth most of the time. All weekend she would be away, trying to get some relief from the stress of living here and then she would come back to find the basement framed and a welcome mat at the top of the stairs.

"I'll take those out and get the car warmed up for you. It's a cold one out there today." He jumped to his feet and grabbed the bags and the car keys.

"You're still in your pyjamas. You'll freeze," she said. But Paulie put his parka on over his pyjamas and his boots on his bare feet and headed out the back door. The snow crunched underfoot and his skimpy pyjamas flapped around his legs in the wind. Theresa's Chevette was parked beside the garage. He sat behind the driver's seat a moment and waited for the engine to rev a bit slower. A Tim Hortons cup sat in the cup holder with a bright ring of lipstick around the rim. He rarely saw Theresa with make-up on anymore. Not for him anyway. Sitting in the cold car in his pyjamas, he thought about this and then didn't know what to think of it. Maybe he didn't deserve to see her with lipstick anymore. Maybe lipstick didn't mean what it used to. It wouldn't be the same if he saw her with it now anyway. He re-adjusted the seat for Theresa and left the car running and jogged back to the house.

Theresa watched Antonina wipe Dustin's face and fingers with the same vigour she used to scrub potatoes. She chattered to him in Portuguese and Dustin beamed at her and clapped his hands and she clapped back. Theresa hated that they talked to Dustin in Portuguese. Some days when she came home and said something to him in English, she could see the confusion in his face when he had no idea what she was saying. Now that he was making some attempts at speaking, Theresa wanted to be sure he spoke English and she didn't want a string of Portuguese coming out of his mouth.

Paulie came back in, rubbing his hands together. Theresa lifted Dustin from his chair and held him out towards Paulie. "Give your Dad a kiss. Then we have to get going."

Paulie puffed out his cheeks and gave Dustin a raspberry on his naked belly and was rewarded with a gutsy belly laugh. He held onto Dustin while Theresa checked her purse.

"Okay," Paulie held Dustin out to Antonina. "Give your Avó a kiss. Bye-bye."

Dustin pressed his wet lips to Antonina's cheek. She smiled and tweaked his cheek. Paulie carried Dustin out to the car. He got him settled in the car seat while Theresa sat in the front. She pulled out backwards into the lane and drove to the corner before she realized she had not kissed Paulie good-bye.

* * * * *

It was a frosty morning. The sky was bright and the sun glared overhead. An inch of fresh, blinding snow covered the fields. Theresa reached for her sunglasses and snapped on the radio. Dustin liked driving in the car. He stared out the window and each time they passed a herd of cows he slapped the window and barked. The farther she got from the city, the more she relaxed.

She thought being an adult would mean having a life all her own, not a life wrapped up in five other people. She had left home three years ago and still wasn't making decisions on her own. All she wanted was for once to have some say in what type of soap her laundry got washed in or what day the beds got changed. Maybe she wanted fresh sheets on Tuesdays and not Mondays. Or for once, to eat dinner on the sofa and not at the table with everyone else. She hated living by someone else's rules. She felt like she hadn't gotten anywhere in life at all.

Relief washed over her when she pulled into her mother's driveway. This was her home, where she had her own bedroom and she knew there would be peanut butter and cheddar cheese and vegetable thins in the kitchen. And her mother, Louise, would leave books like *God Wants You To Be Rich* on the night table for her to read. By this point she might even read it. How many of those books did a person have to read before the money started rolling in?

Theresa dragged her beleaguered body into the house and let her mother get Dustin out of the car seat. All she wanted was to sit in the rec room and dig her toes into the old shag carpet and get a good dose of home while she had the chance.

Soon she was settled into the familiar comfort of the sagging cushions. Here was the place she spent most of her time growing up. Her father left when she was thirteen and her mother worked at the cocktail lounge until two in the morning most nights. A thirteen-year-old didn't need a baby sitter anymore, but her mother didn't let her leave the house either in the evenings when she was at work. So, Theresa spent her time in front of the television watching shows like *Dallas* and *Dynasty* and *Falcon Crest*. It was here that she formed most of her ideas of what life could be. When she wasn't in front of the television, she was in front of the mirror, teasing her hair, trying on her mother's clothes and experimenting with make-up and perfume. Theresa easily learned to ignore the scorched lawn out front and the Corel dishes in the sink and replace them in her imagination with fine china and stunning views of rolling hills or crashing waves. She had imaginary, adult conversations with girlfriends or lovers while she carried around a wineglass filled with ginger ale and nibbled from cheese and cracker trays she prepared for her pretend parties. Her mother would come home to find the remains of these parties and sniffed Theresa's glass for traces of liquor. She didn't know what to tell her daughter who seemed so determined to reach for the stars.

"You better get yourself a good job or marry rich if you want that life," her mother told her.

"I know that," Theresa said. All the women on those shows had rich husbands. As soon as she could, Theresa got a job at the supermarket. She saved all her money and was able to pay for her legal secretary course all on her own. Theresa had chosen that course because of the clothes she could wear. Nurses and teachers always ran the risk of getting dirty somehow and had to wear clothes that prepared them for some kind of vile spillage. She knew enough from her TV shows that those women would do well to have some kind of job since they always ended up cheating on their husbands and ruining their marriages.

Theresa and her mother didn't talk about it that much. Louise couldn't help but think if she herself had a little more ambition she wouldn't have ended up living with a lousy husband she would eventually throw out and have to scrape by serving drinks to his clones at that dismal bar every night. Theresa felt that by talking about it, even back when she was a teenager, that she would be rubbing it in since she knew her life would turn out to be so much better than her mother's. And now that Theresa was living in the city, her life a far cry from what she imagined, she felt like time was running out on her and if she didn't turn this barge around it would run into the muck and be stuck there. There was a desperation to her ambition now, one that hadn't been there before. Things were taking too long. Far too long. Theresa worried that the point had come where it would be so easy to give up and fall in a heap onto the floor and let her husband's family carry her upstairs and plop her spineless body onto the bed. There she could stay and listen to the rest of them go on with their lives, in and out of the back door, in and out of the fridge. And she just wouldn't care anymore what happened.

"How are things at the house?" Louise asked.

Theresa smiled wanly. "Oh, the same. You know. Nothing has changed in that house in years."

"How much longer do you think you'll live there?" Louise clasped a mug of tea to her chest.

"Lord only knows. I didn't think we'd be there this long. But it takes longer than I thought to save up for a down payment. The houses I like are all pretty expensive." Theresa sat with her feet tucked up under her bottom and licked peanut butter off her fingers. Dustin rolled around on the shag carpet. Every so often he would roll over onto his stomach and pull at carpet fibers with his little baby fists, like he would clumps of grass.

"What do you need a big fancy house for? All you need is a solid house on a nice street. They don't cost that much." It was the first time Louise offered any sort of opinion of Theresa's aspirations and she quickly reached for some Bits and Bites.

"I know, I'm starting to think too of a smaller house. We can fix it up with nice stuff and still feel good. You don't have to actually be rich to feel rich, I don't think. Most of the time I just pretend to be rich and it works fine." Theresa laughed. It made her feel funny to admit that but her mother didn't notice. "What I really want is to get out of that house. But I don't think Paulie cares where he lives. He likes being at home."

"Paulie doesn't know anything else. He'll like it fine once you get a house. It'll make him feel all grown up. He's probably never felt that way."

"It's not normal not to want your own place. Or am I abnormal because that's what I want? We both can't be right, can we?" Her mother looked away, not sure exactly how to answer.

* * * * *

It was indisputable how different the house felt with Theresa and Dustin away. Paulie sat at the breakfast table with a worried frown on his face. Anton came back downstairs and sat at the kitchen table to put his boots on. "Come on. We've got to get to the store if we want to get anything done today."

The whole idea had Paulie's stomach in knots but he got up from the table and got dressed anyway. He would go along with it for now and see what happened on Sunday when Theresa came home.

After picking up supplies at Home Depot, they worked all morning to clear enough space in the basement so they could work. A lot of junk had piled up downstairs over the years. Rosa came downstairs to sort through it all and she and Antonina spent the morning bundling things up for the trash. Antonina didn't even break a sweat heaving Paulie's massive hockey bag from one side of the basement to the other. By noon they had still not done any work on the framing but there was enough space to set up the workbench and power-saw. Paulie wasn't sure what Anton had in mind when he saw what little space there was down there.

Anton had safety glasses on and was marking two by fours with a blue pencil. "Measure twice, cut once," he said. "I learned that lesson a few times."

They worked in silence and at the end of the afternoon they had cut all the wood for the framing. Paulie sat on the basement steps and watched Anton lay the pieces out in the shape of the rooms. "You see how this is going to go?"

"Yeah, I get it," Paulie said. He sighed and wondered yet again if Theresa would get it.

An unusual peace settled over the house after supper. One by one the lights went out as the family nestled into their beds. Outside, a blanket of snow muffled sighs of the house and muted sounds of traffic lulled them to sleep.

After everyone had gone to bed Paulie sat in the living room cracking sunflower seeds between his teeth and piling the shells onto the coffee table in front of him. Tomorrow the walls would be up and there would be no turning back. He didn't dare think how long that situation would last, once they moved into the basement.

Paulie's life had changed so fast after he met Theresa. He hardly had time for anything to sink in before they were married and the next thing he knew he was standing nervously in the hospital waiting for someone to come and tell him if he had a son or a daughter. And later sitting on the back stoop with his father, feeling sick already and having Anton pull two cigars out from somewhere and insist on smoking one with his son.

"This is how it always starts," Anton said. "These women have a way of kicking your ass into high gear. Same thing happened to me when you came along. I was young and foolish and not ready for anything and bang, there's your mother in tears on my doorstep. That's where you make your choice. Do I become a man right this instant and take this woman in my arms and tell her I will look after her, or do I wait until it happens again with someone else? You gotta be able to live with yourself, Paulie. Never mind living with her. It's yourself you have to face. You did the right thing. Everything is gonna work out for you now, because you did the right thing."

"What if it's not what I want right now?"

"You make it what you want. It's what you got. You tell yourself you don't want it, you're going to have struggle your whole life. And with one hell of an ache in your stomach. You want this Paulie. Everyone does. You don't think you're ready? Doesn't matter. Ready or not, here it comes. What else are you going to do anyway? You want to fuck other women? Too bad. No one ever promised you a great life. The most you can hope for is a reason to get up in the morning and now you have it. And that's something. Trust me. It's huge."

Anton leaned back and put his arm around Paulie's shoulders. They sat and puffed on their cigars. It made Paulie feel a bit better. A bit smarter and stronger. But, Anton didn't know everything. He thought it was an accident, a funny spoof that happened to so many guys and launched them headfirst into reality. A baptism of sorts. Like there were no other choices in life and it didn't really matter who you ended up with because life dealt everyone the same cards, just shuffled slightly differently.

Now, sitting in his parent's living room, Paulie didn't think he would ever figure out what would make him happy. Getting his car on the road would make him happy, but what for? So chicks would look at him? The kind of girls who went for guys in flashy cars were out of his league anyway. He was thirty-two years old. Maybe guys would admire his car, but what good was that? He wasn't married yet when he got it and now three years later he hadn't even driven it.

He spat out another sunflower seed and felt the sting of the salt in his mouth. He went to the kitchen to get a beer. He was sure he could get twenty grand for it. There was a lot they could do with twenty grand. He could give it to Theresa and let her start looking for a house. A grin crossed his face and he knew what he was going to do. The basement would be a decoy and he would finish the car. Then, in the spring, instead of moving into the basement, he would sell the car and they would move out. Finally, he would be able to give his wife what she wanted.

The bedroom, empty. The bed, vast. Paulie lay down and stretched out, reaching for each corner and fell asleep. When he woke up, he was curled up on the left side of the bed facing the window, the way he woke up every morning.

* * * * *

By Sunday afternoon they had all the framing up. Anton dug out the old propane torch to fix up some plumbing in the bathroom to get the shower installed. He flushed the toilet. "That's a good toilet here. I don't know why I never use this toilet. I always forget it's down here."

Paulie smoked nervously, one cigarette after another. Theresa was expected home for supper. Everyone was excited to show her the basement. The only thing he wasn't sure of was how mad she was going to be and he tried to brace himself for a rough few days.

"Hey, do you ever use this toilet?" Anton tapped the seat with a length of copper pipe.

"Yeah, I do. I use it a lot actually. No one's ever in there."

"You're a sneaky bastard," Anton said.

Paulie and Anton struggled with a pipe fitter. A cigarette was clenched between Paulie's teeth. At a moment when they both had their hands wrapped around the pipe and it was just about to slide in, the propane torch rolled off the vanity and hit the cement floor. A silent stream of gas escaped into the air. Paulie automatically leaned down to pick it up. An ember fell from his cigarette. A flame shot up into his face. "Shit!" He dropped the tank.

"Get out of there, Paulie," Anton yelled from the foot of the stairs. They leapt up the stairs and behind them the tank exploded. The windows rattled and there was the tinkling of glass when the basement window blew. Smoke crept up the stairs. Paulie peered down into the basement. Flames licked at the fresh cut beams. Anton ran to the kitchen sink to fill a bucket with water but they had turned the water off to do the work on the plumbing.

"Get the women outside," he shouted at Paulie.

Rosa was jolted out of her living room slumber. She nearly kicked over the end table as she stood and hiked up her skirt and made for the kitchen. There was a near collision on the back stairs as both Paulie and Anton raced for the phone.

"Get outside. The basement's on fire!" Anton roared, his face red and his eyes wide.

"Get Avó. She's sleeping." Rosa didn't know what to do. Smoke was already curling into the kitchen. Her mind raced to think of things to save from inside, but nothing came to her mind other than to grab a few coats. Anton was yelling into the phone to the fire department and waving frantically for Rosa to get outside. The kitchen was quickly filling up with smoke. Paulie disappeared into the front hall to wake Antonina.

He found her in a deep sleep on her bed, her lips sunken without the support of her dentures. He shook her shoulder. "Avó, get up. You have to go outside. There's a fire downstairs."

Her dark eyes flew open. There was no time for her to retrieve her teeth or her rosary. Paulie hustled her out the front door, where Anton and Rosa stood clutching one another and staring at the house, bracing for what they thought would be a second, more devastating explosion. One that would surely send the house to the moon. Rosa draped a coat around Antonina's shoulders. In the distance they heard the wail of sirens, a sound they heard so often and quickly dismissed, knowing the trouble was somewhere else. They watched, helpless, as the sirens neared and black smoke billowed out the basement window.

The trucks came screaming down the street and shattered the silence of a Sunday afternoon. The firefighters leapt from the truck and cranked open the fire hydrant. The family stood dumbly by as they dragged the hose through the front door. One by one the doors all around them up and down the street opened and curious neighbours stepped onto their front steps to watch. A few ambled over, clutching their arms to their sides for warmth, to find out from Paulie or Anton directly what was happening and then scurried back to tell the onlookers. Cars slowed down and the people inside them stared.

* * * * *

Perry was on his way from Shooters Sports Bar where he had watched an NFL game and eaten his fill of hot wings. He really hadn't paid much attention. His mind was on other things. On the seat in the car beside him were a couple of finance magazines. He thought it would be good to know something about money if he was going to be wining and dining investors for his business. This was what preoccupied him now; getting enough money together to do it.

He was driving down Notre Dame Avenue when the fire trucks roared past him. Out of curiosity, he swung the car into the left lane and followed. It turned down a side street and stopped in front of a small, white bungalow. Already a crowd was gathered on the street and he pulled his car over and joined them. As far as he could tell there was not much of a fire going. Sometimes people panicked at the first lick of a flame. People were crowded around, clamouring for information. Others lined the boulevards, barricaded behind the three-foot snowbanks, holding cups of coffee in one hand and small children with the other. This was probably the most exciting thing that had happened on this street all winter, he thought.

Perry decided against lighting a cigarette in case there was some kind of a gas leak. There were stories of houses blowing up and leaving nothing but huge craters in the ground. Families come home after work and find a hole where the house used to be. Things just blow up sometimes. Urban natural selection.

An old woman was offered a kitchen chair which she waved away. Another car pulled up behind Perry's and a woman leapt from the driver's seat, not even bothering to take her baby out of the back and ran screaming up to the family.

"What happened?" she shrieked in a voice that made Perry's ears ring. He was trying to figure out who lived in the house. At first he thought it was the old woman who didn't want the chair. But now this younger woman, the one who left her kid wailing in the back of the car, seemed to live there. A man around Perry's age was trying to talk to the young woman but she kept screaming. If that was her husband, Perry felt for the guy. His face had been burned by the fire and his eyebrows were gone and she didn't even notice.

Eventually they pulled the hoses out of the house and the ambulance and two of the trucks left. People lingered on the boulevard, not wanting the spectacle to end. He watched the fire chief talking with the family. They must all live there, the young guy and his wife and baby and then the older couple and the old woman. It was puzzling how they all fit in that tiny house.

Perry got back into his car and drove off. It hadn't turned out to be much of a fire after all.

* * * * *

The damage was minimal. The fire chief led Anton and Paulie through the basement. It would have to be gutted and all their work redone. A couple of windows needed to be replaced but all in all they were very lucky nobody was hurt and that they could stay in the house. Their insurance would probably cover everything.

Theresa sat on the sofa between Antonina and Rosa, sobbing while Dustin had hold of her hand and twirled her wedding ring around and around her finger.

"I can't believe this," she kept saying. "What were they doing in the basement? There's nothing down there." She gulped her glass of white port. Everyone was shaken. Paulie and Anton came upstairs and they all drank a small glass of port to calm their thumping nerves

"It's going to be all right," Anton said.

"What the heck were you guys doing down there anyway? Making a bomb?"

Anton left it up to Paulie to tell. It didn't matter anymore what they were doing down there. He sunk down in the easy chair. "Well, Dad and I were getting it fixed up for us to move down there."

"What? Who? Us?" She smacked her knees with her hands. "You want us to move into the basement?"

Paulie and Anton looked at each other, not sure which of them she was talking to. "Whose idea was that?"

"It was our idea," said Anton. "Don't worry. We're going to rebuild. A little fire isn't going to change anything. We want you and Paulie to be comfortable here."

Suddenly Rosa stood. "I've got my ham to cook."

Antonina scuttled after her and left Paulie and Anton to deal with Theresa.

"How could you let this happen?" Theresa shouted at Paulie. "I thought I could trust you. I go away for one lousy night and I come home and my whole life is upside down."

A wail escaped her throat and she ran upstairs. Anton and Paulie didn't move until they heard the bedroom door slam. The house stunk of ash and smoke. Paulie still had soot on his face. His singed eyebrows itched. It was no surprise, her reaction. "Maybe it wasn't such a great idea," Paulie said.

"What do you mean? Because she's upstairs crying means it's a lousy idea? You're the one who wanted to surprise her. Women don't always like a surprise, unless it's something they're expecting anyway, like an engagement ring, or chocolates on their birthday. Why does she hate us so much?"

Paulie shut his eyes. "She doesn't hate you. The life she wants will only ever exist in her head. That's what she hates. That she can't get what she wants."

"What's wrong with this life? She has everything she needs." Anton was perplexed. Everybody hated their life a little bit. It was a given and crying about it was just a waste of time.

"I have no idea," Paulie said.

"Anton," Rosa appeared in the doorway. "Put the water back on. We have supper to cook."

Anton got up and slapped Paulie on the knee. "This is a good life," he said and went to tend the plumbing.

*　*　*　*　*

Theresa lay on the bed hugging her pillow. Her empty plate sat beside her. She had eaten in their room tonight. She stared out the window and wondered what would have happened if she had stayed here all weekend instead of going home. She could have stopped Paulie from starting on such a stupid project and saved the house from almost burning down. Across the hall in the bathroom the water was running. Antonina was going to bed. First she filled the sink, then there would be lots of splashing. The plug would make a plop sound when she pulled it and before the sink was empty she would begin brushing her teeth and spit into the draining water. Even a near disaster wouldn't convince her to break with routine.

After Antonina, Rosa would go in there and have a five minute shower. Then Rosa would knock on Theresa's door and say, "bathroom's free". It drove Theresa crazy.

There was a gentle tap at the door. Paulie came in holding Dustin. "He's getting pretty tired. I think he needs to go to bed."

"Paulie, how could you do this?"

"Terri, listen." He tugged at the bottom of Dustin's shirt. "It was Dad's idea. They really want us to stay and they know we hardly have any space up here. They are trying to make things more comfortable for us. It might not even get done now. Who knows?"

"Paulie, they are trying to make things more permanent for us. If they spend all that money and time re-doing the basement and then in a year we tell them we're moving, they'll be so mad. You know that. We can't let this happen. We have to stick to our plan."

"Terri, the plan isn't working. The plan was for us to get out in six months but that didn't happen and it doesn't look like it's going to happen in the next six months either. This doesn't have to be forever and we will be more comfortable. By the spring you'll be able to decorate. It will be done and you can decorate your new place." Paulie stood at the foot of the bed, bouncing Dustin on his hip who slurped on a bottle of apple juice.

"You must think I'm real stupid," she said. "I am not going to spend all of our savings decorating the basement. You're a jerk, Paulie. A selfish jerk."

"I'm a selfish jerk? My goddamn eyebrows are gone. All you have yammered on about is how awful I am to try to make your life a little more pleasant. I nearly got killed today and you have not said one word of appreciation that I am still alive."

"Oh, just go away." Theresa threw herself sobbing, face-down into the pillows. Paulie put Dustin in his crib, covered him with a blanket and went back downstairs. He was not up for consoling her tonight.

Watch you don't fall

Dustin snored in his crib. Theresa turned on the television and waited for her brain to shut down for the night. A good sleep was what she needed right now. She was tired of thinking and wished they would put *Falcon Crest* back on the air so she could divert her attention to something good. At least the men would have to wait now before they could get working on the basement again. The insurance money had to come through first. Across the hall she heard the toilet flush and a few seconds later it flushed again. Beautiful. Just beautiful, she thought.

Chapter Seven

Fat, cold snowflakes fell heavily and clung in thick clumps to every branch and every ledge. The clouds hung low, the colour of pigeons, and a wind blew steadily from the north.

The Wiltshire Hotel on Main Street stood between a discount clothing store, housed on the main floor of an old warehouse building, and a vacant lot, littered with non-refundable bottles of solvents and glue and a lot of broken glass which jutted through the fallen snow. The building stood frail and defenceless as snow pelted against the windows. In 1928 it was partially destroyed by fire after which the owner spent fifty thousand dollars renovating the building, adding four storeys along with a billiard room and a saloon. The top four floors were still boarded up and vacant. Ruby, Darren and Walter now spent their days in the old saloon, wary of some outlaw stranger to come bursting through the swinging doors with an ill wind at their heels.

The Wiltshire was one of a few remaining relics from the twenties along north Main Street. Back in the day when Main Street meant something other than debris swirled around by an unrelenting wind. When business was brisk and commercial travellers, agents working for eastern manufacturers and wholesalers, criss-crossed the country by train, buying and selling and negotiating deals. They stayed at the Wiltshire, drank in the beverage room, ate in the massive dining room on the second floor, walked up the street to the bank in the morning and shook hands all around.

Now the only businessmen around were drug dealers, pimps and bootleggers. People locked their car doors when they drove down here and shook their heads at the derelicts as they passed by. The whole area should be torn down and re-built, was what most people said and that was what slowly was being done, even though the derelicts weren't taking the hint.

It was a typical first class hotel when it was built in 1920 by Archibald Wright. A room cost two dollars and fifty cents a day. There were seven storeys with twenty-five rooms and four bathrooms on each floor. The lobby, with its ornate columns and cornice work, took up half the first floor. White and black tile dotted the floor. It was meant to be easy to clean when people brought the snow and slush inside and the heat melted it into puddles of water and grit. Today, close inspection of the floor and walls revealed dark brown mold which slowly ate away at the integrity of the walls. It was a dingy lobby lit by a couple of bare bulbs where once a crystal chandelier shone brightly.

On the second floor was the grand dining room with red cedar wooden beams and columns and a frescoed ceiling. The doors had been shut and locked years ago, probably after the very last party and nobody had gone in there since. Neither Perry nor Carmen had ever seen it. Walter claimed to hear parties going on there still. It was a remarkable building in its day, vital and pulsing with the industry and opulence of the pre-depression years.

Just two blocks from the Wiltshire Hotel was the cultural hub of the city, the Centennial Concert Hall, where the symphony, the ballet and the opera performed. The Manitoba Theatre Centre, the museum and City Hall all occupied the area just south of the rundown stretch of hotels and rooming houses. There is a tense mingling of two worlds as concert-goers drive cautiously through the shadowy streets, in search of a parking spot under a street light. They could always pay and walk through the tunnels, but many put on a brave face and scurry back to their cars after the show and hope their anti-theft contraption has done its job. They lock themselves inside and pray for green lights and hope the bums don't see them staring.

The vacant lots were growing in number along Main Street. Some of the buildings, the rare ones which still were structurally sound, or offered unique examples of architectural style, were spared and renovated. The Wiltshire was not among the chosen. It would continue to shudder and sag until a decision was made to do away with it. Until then, the people whose lives brought them here, carried on within and did not notice the slow decay. It was not an eyesore, not a dangerous structure, not a relic from the past. To them the building remained central to their lives.

The inside of the building was a mystery to most people. The lobby was now encased in plexiglass and caging. Bars and giant bolts blocked access to everything, including the toilet. The bottles behind the bar were padlocked behind chain link fencing and the cash box never had more than twenty dollars in it at a time. Traces of the hospitality industry the hotel once represented were scarce. Only the smell of coffee gave any hint that human life could still be supported here.

* * * * *

Perry hoisted the antique ashtray up the back stairs and dragged it through the kitchen to his office. He had found it on the weekend at the Good Will store. It was a beauty. A pink marble base and solid silver details. The stem was a rimmed silver and then the ashtray was the same pink marble with a silver tray. It weighed at least fifty pounds. He stood it beside his desk and then sat down and sipped a Mountain Dew as he admired it. It was perfect for his office.

Aimlessly, he flipped through a copy of *Business Week*. He didn't understand any of it and had no idea where to begin, but he enjoyed the ads at the back for the villas in Tuscany and Provence. The CEO of some big investment company was on the cover, jowly and smiling, arms crossed and perched on his desk. They always made them look like that. Like making millions was the most relaxing job on the planet. He also had the *Financial Times* and the *Wall Street Journal*. He was actually thinking about investing, which was why he had all the magazines, but they did little to tell him what to do with his money. He tuned the television to the news station and waited for the financial report.

Slowly, he was pulling his new image together. The suit he wore was the third one he had bought in the last week. The fabric was a light grey with subtle pinstripes. He was getting used to wearing suits and even enjoyed throwing different ties onto a shirt to decide which one to wear. He had found his graduation ring and wore it on his pinky finger. It had a deep red stone and a nice weight to it. His face felt smooth and clean now that he rid himself of a ten-year-old moustache and had assumed the habit of shaving every day. Today he turned the computer on for the first time in months and enjoyed the hum it added to the rest of the ambient sound.

These days he drove to work among the sullen masses and gloated. Those people were exhausted before their day began. Why? Because they let life trample over them. Life defeated them a long time ago and now they were being dragged through some crap that stunk and they woke up in agony and couldn't shake the shit from their fingers.

Bettina von Kampen

There was no way Perry was going to ever drive around feeling like that. He was lord of the manor. He was his own boss, a high roller, a heavy hitter, a man of steel. All day he spent with his money magazines and thinking business. Yes, life was on the upswing.

He tapped his cigarette into his recently acquired standing ashtray. Very retro, very chic. Very gangster, he thought. He swung back in his chair and put his feet on the desk. Smoke hung over his head in a puffy cloud. The heaters hissed. The smell of hot dust filled his nostrils. On his desk lay a single, clean file folder on which he had carefully written Grand Beach Uptown. There was nothing in it yet. Everything was still in his head. But he knew it was going to be huge. Soon he might even tell someone about it. Someone who would see what he was getting at. He needed to know if it was a valid idea or not. How else would he get anywhere if he didn't have ideas like this? Surely there would be others out there who wanted what he wanted. A chance to see women in bathing suits in the winter. He smiled and leaned back in his chair. A little fantasy never hurt anyone.

* * * * *

All the lights were on inside the hotel at ten in the morning. Carmen hated this time of year, when the hours of daylight spanned only a fraction of the day. She banged at Walter's door. It rattled on the hinges. The doorknob hung loosely in its casing, so Carmen was careful when she tried the door. It was open for once, but he had the chain across. She knocked again and called through the gap, "Hey Walter! Time to get up. No hibernating allowed."

A growl erupted from inside. Walter shuffled to the door and let Carmen in. There were piles of newspaper stacked up against the wall next to the closet.

"What are you doing with all of those?"

"I had 'em in my closet but I had to get in there last night to hide so I had to get the newspapers out."

"What were you hiding from?"

"That asshole down the hall never paid his money. The guy came for him last night. Banged on the door for an hour and then came down here and banged on my door. I had to hide."

"I've told you Walter. There's no else that lives on this floor. Just you."

Walter fell silent and looked suspiciously at Carmen. She held a sock out towards his foot and without paying any attention to her, he raised his foot gracefully towards the outstretched sock.

"You have to let me at that beard of yours one day. You still have egg in there from yesterday." She brushed at his beard until the bits of egg fell out. "You saving that for something?"

There was egg in his harmonica too. Every few days it would cease to make a sound and Walter would bang it on the table until Carmen came and took it to the kitchen and pried the crusties out with a skewer.

"Maybe we should start feeding you something other than eggs. Something that's easier to clean three days later. What else do you like?"

"Schmaltz." Walter was on his feet now. He stood in front of the mirror and gazed at his reflection. With his better hand he smoothed over tufts of his beard which stuck out at odd angles. He wore a dark green hunter's cap and folded the ear flaps up.

"What the hell is that? Schmaltz?" Carmen stood and waited for him by the open door. She rubbed her shin on the back of her other leg.

"You put it on toast and eat it. It's fat. Chicken fat makes the best schmaltz. Leave it sit a day and it gets hard and then you can spread it on toast. It's the best thing you'll ever eat. You never go hungry as long as there's schmaltz."

"Yeah, sure. If you don't die eating it. There's probably enough schmaltz grease in the kitchen to lubricate a tank but I think we better stick with eggs for now."

"You've got schmaltz in there and never told me?"

They were on the stairs now and Walter's chatter gave way to panting as he inched his way along the railing. The cold had settled permanently into his bones. Once Carmen had him settled at a table with his eggs and had squirted ketchup wherever he pointed, she put another cigarette to her lips. Perry came in to refill his cup. He had on a new suit and held his hand up to the light to show off his ring.

"Accessories now. I'm impressed," Carmen said. She shook her lighter and tried to get a flame. "You've almost got that porn star look down to a T. You slick your hair down like that with schmaltz?"

"What the fuck is schmaltz?" He pulled his lighter from the inside pocket of his suit and held a flame to Carmen's cigarette. There was no point in arguing with her. Ignoring her would at least still get things done around here. Anyway, it meant little to him if she was impressed or not. Carmen would be a hard sell. He knew that.

"Ask Walter. He's the one up on fine foods." She waved her cigarette at him. "Thanks."

It seemed to Perry that Carmen survived on cigarettes and coffee and the sweet pickles she dug out of the gallon jar in the kitchen and ate by the saucer full. She was skinny as a twig, leaning against the bar on bony elbows which could drill through the mahogany, her legs twisted around one another like pipe cleaners. Her skin had an unhealthy, sallow hue, a blend of the caffeine and smoke that flowed through her veins. She dyed her hair a different colour every three months, which was the only visible attention she gave to her looks. Right now it was a dark brown. She wore little make-up, but her nails were always painted. Many times Perry had offered her a joint or two to take home on the weekend, but she never took them. "Did enough of that in my youth," she'd say. "And worse."

She was around forty or at least that was Perry's guess. She lived alone in one of those four storey, yellow brick apartment blocks with warped aluminium frame double-pane sliding windows. Hers was the middle of three identical buildings, way up on Main Street, almost in the Maples. From what Perry could deduce, she worked at the Wiltshire during the week and spent her weekends washing Walter's piss-soaked pants and fiddling with her hair. She must have had some wild days when she was younger to settle for this now, and not even take him up on his offer of free weed.

"Any plans for the weekend, Per?" She noticed he was smoking something other than his usual Players Light. It was one of those long, thin cigars. The kind that came individually wrapped. He was having a hard time keeping it going and coughed clouds of thick smoke into the air. "You know you're not supposed to inhale those things, right?"

"No shit." He didn't have a clue. "I got these from A-1 on the corner. They've probably been sitting there since the depression."

In the corner, Walter imitated Perry by coughing and hacking and waving away imaginary plumes of smoke. Perry scowled at him and stubbed out his cigar.

"Is it Cuban?" Carmen picked it up out of the ashtray and twirled it under her nose.

"It's a Pom Pom Opera. I have no idea where it's from. I just wanted to try it."

"Shit, Perry. I don't know if you're becoming a pimp, a porn star or a peccadillo."

"What the fuck's a peccadillo?"

"Hell if I know. I just heard that somewhere."

Perry smoothed out his lapels. "I just think this is closer to the real me. I am a business man and I have a few deals going on right now and I thought it would be better if I dressed for success."

Carmen's eyebrows arched. "What business deals? You mean the pot? That's not business. That's crime. Are you trying to be some kind of mafioso guy?"

Perry ignored her. "Can I get some lunch?"

There was a moment of silence as they both watched the smoke swirl in the air.

"You better not start carrying a gun or I quit." Carmen stubbed out her cigarette and disappeared into the kitchen.

Perry saw Walter still scowling at him. "How about you Walter? You ever want anything to change?"

Walter stared at the corner and he muttered something Perry didn't understand. One thing changes around here and he'll go ape-shit for sure, Perry thought. This place had become his institution without him having to suffer the trauma of being put in one. It just grew around him like moss. Perry shuddered at the thought.

Carmen brought Perry a cheeseburger and fries smothered in chili. He ate while Carmen pecked around the edges of his fries.

"Need a ride home tonight?" he asked.

"Sure, I've got Walter's stuff to wash." Perry wrinkled his nose. At least his car had a trunk. A vehicle with a trunk was imperative for a drug dealer. And when it came to Walter's pants, Carmen used a pair of rubber gloves to handle them and sometimes she wore a surgical mask; there were serious fumes in those pants.

Perry didn't know why Carmen did all that stuff for Walter. She treated him like he was her grandfather or something. But, it was none of his business. Whatever made her happy. Without Walter to bug during the day, Carmen probably would go work somewhere decent and Perry needed her here. She was good at keeping people away from his office, tolerated his business and put up with Tibor and Harv on the days they hung around drinking beer and switching channels on the television. Carmen was what his mother would have called a good egg.

"Any more news about the hotel?" Carmen asked.

"You mean about Bradley selling it?"

"Yeah. Is it for real this time?"

"No sign yet." Perry pushed his plate towards Carmen and reached for his half smoked cigar. "I wouldn't worry about it. He was drunk."

Carmen drove a French fry through the remains of the chili. "Right," she said as Perry coughed out a cloud of pungent smoke.

A banging noise erupted from the corner. Walter was trying to knock egg out of his harmonica. He gripped the harmonica between both hands and brought the instrument down on the table top with a double-fisted hammer swing. For a feeble old man, he was able to make a lot of noise.

"Give it here, Walter. I'll clean it up." Carmen picked up the harmonica and squinted into the reeds.

"Hurry up," yelled Walter. "I'm gonna need that any second."

Walter had spotted Donald outside and needed the harmonica to bleat out a few notes to herald Donald's entrance. This always visibly bothered Donald and Walter hated to miss a chance to get under Donald's skin. He blatted out sounds like a traffic jam or a hog squealing and watched the red tide rise up Donald's neck.

Donald stood on the corner across from the hotel and blinked snowflakes from his eyes. Ever since that City of

Winnipeg sign appeared on the door of the hotel, he had been living on the edge. He spotted it there one morning at the beginning of December and decided to take action. It was a notice of eviction for the Wiltshire Hotel. Just beneath it hung another one, almost identical except it was a notice of demolition. Both notices were folded up in his coat pocket. They were never left unattended and for weeks now he had been carrying them back and forth between his home in the rooming house and the hotel. This was Donald's secret weapon. He didn't know yet how he would deploy this weapon, he just knew it was a good thing to have. The date for the eviction was March 27. Three months from now and those dumbasses in there had no idea the roof was about to fall in on them. He chuckled and waved his Burmese walking stick at the traffic signal as he stepped off the curb. It was great fun to have one over on them.

In his satchel he carried his supplies for the day. A sheaf of paper, glue, scissors, an assortment of glitter and ribbon and a variety of women's magazines. Everyday he came to do his work at the Wiltshire. He produced one to two collages a day. Sometimes he left one for Carmen as a tip and the rest he took home and placed in his portfolio. In the summer he wandered among the tourists in Old Market Square or down at the Forks Market and sold them for ten dollars each.

He crossed the street and stopped to peer through the door. Perry and Carmen were eating. Walter was in there, of course. Walter never went anywhere. He was banging his harmonica on the edge of the table. Always trying somehow to get Carmen's attention. Donald knew Walter wasn't as helpless as he made out. He used to be a hobo and hobos were not a helpless bunch. Even with his crippled hands, the guy could still make a nuisance of himself. No sign of Ruby or Darren. No sign of panic. They still didn't know. A surge of excitement built in Donald's chest. Every day he was faced with the decision of whether or not to spill the beans, but keeping the secret was too much fun and he hadn't yet said a word.

"What's Donald doing out there?" Carmen spotted him with his hands cupped on either side of this head to see through his reflection.

"Some dumb ass thing," said Walter. He grabbed for the harmonica "Give it here. I need it."

"Here, this should do." Carmen picked one more egg flake out and tapped it over his plate. A few more crumbs fell out. "Try blowing a tune."

Walter hummed into the reeds and a high pitch whine came out.

"Beautiful," they both said at the same time.

Donald entered the bar to a trumpet blast from Walter's harmonica, but today he barely batted an eye. His mind was filled with visions of the whole bunch of them sitting in there, idling away, completely oblivious to the wrecking ball swinging towards them and not noticing anything until the first bits of plaster rained down on their heads. Maybe some bits would get stuck in Walter's harmonica and Carmen would have to come to his table to get them out. By the time she realized it was plaster and not eggs dropping onto the table, it would be too late. The ceiling would collapse on top of them and they would all be goners. How utterly tragic.

He made his way to his table and gave Perry a sidelong glance. Perry was looking at him through a cloud of cigar smoke. Donald coughed and waved his hand in disgust and Perry coughed an exaggerated cough and waved back with a mocking gesture. There was a distrust between them that neither could trace to anything specific, just that each thought the other was out to get him in some way. The suits stumped Donald. He couldn't figure out why suddenly Perry was trying to impress everyone. Usually, Donald was the only one in a suit and he didn't like the competition. Soon enough though, Perry would go down in the rubble like all the rest in his fancy suit and cheap cologne.

Donald hung up his coat and set his satchel down on an empty chair. He didn't have the energy to work today and went ahead and ordered his vegetable soup with extra crackers and buttered toast. Perry and those damn suits were throwing him off. There were five unfinished collages in his bag and he had no inclination to finish them. This, to an artist, is a disturbing trend.

From time to time he fingered the papers in his pocket. None of them knew a thing. His soup arrived and he tucked his napkin into the front of his shirt and dug in. His eyes darted around the room. Walter had fallen asleep and Carmen was in the kitchen. Having finished his lunch, Perry too had disappeared into his office to wait for his goons. All of them going about their lives like nothing was wrong. Donald giggled into his soup until his eyes teared up in the steam.

"Walter, is there someone staying on your floor? I swear I saw someone looking out a window at me from up there."

Walter sniffed and ignored him, but Donald could see there was a slight twitch in his hand. Walter spooked easily.

"Did you hear anything last night?" Donald persisted. It didn't matter that Walter didn't answer. The seed had been planted and would fester all day.

Donald left early. Today was not the day for them to find out. It was still snowing when he headed for home. Big, fat flakes melted on his face and when he licked them off his still salty lips, they tasted sweet, even though when he looked up at the sky, he wondered what poison might be in them. He continued licking all the way home anyway. It was hard not to.

Chapter Eight

Three weeks after the fire and the house still smelled of smoke and ash. Theresa sat at the kitchen table and scanned the real estate news and sipped a glass of orange juice. A few remaining Cheerios bobbed in a bowl of milk beside her. Ever since the fire Paulie had been trying to convince her the basement wouldn't be so bad but she would have none of it. She sat with the newspaper each morning and circled houses they could not possibly afford and jobs Paulie was not qualified for and left it out on the table. She spent a lot of time in their room and Paulie spent a lot of time downstairs in the living room. Most nights he came upstairs after she had fallen asleep and crawled into bed and clung to the outer edges of the mattress.

With this tension gnawing at the threads of their relationship, Theresa even briefly thought of packing up and leaving him but what were the alternatives? Move home and marry someone who worked at the plant and had a rifle rack on the back of his pick-up and drank kegs of beer with his friends every weekend? Move out and live life as a single mother, one of those droopy breasted women with broken glasses who pushed their Kool-Aid drenched babies around playgrounds in folding strollers and used baby wipes for everything? She hadn't had sex with anyone but her husband. Paulie and his predictable cock, rolling her over when she was already half asleep and couldn't wake up enough to muster any excitement for herself before he was finished. Those spasms of ecstasy and all the back arching and shuddering were beyond Theresa's grasp. An unsolvable riddle. Something thin and beautiful women experienced with tall, chiselled men. Deep down, Theresa felt deficient, physically somehow not fit enough to feel what they felt.

Anton came into the kitchen and looked over her shoulder. "There's one. Three million on Wellington Crescent. Seven bedrooms. Hey, we could all move in."

Theresa slapped the paper shut and stomped upstairs. It was a relief to get ready for work. Her freshly pressed outfit hung in the closet. Today was only the second time she was wearing it, a teal blazer and grey skirt. It made her feel very smart and sophisticated. She dressed with care, smoothed her skirt over her thighs and checked for panty lines. A little make-up and a squirt of Obsession and she returned to the kitchen to get her purse and keys. Anton had taken her chair at the table and was flipping through the classifieds. Paulie sat beside him, drumming his fingers on the table. They both looked up at her when she entered.

"What are you doing today?" She knew they wouldn't do any more on the basement until the insurance money came through.

"Probably work on the car, I guess," Paulie said. "Keep busy somehow. I'll check the job ads once Dad's done with the paper. Oh, I have a game tonight. Late. 11:30."

He had figured out to beat her to it. Besides, he really was going to check the ads. Antonina cracked pecans at the counter, her granite hands gripping the nutcracker and each crack amplifying the silence at the table. Theresa buttoned up her coat and smoothed her hair down. "Tell me when you have an earlier game, I might come watch sometime."

Theresa squeezed Paulie's hand as she leaned over and kissed Dustin who chewed a piece of bacon. "You be good with your Avó. Don't get that on my scarf."

"Adeus," said Antonina, not getting involved.

"Adios amigos," Theresa said.

In the car, Theresa's mind shifted to work. She had worked at the law firm for nearly four years. Last year they had moved the office from a strip mall on Sargent Avenue to a big building on Broadway. The location was more prestigious, being two blocks away from the law courts, and business had picked up as a result. In her work clothes, driving along Portage Avenue with a cup of coffee steaming beside her and a briefcase on the passenger seat, Theresa envisioned herself transformed into a role something like Christine, the young and talented lawyer on *The Young and The Restless;* someone who had important work to do and was paid a lot of money to do it.

She pulled her car into the parking spot reserved for her, number six, and stepped carefully out of the car onto the icy ground.

"Hey, Vera," Theresa said once she got inside. She hung her blazer on the back of her chair.

"Morning, Terri." Vera didn't look up. She was focused on a Free Cell game on her computer.

"What game are you playing?" Theresa turned on her computer.

"781," said Vera. She snapped her gum between her teeth. "I already reset it once."

A moment later, Theresa had the same game on her computer screen and was quickly clicking and dragging cards all over the screen. "Done," she shouted. She kicked her boots onto the floor and slipped into a pair of tan pumps.

"Damn," said Vera. On her desk she had a glass of water and a bottle of Motrin. Theresa watched her pop two pills into her mouth followed by a big drink of water. "They still working on the basement?"

"No. They're waiting for the insurance money. Thank God. Now Paulie is working on his car again. Don't ask me why."

"Men." Vera said and huffed. She wore her tinted glasses today. Her lipstick clumped on her dry lips and there were traces of it on her teeth too. Vera and her boyfriend BJ tied one on at least three times a week. "It's either get drunk and have sex, or fight," Vera explained. "There's no in-between with us."

There was a pile of documents on Theresa's desk which she had to tend to today as well as ten or eleven files which needed the accounting done and invoices sent out. She kept track of Larry's appointments and noticed he was expecting Tibor right at nine. Theresa cringed. Tibor must have been in some kind of legal trouble because he came to the office once a week to meet with Larry. He leered at both Theresa and Vera and everything he said, no matter what, was made unpleasant by the smell of his breath.

Theresa would be at her desk all day today, typing. That was her main skill. For that talent she earned eleven dollars an hour while Larry sat in his office and did God knows what and made three hundred dollars an hour. She got out once in awhile to run across the street to get Larry a sandwich, but mostly her days were spent at her desk, hunched at the computer or on the phone. Most of the work involved photocopying, faxing, phoning and typing. Theresa was good at it, organised and efficient and ahead of most deadlines. It helped motivate her to have a small crush on Larry. He was a great dresser and didn't shy away from the Drakkar Noir. She could smell it now, even with Larry across the room in his office. She tried to get Paulie to wear cologne one time but Anton wouldn't let up with the faggot jokes.

A dishevelled Larry stumbled through the door. He hit his shoulder on the doorjamb and walked towards Theresa rubbing his arm. Today he wore his pale blue shirt and yellow tie, an outfit Theresa didn't particularly like on him. She thought it made him look smarmy. She preferred him in white shirts with light coloured ties. Her crush on Larry was more of a distraction than an emotional attachment. Her fantasies about the two of them tangled on the floor of his office gave her a break from anticipating the long evenings at home listening to Rosa and Antonina mutter back and forth. She knew Larry loved his wife and quite often just when Theresa was off and dreaming of grabbing Larry by both butt cheeks, the phone would ring and she would turn beet red as she transferred his wife's call through to his office.

Vera fooled around with Larry's partner Marshall once and nearly quit her job because of it. Somehow, she ended up getting a raise to fifteen dollars instead. She had no explanation for that and largely steered clear of him now.

"Terri," Larry said. Only he and Paulie called her that. "Has Tibor called? I was expecting him at nine."

"No, no calls yet."

Larry always got worried when Tibor didn't show up on time. Some days he missed his appointment all together and that made Larry irritable and Theresa had to be extra pleasant for the rest of the day.

"I'll let him in when he gets here," Theresa said. Larry turned to go back in his office.

"Oh, I almost forgot," he said. "Next week sometime you're going to have to go down to the Wiltshire Hotel for me. I can't get anyone on the phone down there. The notices went up before Christmas and we have to make sure everyone there knows what's going on."

"What's going on there?" Theresa perked up at the thought of having something new and important to do.

"The place has been sold and slated for demolition. Everyone has to be out end of March and I have no idea if anyone down there knows that. Hell, I don't even know if anyone works there anymore."

Larry never asked her to do any field work. It was always him that went to these meetings with clients. Now he was asking Theresa to do some real legal work. The thought of carrying her briefcase into a meeting with a client and discussing the case sounded thrilling to her. Maybe this could even lead to a raise, if Larry started asking her to do more things like this.

"Sure, where is it?" She had never heard of the Wiltshire Hotel, but it sounded fancy.

"Up on Main Street." He loosened his tie. "Not the best part of town, so you might want to take a cab rather than risk getting your car ripped off."

He leaned against the door jam and crossed his legs, knowing full well the effect this *GQ* super-model pose had on his secretary. He may be a devoted husband, but he had his vanities too and liked to indulge once in awhile. A man feels much more confident when more than one woman thinks he's hot and he could tell by the way Theresa averted her gaze that he still did something to her.

Theresa fingered the buttons on her blouse nervously. "Is it safe for me to go at all? What if I get mugged or something?"

Larry chuckled. "It will be broad daylight. Get the taxi to wait for you. The guy you want to talk to is Perry Storch. He's the manager. Call ahead, make sure he's there and then go."

"Can't I just tell him on the phone?"

"It's better to do this in person so there can be no dispute later on. There's a couple of forms to sign. They should be happy they're getting evicted. The place is a dump."

He turned and went back into his office and Vera made a patting motion with her hand over her heart and threw a kiss after him. She grinned at Theresa who blushed and plugged the Dictaphone into her ears and turned her attention to her work.

Theresa and Vera worked back to back for the rest of the morning, pausing every hour or so to get coffee and play a game on the computer. At noon they leafed through the yellow pages and ordered lasagne and garlic bread from the pizza place down the street. They ate at their desks and ignored the phones when they rang. Theresa told Vera about the Wiltshire.

"Down on Main? There's a lot of hookers down there. All the streets are named after them."

"What? Are you serious? Why is Larry sending me down there?"

"He's probably afraid to go. He might get popped." Vera laughed at Theresa's expression. "Don't worry. It'll be daylight. The crazies only come out at night. You'll be fine."

For the rest of the afternoon, Theresa worried about her trip to the hotel. She would have no problem going to a nice hotel, or even a motel. But that part of Main Street was known for the bums and native people who were always high on gas or glue and would kill for it. She had no idea how best to prepare herself when she went.

Instead of driving straight home, Theresa took a long detour down Main Street so she could see the Wiltshire from her car. She locked her doors and drove north on Main Street. Traffic was heavy and huge amounts of exhaust chugged into the air from all the cars. The light was fading and the streetlights came on, instantly making everything seem darker. Theresa began to second guess her decision to drive down here in the dark, but there was no way to turn around. She followed the traffic past City Hall and the museum and into the run-down stretch of Main Street where she would find the Wiltshire Hotel.

Most of the buildings were boarded up. The sidewalks were lined with dirty snowbanks and not many people were outside. In one doorway sat a motionless figure, huddled deep in the corner. Theresa shuddered. If the drunks were passed out on the sidewalks, then the ones inside were sure to be awake and belligerent. People got stabbed along this stretch of Main Street all the time. Most of the incidents didn't even get coverage in the newspaper unless someone was killed and even then it was only an inch or so of space.

The Wiltshire was built with red brick, grimy and brown from layers of exhaust and dirt. The windows of the building were opaque with dust. It was impossible to tell what was going on inside and if she didn't know any better she would have assumed it was condemned and deserted already. A native man sat in the bus shelter in front and stared at her as the car crept past. She quickly looked away and so she failed to notice if there were any notices posted on the front door or not.

She circled around the back in time to see a skinny woman throw out the garbage. A cigarette dangled from her lips and she paid no attention to Theresa. The heavy steel door slammed shut behind her. Something must still go on there, Theresa thought, if there is garbage to be thrown out. Idle places wouldn't generate much garbage. She was curious about the woman. It didn't seem like the kind of place a woman would be safe. Maybe she was armed. Maybe they were all armed and Theresa would have to go in and have no way of protecting herself if someone pulled a gun from somewhere. It was a good thing they were tearing places like this down, she thought.

There was a black Monte Carlo parked in a spot reserved for the manager. It was spotless and gleaming, even the tires had been polished. The car seemed out of place behind such a dilapidated old place, but the sight of it put Theresa's mind somewhat at ease. At least the manager might turn out to be normal.

She navigated the car around the block and back onto Main Street and headed for home. It was a relief to turn onto Portage Avenue and see the big yellow B lit up at the Bay. Soon, she turned into her car port and saw the light from the kitchen. For a moment it felt good to be home. The image of the drunk in the doorway flashed through her mind as she hurried through the back yard towards the house.

* * * * *

Upstairs, Theresa clicked on the television on top of the dresser. Miguel was bringing Nikki a pitcher of iced tea into which she poured some gin when he wasn't looking. Nikki had started drinking again because Victor left her for a poor blind girl from the country. Poor Nikki.

Theresa wrestled with the dresser drawers. There was barely enough room between the bed and the dresser for her to get the drawers open. Dustin's crib took up one corner, then their bed and the dresser and that was all the space there was other than the chair in the corner that was forever heaped with clothing.

It was quiet downstairs and Paulie wasn't home yet so Theresa lay down on the bed and watched Nikki get drunk. It didn't strike Theresa as anything so terrible. Nikki drank three glasses of the gin-laced iced tea out of the pitcher and eased herself onto a day bed looking placid and content. Theresa decided to do the same.

She got off the bed and crept to the top of the stairs and listened. Antonina and Rosa had *The Price is Right* on in the living room and she could hear Dustin babbling. She stole downstairs and quietly took two cans of beer from the fridge. The entire bottom shelf was filled so they wouldn't be missed. Without the women noticing her, she crept back upstairs and plopped herself down on the bed. The first can opened with a satisfying hiss. She slurped the foam from the top and took a big gulp. Half way through she could feel the numbing pleasure in her thighs and at her temples. The rest of the beer went down easily. Theresa opened the second can, then settled amongst her pillows and watched the drama unfold on the television.

Now, there was a house. If Theresa had a dream house it was the Newman ranch. Nikki's living room was bigger than this whole house. And now that Victor was gone again, she had the whole thing to herself. One day, Theresa and Paulie would have a nice big house like that. With so much furniture it only got sat on when they threw a party or something. One day.

"Theresa, come downstairs and set the table." Rosa's voice jolted Theresa out of her daydream.

Theresa pretended not to hear. The beer had her feeling heavy and lazy. She stayed another five minutes and watched the end to the show. Nikki was about to stumble drunk into the pool, but that would have to wait until tomorrow.

"Theresa!"

"Good grief, I'm coming already." The kitchen smelled of fat and onion. It even smelled that way when they weren't cooking. "You know all that yelling is going to make me mental. Why do you always have to yell?"

"If I don't yell, nobody listens." Antonina replied. Theresa's voice was slightly slurred. Antonina gave her a suspicious look.

"What? I had a beer. Okay? Paulie and Anton drink all day long and never get any guff from you so don't give it to me." Theresa leaned heavily against the counter. Being drunk felt a lot different once you were on your feet. "I've had a long day."

There was a bucket of water on the floor with potatoes bobbing on the surface. Antonina cut a wedge of raw potato and gave it to Dustin who sat secured in his high chair.

"Raw potato? That's what you feed pigs. Give him a cracker or something." Theresa got the box of Ritz down. Behind her back, Antonina gestured feeding potato to Theresa as Rosa watched and covered her laughing face.

"He eats too many crackers. At least he has to chew a potato. Here, you want a piece."

"No, I'll wait till they're overcooked and salty. I'll have a cracker though."

Rosa poured coleslaw dressing on a large bowl of shredded cabbage and handed it to Theresa. "Here. You mix it up."

Theresa took the bowl and sat down at the table to toss the salad. Rosa worked around her setting the table. "Can't you do that over there?"

"There," Theresa said and plunked the bowl in the centre of the table. "I'm done. What are we having anyway? It smells funny."

"Kidneys and potatoes and beans."

"My favourite."

Antonina banged the pot on the stove and turned around. "You can make supper sometime. You make what you want and see how we like it."

"Maybe I will." Theresa moved the placemat in front of her and rested her head on her arms. "I'm so tired."

Antonina scowled.

Paulie came through the door. He clunked a bag from Canadian Tire down on the counter.

"What's in there? A carburetor?" Theresa lifted her head up. Antonina was smiling again. It was beginning to get on Theresa's nerves the way Paulie inched his way out to the garage every night after dinner to tinker on his car.

"As a matter of fact, it is a carburetor. Would you like to see it?"

"Sure, I'd love to see your new carburetor. You must be very proud." Theresa giggled sarcastically. "Maybe you can find a job at Canadian Tire in the carburetor department. I'm sure they could use a man like you."

Paulie put the car part on the table. Theresa reached for it and turned it over in her hands. "Hmm, I don't like the colour." She got up, knocking the chair backwards and went to the back door. She swung the door open and flung the carburetor into the snow.

"What the hell is wrong with you? That cost nearly two hundred bucks. Jesus." Paulie ran outside after it and scooped it out of the snow and brought it back inside.

Rosa and Antonina stared at Theresa while Paulie swore and tapped the snow off the package into the sink. Theresa didn't care. Her head felt like it was filled with lead and nothing that was going on made any sense anyway.

They sat down to supper and ate in silence. Theresa felt the start of a headache at her temples. After supper Rosa patted Theresa's hand. "You go up to bed. We'll play cards tomorrow night."

On some level, Rosa understood Theresa's frustration and sympathised with the situation. It was difficult to like her sometimes, but Rosa at least understood. Theresa nodded wearily and left the kitchen.

"She had beer," Antonina told Paulie as though drinking two beer was the most evil act imaginable. Paulie listened, a beer inches from his lips.

Rosa remained silent and went about clearing the table. Paulie put on his coat and took the carburetor out to the garage.

He turned on the light and pulled up the hood of the car. Slowly and precisely the engine was starting to look like an engine once again. He was anxious to get to the exterior. To grind down all the rust and make his baby lemon custard yellow once again. Most Barracudas were either orange or lemon. Some guys got theirs painted black, but the hardtop was already black and Paulie liked the contrast. But, first things first. If the thing didn't run, it wouldn't matter how pretty it looked, he'd never get twenty grand for it.

He could see his breath. The garage was heated, but not nearly as cosy as the house. He wore his quilted jacket liner and boots. There was a coffee maker and a mickey of Canadian Club stashed behind the charcoal briquettes. Everything a man needed to keep warm. He sat in the old armchair and warmed his hands by the heater. After a few belts of the whisky he got to work. There was still a lot to be done, but if he did a little everyday it would be done before they called him back in to work.

* * * * *

Theresa's head pounded and the high from the beer was replaced with a sense of loathing for everything under this roof. Her life had become dimmer, less lustrous than she imagined. What she had imagined for herself was something richer, more flashy and sleek. What she got was dull and stupid. She needed a jolt to rocket her into some other life. The trip past the hotel hadn't helped her mood much. She was not one to dwell on her good fortune and didn't like it when others less fortunate than her made themselves apparent. She wanted more and if other people had less she had a hard time being thankful. What a person wants is all relative.

She lay in bed and waited for the aspirin to take effect. Dustin breathed noisily in his crib.

Eventually, Paulie stumbled up the stairs and fell into bed drunk and naked, his hand clamped around his semi-hard penis. He wriggled in between Theresa's sleepy thighs and then, in the middle of a silent night, they made love. It was over moments after it had begun and they each rolled away from the other. A sad emptiness lay heavy on the bed between them, like some lost memory neither of them dared to recall.

Chapter Nine

Another grey day dawned and the traffic crawled sluggishly through the streets. Perry drove down Main Street with the remains of rush hour traffic. There was a Coke from yesterday in the cup holder. He lit a joint and listened to the radio. This morning he had to retrieve two dead fish from the aquarium and flush them down the toilet. Something always made him afraid they weren't really dead and would swim back up and he'd come home to find them breeding in the toilet bowl. The more he neglected those fish the more they seemed to thrive in the murky environment of the tank.

The light turned red and he eased the car to a stop. His mind was in synch with the bass line of a Pretenders song and he thought about the beach. Everybody loved to think of the beach at this time of year. Today he was going to work on a budget and think about how many staff he would need to hire for his venture and how little he could get away with paying them so that he could get stinking rich. Maybe he would give up the dealing all together. It wasn't as exciting as most people thought. There were no parties every night with people dropping by with bottles of gin and girls in skimpy clothes hanging around and packing the bong for you.

It was a drag waiting around and getting paranoid about everybody and being tied to a phone. At least he had

Tibor and Harv to do the dirty work. He didn't have to deal with the customers anymore. Pot smokers could be a big pain in the ass. The worst were the cokeheads who needed the pot to get them high before they came down, because coming down from coke was one of the most dismal experiences there was on the planet and people would do anything to avoid the confusion of reality hitting them between the eyes like a 747.

The bus in front of him spewed thick grey exhaust into the air and Perry instinctively held his breath. He turned down Bannatyne Avenue and pulled into the parking lot behind the hotel. The Doors were on the radio, "Love Her Madly", they sang. He turned off the ignition and sat in the car. He stared at the back of the hotel. The brick was nearly black from years of pollution battering at the walls. He wondered if he had it in him to be anything other than a drug dealer. Every single person he knew was a pot smoker. He couldn't turn around without getting a cloud of smoke blown in his face. The only kind of training he ever had was two years of wood shop in high school where he made five cutting boards and one sign for his aunt's needlepoint shop, Pins and Needles. He didn't even know how to fix the taillight on his car and had to take it to Canadian Tire where they told him his oil pan was leaking and his air filter was clogged and so a five dollar light bulb ended up costing him two hundred and fifty bucks.

He spit on a scuff on his shoe and wiped at it with his thumb. His thumb turned muddy brown and he instinctively wiped it on his pants and left a smudge on his left thigh. That's how it went. Even with the mild buzz he had going, he couldn't shake the funk he felt settling into his brain. Especially because he knew these funks always ended the same way: his supplier would call with some grade A weed from the mountains in BC and Perry knew if the grade was better, the price could be jacked up a bit because every pothead thought themselves a connoisseur and every connoisseur was willing to spend a bit more for a better product. So, Perry got caught in the circle. At least his job was easy. It was Tibor and Harv that had to put up with the customers, poring over every bud, twirling it under their noses like a cork from some bottle of French wine. Wanting to try some for free before they bought it. Then telling them, "Hey man, that wasn't Purple you sold me last time. It tasted more like Time Warp. What do you have today?" Like they know better than the dealers what's in the Zippy bag. God, the drug trade had become elitist somewhere along the way. People weren't satisfied anymore just to get the stuff. Tibor had a lawyer he sold to and the guy dropped everything when he showed up and spent ages picking through the buds. The customer was becoming demanding. That's why Tibor and Harv loved the kids so much. They could sell them shake with a few leaves thrown in and the kids would go away happy.

It was good to have something else on the go. Something that was just for him and didn't involve breaking the law and relying on his friends to make his money. A legitimate business proposition. He was just waiting for the right person. Someone with a bit of a nest egg they might want to invest in a sure winner. He kicked the car door open and stepped out into the parking lot. The back of the hotel loomed up above him, casting a dark and cold shadow across the pavement. He liked the feeling of the fabric of his new pants against his legs, the way it swished against his skin. It immediately gave him a sensation of power. People should pay more attention to the fabric they wear, he thought. It can really make a difference in your mood.

* * * * *

Carmen had her head buried in the freezer, a bucket of sudsy water on the floor beside her. A large fly buzzed laconically by the windowsill. There were always one or two super flies which survived the deep freeze of winter and emerged sometime after Christmas to languish in the weak rays of the sun.

"Morning, Carmen," Perry said, unbuttoning his leather jacket. His eyes fell on Carmen's behind and took it in a moment.

"Hey Perry," she said righting herself. She pushed her bangs out of her eyes. "Someone called earlier and asked for you and I have a weird feeling it was the health inspector so I thought I better get things cleaned up in here."

"Sure, sounds good. I'll be in my office."

"Are you expecting Harv and Tibor today? I don't want anything going down while the health inspector is here."

"No, I doubt they'll be by. I've got some other stuff to work on. Call me if you need me."

Perry hustled through the bar and went to his office. He reached into the fridge and fished out a Mountain Dew. The lights flickered and buzzed as they came on. He breathed the musty air and smoothed his tie. Today he was going to accomplish something. He turned on the computer. While it was booting up, he took all the cash out of the safe. Nearly two thousand dollars. Perry laid it out on the desk, counted it and put it neatly in his wallet. Money made all the difference in the world. Those people who said money didn't matter probably never held two grand in their sweaty little hands before. The indoor beach folder lay under some magazines on his desk, still empty. His enthusiasm for the idea seemed to depend on the amount of THC in his system. He held it a moment, ready to trash it and then decided to keep it awhile longer. Give it some more thought when he had the energy for creative thoughts.

He sat, staring at the computer screen, feeling the thickness of the cash in his pocket. He flipped to the business section of the paper and read the headlines about mergers and take-overs and billionaires in Japan. He scanned the columns of tiny numbers in the daily closing rates. It was a complex code. One he didn't have the patience to try to understand today. Not when there was another code he had a deeper understanding of. And rather than reading about making money, he could go out, have a few beers and actually make some money. He grabbed his jacket and went back to the kitchen.

"If Harv and Tibor show up, tell them to come back tomorrow. I'm going to the casino."

"Are you coming back here today?"

"Maybe. If I make a million then I'll be back to give you half."

"That'll be the day."

"It happens you know. People win big on the slots. It's what keeps them coming by the busload."

"No, I mean you sharing some of your money. That's what'll be the day."

Perry pulled his wallet out and flicked two twenties onto the table. "There. How's that for generosity."

Carmen smiled to herself. There was no new Perry. He was the same self-congratulatory, scheming rat he had always been, just better smelling and better dressed.

"Thanks Stork," she said. It was the least she could do after he handed her forty dollars for nothing.

"You're welcome. See you later."

Carmen went back to her scrubbing and Perry steered the car towards the casino.

* * * * *

Donald had finally chosen his time. Today was to be the day that he revealed to the ignorant masses at the Wiltshire Hotel their fate. His heart pounded with excitement as he dressed to go. The notice was crumpled in his coat pocket, where he checked for it repeatedly, in case he needed proof, because they probably wouldn't believe him when he told them. They were thick in that way and he fully expected some resistance to the idea that their existence was about to cease.

For a couple of weeks he came and went, enjoying the secret and choosing his time to spring it on them. It was only fun for a while and then it got boring. There were no inexplicable events happening that left everyone scratching their heads wondering what was going on. Nothing for Donald to grin about or gloat over. In fact, he couldn't see any indication at all that the hotel was going to be destroyed. Everyone was as complacent as ever. They sat there endlessly, as though time meant nothing and would sit there until the very day they came with the bulldozers, tripping to oblivion, they would tumble into the rubble heap still swirling their coffee and humming a meaningless tune.

The whole night previous, Donald sat on his bed eating slice after slice of bologna and gulping down cream soda and went through them one by one. Ruby probably wouldn't get it and if she did, wouldn't care. She was too tough to be a woman. News like that wouldn't phase her. Donald suspected she had been through much worse. Once the hotel was gone she would end up in some other hotel and not even know where she was. There was no sense in telling her. With a secret this good, he wanted a reaction and Ruby would glance at him like he was nuts and get right back to her bags of garbage.

Carmen would immediately worry about Walter and Donald wanted her to stop her fussing over Walter. Telling Carmen would be no fun at all.

Darren never spoke and Donald wasn't sure if Darren would fly out of his seat, grab him by the collar and slam him up against the wall or just fall asleep. He wasn't about to find out what creature lurked behind those dull eyes.

Perry, the weasel, the two-bit drug dealer. Donald didn't trust Perry. He might keep the information to himself and use it later for his own gain. And that left Walter who had been Donald's first choice all along.

He hardly slept. The scene played itself over and over in his head all night long. Every time he got to the part where the news registered on Walter's horny-toad face, Donald howled with laughter and had to press his hand over his hernia so it wouldn't bulge out any further. Hopefully, he would have a moment with Walter all to himself.

So, he had chosen today for no other reason than he was about to burst if he didn't tell someone soon and besides, that place was getting dull, duller, dullest. Everyone sat in the same spot, the television tuned to the same channel. Everyone wore the same thing. Even Perry's suits were repeating now. The days resembled one another with uncanny precision. Anyone peeking through the windows from the outside for a full week would quickly lose track.

* * * * *

At the same time that Donald was buckling up his galoshes, getting ready to change the course of history, Theresa was listening to Larry as she got ready to go.

"Just get the guy to sign the papers and leave. The taxi will wait for you. It shouldn't take more than half an hour there and back. An hour, tops."

Theresa waited inside the door until the taxi pulled up. They drove up Main Street. The distant sky was grey, more snow on the way. Winter had a way of blasting its way in on the prairies over and over again. The wind from the north had a cruel arctic bite. The woman who had answered the phone at the Wiltshire said she expected Mr. Storch in today and so Theresa hoped to be back at the office before noon.

She watched out the window as the taxi took the same route she had taken the other day. It looked much grimmer in the daylight with more decay and garbage visible. There were more people around too, shuffling and weaving along the sidewalks in groups, wearing dirty clothes and no hats. In front of one hotel a fight had broken out between two women. A man with no front teeth stood by and laughed at them. Theresa hoped that nothing was going on outside the Wiltshire. She noticed a slight trembling in her hands and wrung them together to make it stop. The cab swung around to the other side of the street.

"Here you are," the driver said.

Theresa peered out the window at the building. "This is it?"

"The Wiltshire Hotel. Winnipeg's finest." The cabbie clicked off the meter. "Seven-fifty. You want me to wait for you?"

"No," she said, her voice wavering. "I'm not sure how long I'll be." She handed the driver his fare and stepped out onto the street.

* * * * *

Donald set off towards the hotel, taking his usual route up Elgin, making his way to Old Market Square and then cutting across behind the Leland Hotel. He rounded Main Street just in time to see Theresa step from the cab onto the curb. He eyed her curiously, clearly a stranger to these parts of town. Was she getting out at the hotel? It was hard to tell with the wind making his eyes tear up.

It was not until this juncture that it occurred to Donald that someone else might know about the hotel. He immediately did not trust the woman who stood in front of the hotel and scanned the door from top to bottom. She carried with her a slim, tan briefcase and wore dressy boots and a long coat. She must be the real estate agent. Donald broke into a murderous trot as he realized he was about to be scooped.

Theresa stared at the front of the Wiltshire Hotel. Up close the decay was even more apparent, with entire chunks of brick gone. It was a wonder no one ever got hit on the head with flying debris. The street was littered with shards of broken glass and Final Net hairspray bottles. A single light bulb shone in the lobby. The hotel's name was spelled out in gold and black stencil in the window above the door. The door handle was reinforced with a plate of steel and the window was covered with a metal cage. For Theresa the concern was more with getting out alive than with getting in. There was no notice posted, as Larry said there would be. An oversight long forgotten and buried by some city worker. Theresa braced herself to be the bearer of the news. A cluster of people shuffled towards her and Theresa hastened to get inside.

Out of nowhere a man appeared as Theresa reached for the door handle and startled her so much that a high pitched yelp escaped her. Huffing and wheezing he lunged for the door and wrenched it open, glaring at her before he lurched into the hotel and left Theresa standing on the sidewalk as the door swung shut.

She took a deep breath. Just another Main Street crazy, she thought, trying to reassure herself. Nobody else was around. Nothing to do but get inside.

The door to the hotel was heavy and dragged on the floor where grooves had been etched into the floor over time. She gave it a push to get it to close again. Her heels echoed on the tile floor as she made her way down the hall. Through the doorway to the bar she glimpsed a few people, one of whom was the man who nearly knocked her off her feet at the front door. All eyes were on her. They were waiting for her to come in and explain her business.

The manager's office was just past the bar and so she walked past the staring eyes thinking that would be the most likely place to find Mr. Storch. The door was closed and she couldn't see inside because of the frosted window. She knocked twice and got no reply. The place was silent except for the sound of the television coming from the bar. She didn't hear any voices even though there were at least three or four people in there. Haltingly, she trod towards the room.

She pushed open the door and peeked inside. They had been expecting her. Everyone in the place had their gaze riveted to her face. As she let her eyes roam around she saw that there was an old native woman at one table and an old miner or something seated at another. None of them seemed to have anything to do with the other and each had an assortment of stuff strewn across their table. Right now their attention was on her. They waited, not taking their eyes off her, for Theresa to speak.

It was alarming and she didn't know what to make of these people. She eased her way into the room and stood leaning up against the door behind her. Thankfully, the waitress then appeared through the kitchen doors. It was the same woman Theresa saw the other night throwing out the garbage. She carried a plate of eggs over to the Klondike man and placed an identical plate in front of the other man. When she spied Theresa standing frozen by the door Carmen said, "Health inspector, right? I had a feeling you'd be dropping by today. Come on in. Everything's spotless."

"Um, no," Theresa sputtered. "I am actually here to see the manager. Mr. Perry Storch."

"He's not here." Carmen said in a dismissive tone, now that Theresa turned out not to be the health inspector and

Carmen had busted her butt all morning getting the grime out from behind the fridge.

"But when I called someone told me he was here."

"That was over two hours ago and at that time Mr. Perry Storch was in and now he is out."

Theresa tried to ignore the hint that she was being hustled back out the door. It wasn't up to them if they wanted her here or not. It was a public place and she had every right to be standing in their space. It wasn't like she had invaded their living room during a wake or something. Besides, she was here on official business.

Carmen busied herself cutting up the toast for Walter, who Theresa now noticed was horribly crippled with arthritis.

"Do you know when he might be back? I'm with the legal firm handling the sale of the building; Taylor and Lambert."

"You a lawyer?" Carmen gave her a sceptical look. If this woman was a lawyer, she had on pretty cheap boots.

"Yes," Theresa said. "I'm a lawyer." She wanted this skinny woman to stop sneering at her. It made her uneasy and Theresa didn't know why she already had everyone's guard up.

"You can wait if you want. He just went out to get me some change." Carmen wasn't about to tell this lawyer that Perry was at the casino. It was still part of her job to cover for him. She would probably wait ten minutes and then Carmen could apologise and get her out the door. "Have a coffee if you like."

Theresa looked around for a safe place to sit. The people didn't look that dangerous and the coffee smelled fresh and inviting.

"Okay, I'll wait a few minutes." She didn't want to have to come back "Maybe you can help me. We need to know how many people live and work here."

Carmen gave her a puzzled look. "Wait a minute. Did you say the hotel was being sold?"

"Well, I'm really supposed to deal with Mr. Storch. There was supposed to be a notice on the door but it must have been forgotten."

"Jesus Christ."

In the corner, Donald gasped and then coughed spasmodically. Both women turned their heads to see if he was all right. He sputtered and waved them off.

"Maybe I will wait for Mr. Storch. If you think he'll be right back."

"Make yourself at home. I'll get you a coffee."

The waitress was thawing a bit. Theresa sat at the end of the bar and faced the room. She noticed Walter cupping his coffee with those gnarled hands and wondered how he looked after himself. The other man had stopped coughing and now stared hard at Theresa from the two tables he occupied. One had bits of paper strewn across it and the other one he used for food. A plate with the hardening remains of the breakfast special sat next to him. The man was mad about ketchup. Theresa averted her eyes. Even if he was crazy, he was freaking her out a bit with those buggy eyes and insane glare. What had she done to him?

Carmen poured a coffee from behind the bar. "So, the old fart finally decided to unload the place. I know, I know. You can't say anything. Just tell me. How long do we have here?"

"Well, that's what was supposed to be on the notice," Theresa said. "Some mistake at city hall. They'll be getting a call from me about that."

Theresa hoped she sounded like she had some authority. She noticed Carmen waiting for an answer. "I really shouldn't say too much but I guess if the notice had gone up like it was supposed to you would know anyway.

You all have to be out by the end of March. They're tearing the whole thing down."

"Wow." The news was sinking in and Carmen lit another cigarette. "You smoke?"

"No thanks. Sorry to be the bearer of bad news."

"Aw, shit. Everything will work out. I really am not surprised though." Her gaze and her thoughts drifted out the front window. Out by March. That was still a few months away. Anything could happen in that time. Was it for real this time? One thing was for sure. This was the first time a lawyer came to deliver the news. Before it was always just Perry spouting some gossip from the dude in the Bahamas. Tearing the whole thing down. It was hard to imagine.

"What's he doing over there?"

Donald was frantically snipping up a magazine and Theresa couldn't figure out what on earth he was up to. At least he had stopped staring.

"Donald? He's working on his pictures. Comes every day and makes himself at home. Eats his meals here. Goes home after four sometime." She wiped down the counter in front of Theresa. A cigarette smouldered in the ashtray with an ash at least an inch long.

The place was strangely fascinating to Theresa. She watched the man whittle pictures out of his magazines with a large pair of scissors. Beside him was one of those clear bottles of glue with a red nipple where the glue came out. He worked with the diligence of a five year old, rarely looking up to see what was going on around him. The next thing Theresa expected to see was liberal sprinklings of green and gold glitter. Over in the corner the other one's eyes darted around the room over the rim of his coffee cup which he held in both hands up to his mouth. Coffee stained the front of his shirt. It was like day camp, Theresa thought, for down and out old people. Maybe next time she could bring Antonina with her for a plate of runny eggs and thin coffee. It wasn't much different from what she expected the place to look like. A beam of light struggled through the dusty window and illuminated the dust and smoke swirling in the air. The brown carpet was hard and worn. Everything looked sticky, the tables, chairs, door knobs. A greasy film clung to everything and Theresa was sure she would be stuck to her chair when the time came for her to get up. It was a good thing she wasn't the health inspector.

"What about him?" Theresa pointed at Walter.

"Walter? He lives upstairs. Has forever."

Walter had not taken his eyes off Theresa and he was staring at her now as Carmen spoke. It was unnerving the way these loopy street people stared, as if they wanted to infuse some of their lunacy into her before she left.

"Hello," she said, since she was talking about him and he knew it. Some kind of trance was broken and abruptly he got to his feet and headed for the door.

"Walter, where are you going?" Carmen called after him.

"Upstairs. I gotta get upstairs. There's something stifling in the air down here." He glared at Theresa and heaved the door open.

"All right then. I'll see you tomorrow."

"If you're lucky."

They watched him disappear around the corner.

"That was weird," said Theresa.

"Not really. He's a paranoid little man and we don't get visitors in here often. You freaked him out, that's all. Don't worry about it." Carmen stubbed out her cigarette. "I gotta get back to work. Stay as long as you like. He should be back soon, but sometimes he gets sidetracked."

The Young and Restless came on the television and Theresa forgot all about Walter and turned her chair to watch. She became absorbed in the affair Jack and Ashley were having behind Brad's back. Theresa came to the end of her coffee and the end of the show and still there was no sign of Perry. No sign of Carmen either who had stepped into the kitchen and not come back out. Perhaps it was time to leave. The man with the pictures hadn't stirred for awhile. Theresa pulled her coat on and tiptoed out. The news was delivered. She had done her job. Tomorrow she would return and finalize things with this Mr. Storch.

Chapter Ten

Theresa got back to the office just before noon. This was the quietest time of year along Broadway. The last of the hot dog vendors packed up around Halloween and they didn't usually return until the snow had melted away. Now there were only three foot snowbanks in their place. All summer long this was the place to eat. Along the tree lined sidewalks of Broadway at noon the office buildings spilled out hundreds of men and women, tired from their mornings inside under the harsh lights. They lifted their faces to the sun and breathed in the smell of fresh air and grilled franks. They mingled on the cement risers, sipped 7Up and chewed on their foot-longs, the men in their suits and the women in short skirts. It was an al fresco pick up joint. Many affairs began alongside the fresh cut chip wagon.

Now there was only the Subway where they could step out for sandwiches. Theresa went in and ordered a meatball sub and a bag of ripple chips. She felt hungry and a bit over-stimulated from her morning. She spied Larry and Marshall hustling across the street. They got in line behind her.

"How'd things go this morning?" Larry asked as he viewed the menu even though he must have known it by heart.

"He wasn't there. I had to sit in that dingy place and drink three day old coffee out of a chipped cup that could have been washed in the toilet for all I know and wait for the guy. He never showed and now I have to go back."

The guys ordered their sandwiches and turned to Theresa. Hunger was sharp at this time of day and they couldn't focus on much other than their food.

"There's only that Mr. Storch and the waitress who work there and one old man who lives there. How can that place be making any money? Half of it is boarded up already. I mean, there were other people there, but they were the day people, making crafts and staring into space. It's weird, I tell you. I feel like I've been to the twilight zone."

Larry smiled and his eyes crinkled in that way Theresa liked so much, even though she knew he was half laughing at her. She sat at a booth and unwrapped her sandwich. Vera appeared from the bathroom and resumed drinking her coffee. She pulled her sweater coat tight around her. She had her sunglasses on even though the sky was overcast.

"How did it go this morning?" she asked.

"I have to go back in the morning. The guy wasn't there."

"Typical," said Vera, eyeing Marshall and Larry as they ate their meals.

* * * * *

Later, back at the office, Tibor finally showed up for Larry. His hair was unwashed and he had spilled something down the front of his jacket. Theresa cringed when she saw him. His fingers were yellow from tobacco and he never tied the laces to his giant basketball runners. He made Theresa uncomfortable even when he wasn't around. The dread of his walking through the door at any time was a stress she would rather not deal with. He tromped in and didn't bother to speak until he was at Larry's closed door. "He in here?" he grunted at Theresa.

"Just a second. I'll see if he's busy." She hated the way he waltzed into Larry's office as though he were the one and only client and took some small pleasure in making him wait. He never made direct eye-contact with her and made no attempt to be personable or pleasant. He probably knew how uneasy he made her and revelled in it. She didn't even know what he was doing here. Larry never asked her to prepare anything or type up any paperwork for him. Maybe he was a black sheep brother who Larry gave money to.

"Send him in," Larry said with that same relieved look he always had when Tibor arrived. It was really the strangest thing and Theresa could not figure it out. She went back to her desk, relieved that for the rest of the week she wouldn't have to worry about Tibor coming through the door.

* * * * *

Antonina glanced at Theresa when she came in the back door and headed directly for the refrigerator.

"Don't you ever leave the kitchen?" Theresa asked from inside the refrigerator.

"There's lots of work to do, feeding everybody." She was hunched over a pot of water that sat on the floor between her feet, her elbows rested heavily on the tops of her thighs as slices of carrot cascaded into the pot from the deft hands. This was the way she mostly sat, hunched over some sort of work. Later in the evening she would sit by the television under the light of a lamp and darn socks from a basket by her feet. Everyone was welcome to place their tattered socks into the basket. It was the first time Theresa ever encountered anyone who darned socks and she learned to put her socks in the basket rather than the garbage, because Antonina would retrieve them and mend them and then they would appear all fixed up on their bed in the evening.

It was true about the time she spent in the kitchen though. When Theresa left in the morning, Antonina was usually peeling potatoes for lunch and when she got home, there she was in the same chair, scraping carrots. There always seemed to be a pot of water boiling on the stove and one on the floor by her feet. Antonina's brow was bathed in perspiration sixteen hours a day.

Theresa's head was stuck in the fridge as she rummaged around for the Cheese Whiz. Antonina eyed her bottom and thought not so kind thoughts. Theresa found the Cheese Whiz behind a bowl of boiled eggs.

"Guess what I did today, Avó." Theresa was excited to tell someone about her day and Antonina was the only person home.

"What?" The pot on the stove bubbled furiously and droplets of water spattered and hissed onto the element.

"I had coffee with some homeless people today. Downtown in an old hotel. What do you think about that?" Theresa fixed a few pieces of celery with Cheese Whiz and arranged them on a plate. Antonina didn't seem to have heard her.

"You'll spoil you supper," said Antonina, knowing that no amount of celery and cheese spread would spoil Theresa's supper.

"No, you'll spoil my supper with all that salt. What are you boiling up for us tonight? Pig knuckles."

Antonina scowled at Theresa. She understood more than Theresa knew. "There's nothing wrong with salt. You Americans say you don't like salt or fat or sugar but you make artificial salt and fat and sugar, so you must like something. Maybe you can make supper tonight."

"Well, you have a point I guess. Yeah, I'll make a nice supper. You'll love it." Theresa crunched down on her celery and chewed quickly. She was starving. "You haven't said anything about my day."

"You didn't go to work?"

"It was work. I had to go downtown to an old hotel and tell the people it was going to be torn down."

"What?" Antonina furrowed her brow. She had a hard time understanding most of what Theresa said. The girl spoke so fast and even if she slowed down, it was hard to figure out her point.

"Why don't you ever listen to an English station?" Theresa said, meaning the little radio the women listened to, tuned into the Portuguese station all day long. "You might learn something."

"You listen long enough, you learn something too."

"We live in Canada. There's no reason for me to learn Portuguese, por favor."

Antonina started to say something else but Theresa had her mouth full and was halfway up the stairs. Whenever Theresa felt like the odd one out, she thought of Antonina. At least Paulie had chosen her. It wasn't like Rosa and Anton had much choice but to bring the old lady along to Canada. No wonder Antonina lived to rule. There was definitely a strange dynamic in the house, what with Rosa living under the watchful eye of her mother-in-law and then Theresa, subject to both of them; a mother-in-law double whammy.

Theresa knew deep down inside Rosa was on her side. Out of everyone in the house, Rosa seemed to understand how she felt. Maybe she didn't always show it, since she was still, after all these years trying to prove herself worthy of that slob, Anton, but there were times when compassion was transmitted in Theresa's general direction. Usually when Rosa sat soaking her feet and her guard was down. Who was she supposed to side with? The daunting, judging mother-in-law or the struggling to please daughter-in-law? Somehow Anton and Paulie remained oblivious, surrounded by doting wives and mothers and grandmothers, all of whom felt caught in the middle by some unseen net. Three people in the same boat could cause a lot of upset.

* * * * *

Antonina eyed the Cajun spice mix with some suspicion.

"That's all?" She said, pointing a crooked finger at the salad.

"What do you mean? There's chicken that goes with it. Hot, spicy chicken."

"Chicken and salad? That's all?"

"It's called Cajun Chicken Caesar salad. It's from another country. I'm going to warm some buns too. What else do you want?"

"The men won't feel full with salad. They need some more. Boil some potatoes." Antonina fidgeted in her chair. It was torture for her, to sit by and watch someone else cook. The things Theresa cooked were too far out for Antonina's palate. There were always additions and modifications. When Theresa made vegetarian lasagne, Rosa threw some minute steaks in a frying pan after Antonina whispered frantically in her ear that there wasn't going to be any meat. When she made tortellini with pesto sauce they all hated it and had red snapper instead. Now, Theresa found herself heaving the giant pot onto the stove and peeling potatoes so there would be plenty of starch and something to throw some salt on when they all sat down to dinner.

"You always hate what I cook. You complain when I don't cook and you complain when I do. There's no pleasing you. It's good for you to try something new for a change.

What kind of life is that when you won't even try a different way of cooking chicken? Sheesh."

Antonina shook her head and muttered something in Portuguese.

"Are you swearing at me? I wish you'd speak English once in awhile."

Antonina made a derisive noise in her throat and stared out the window. Her fascination with warm chicken served on cold salad overcame her and she reached over and helped herself.

"You like it?"

Antonina chewed the way she did when she wiggled fish bones to the front of her mouth. "That's supposed to be cheese?"

Theresa dipped her little finger into the Caesar dressing and held it out to Antonina. "Here, try this."

Antonina tentatively stuck out her tongue. Her mouth puckered and she smacked her tongue to get rid of the taste. She took another bite of her celery stick.

When time came for supper, Antonina took one bite of her chicken, gasped and bolted to the sink. Tears streamed down her reddened face. She ran the cold faucet full bore and spit repeatedly into the sink. Dustin chortled at the sight of her scooping water into her mouth and letting it run out again. She leaned heavily on her elbows and turned to shake her head at Theresa.

"Okay, I get it. No more Cajun chicken."

"What are you trying to do," Anton said. "Kill the old lady?"

"It's not that spicy. It's just a mix." Theresa helped herself to what was left of Antonina's plate. The kettle boiled. Antonina soothed her scorched windpipe with peppermint tea.

After supper Rosa and Theresa sat at the clean kitchen table and played Crazy Eights. Paulie was at hockey.

Watch you don't fall

Upstairs Antonina gave Dustin his bath and the splashing could be heard all through the house. Rosa had her feet soaking in a tub of warm water and Epsom salts. There was a piece of frozen chocolate mousse cake in the fridge leftover from dessert that Theresa was trying to ignore. She hovered between ten and fifteen pounds overweight. It was what happened after women gave birth. Sometimes they never regained their figures and Theresa thought she was one of those. No matter how hard she tried, the food always won.

"Do you want to split that cake with me?" she asked Rosa who was shuffling the cards.

"Yeah, get it out. We'll share it."

Theresa brought the cake to the table with two forks and the women each took bites in turn until it was finished. Rosa didn't care about her weight. Her breasts alone probably weighed thirty pounds. She liked to sit with her arms folded and her breasts resting on them so that they were completely concealed. Theresa decided that until the day came when she found herself heaving her breasts up onto folded arms, she would not consider herself fat.

"You have to go back to that old hotel tomorrow?"

"Yeah, one more time to finish things up. The guy I was supposed to see wasn't there."

"Well, you be careful down there. There's bad people in that part of town. I see it on the news all the time." Rosa picked her feet up out of the warm water and rubbed them dry with a pink towel.

"The people I saw today couldn't hurt a flea. I swear, it was like day care for old people. They should all be in nursing homes, not bars. It's not very stimulating for them. All they do is stare out the window and watch television all day. No wonder half of them talk to themselves."

"They are crazy people?" Rosa asked, a bit fascinated that Theresa would have witnessed insanity first hand.

"Sure, I guess kind of crazy. Not in a bad way though. More like they forgot whatever it was they were supposed to be doing and ended up in this hotel and started to make things up as they went along and pretended everything was normal. Maybe if you do that long enough it becomes normal. That's why crazy people don't care that they're crazy, because they all think they're perfectly normal. Heck, the way they were looking at me today, I thought I was the crazy one."

Rosa laughed at that, baring her overlapping teeth. And Theresa laughed too. Crazy, she thought and shook her head.

Chapter Eleven

They were all there again, the next day when Theresa arrived at the hotel; the big man and the crippled man, Walter. There was an old native woman there today too with cigarette butts spilling out of a coffee tin. The stench of old ashes reached Theresa's nostrils and made them pucker. The big man was asleep in his chair, the same plate of cold breakfast beside him. He hadn't yet started on his pictures. Walter snoozed in his corner and hadn't noticed her entrance. "Well, you're back," Carmen said in an almost welcoming tone. "He's in today. I'll go let him know you're here. Help yourself to a coffee."

"Thanks," said Theresa, smiling broadly. The place felt more familiar. She was proud of herself for shaking her fear from the other day. She even sat down at her place along the bar and waited for Carmen to return. A large figure appeared at the door and stared right at her. He had stringy long black hair and wore a pair of potentially lethal cowboy boots. His eyes drooped from what Theresa assumed was drugs or glue. She cleared her throat and said in a shaky voice, "Hello, are you Mr. Storch?" She couldn't believe this was the man she was supposed to deal with. A cackle arose from behind her. The native woman was just about to keel over from laughing and Theresa realized she had made a mistake. "Sorry," she said to the man who still stood and stared. Theresa frowned. "I made a mistake. Sorry."

He nodded once and went to sit at a table by the window. There was still no sign of Carmen and Theresa was getting nervous. She didn't want that huge native man to pull a knife out from somewhere and go berserk. But, he sat quite still at his table and did nothing and that was just fine by her. She kept her eye on the door, listening for the sound of Carmen's footsteps, willing her back into the room.

* * * * *

Stork had Tibor and Harv in his office. Water lay in gritty puddles all over the floor where they had tracked it in on their shoes. They were annoyed with him because he wasn't letting them light up this morning. Carmen had told him about the lawyer and the hotel. He was worried she would show up again today and he wanted to get these guys out of his office before that happened. He was supposed to be the manager here and it wouldn't do much good to have Tibor and Harv in his office for no reason. Dressed the way they were it would be hard enough to explain even without the pot smoke in the air.

He had to explain to them the whole deal about the hotel even though he was waiting to hear it straight from this lawyer or whatever she was. Hopefully she would have legs like Michelle Pfeiffer. Hell, if she had anything of Michelle Pfeiffer's that would be awesome. Tibor and Harv didn't seem to care. They were still giddy over Perry's suits.

He checked his watch. All the baggies of weed on his desk were making him jittery along with Tibor and Harv sitting in there like a couple of high school drop-outs. The discussion about dress code was over. They sat and stared at him, not knowing if he was kidding or not. "I don't have any clothes like that," Harv said. "You want us to wear suits to sell pot?"

"Who's going to trust us wearing suits when they come to meet us behind a gas station? I think we dress just fine." The two of them waved their arms around gesturing like it meant something. It was making Perry crazy. He was getting nowhere. If he had his way he would get rid of them and get two new guys and train them from the ground up. But Tibor and Harv had been with him since the beginning. They were the only guys he could trust. It would take ages to build up the same level of trust with somebody new.

"You could wear a suit when you go to that lawyer's place. What do they think when you come in there looking like that?"

"They think I'm a client," Tibor said, sucking on a toothpick.

"All right, all right. Stay in your BMX shirts and jungle pants. I'll wear the suits." He slapped his hand on the top of the desk, trying to exude some sort of authority in their general direction.

Carmen tapped on the door and poked her head in. "That lawyer's here."

He sat bolt upright in his chair. "What does she look like?"

"Oooh, she's a hottie." Carmen grinned. Right away Tibor and Harv perked up. "Kind of a cross between Marilyn Monroe and Pamela Anderson. Should I send her in?"

Perry scooped up the baggies and shoved them at Harv. "Come on. Get this stuff out of here."

"You gonna try to get it on with the lawyer?" Harv whooped.

"She's here for me to sign some papers, okay? And if there's time I might discuss a business proposition with her."

149

"Yeah, right. You're all serious business now," Tibor said.

Perry grinned. "And if there's still time and I like what I see, yeah, I might get nasty with her too."

"I knew you hadn't changed that much," Tibor slapped him on the back. "See you later man."

"Yeah, I'll get Jeeves to bring the car around." Harv said, trying to sound English but not even coming close. "See ya, Stork."

"Excellent," Tibor said.

The guys stuffed the bags into their pockets until they bulged. Perry shook his head. It was a wonder they didn't get caught. One bag fell out of Harv's pocket on the way out and Tibor kicked it across the floor in time for Harv to step on it and squish it. "That'll be one for the kiddies," Harv said. He scooped it up and jammed it back into his pocket. He squawked twice and then they were gone.

"Shit," Perry muttered. He lowered himself into his chair and smoothed out his pants. Something told him to be ready for anything. He tried to think if he ever had met a lawyer before. They weren't exactly in his social circle. All he could think was how much money they made. Lawyers were even bigger scammers than drug dealers. He wished he had a view of the parking lot to see what she was driving. He wondered if he could get some money out of her somehow. See if she wanted some pot. He could overcharge her by some ridiculous margin.

* * * * *

Walter woke up and saw Theresa sitting there. He yelped in fright. She had slipped in without him knowing. Theresa's cup clattered onto the saucer. She whirled around and blurted out, "Why did you shout like that? You gave me a heart attack." Flustered and annoyed she gulped the rest of her coffee, thankful she hadn't spilled it everywhere. "What kind of a person yells like that?"

Walter's face turned ghostly white. He stared hard at Donald, who hadn't budged from his spot with all the shrieking going on. Theresa ignored him and wiped up the coffee.

It was immediately apparent to Carmen that something was not right. Walter sat paralysed in his corner, his mouth open and his eyes wild. The room was oddly silent, absent was the usual hum and clatter of scissors, cups and cutlery.

"What the hell is going on down here? What's the matter with Walter?" Carmen said. Walter's hands shook as his eyes moved from Theresa to Donald and back and forth and his mouth bobbed open and closed like a fish.

"I think I might have upset him when he woke up and saw me here. I nearly spilled coffee everywhere."

"Well, that might explain it," Carmen said. "He's not very fond of strangers." Usually it was Donald who upset Walter, but he was fast asleep in his chair. Maybe that lawyer had upset him again. You never knew with Walter what would set him off.

"What's happened to you now, Walter?" Carmen approached him with some caution.

His breakfast was half eaten, his beard littered with crumbs and egg.

"Look at him. He's a goner. That woman did something to him. Came in here and put a spell on him." Spittle flew from Walter's mouth.

"Walter, get a hold of yourself. He's sleeping. If I had a dollar for every nap you all took in these chairs, I'd be a rich woman. Hey Donald. Look alive." Carmen went over and shook his shoulder. His body felt rigid and heavy. "Donald, are you all right? Holy shit. What happened?"

Theresa's heart thumped in her chest as she sat in stunned silence. She watched Carmen for some kind of a signal. Carmen had her ear up against Donald's chest. His body reclined into his chair, his mouth open and his eyes shut.

"Somebody call an ambulance," Carmen yelled. "He doesn't have a pulse."

"I didn't do anything," Theresa stammered. "I don't think I did."

"You, lawyer lady, the phone is behind the bar. Call an ambulance. Oh my God. I think he is dead."

Theresa stumbled towards the bar and with a shaking hand dialled 911. The operator on the other end paused when Theresa told her they were at the Wiltshire on Main Street. "Is he already dead?"

"I think so. I'm not a doctor you know. I'm a lawyer. It might be best to get an expert opinion."

"We'll send the next available car."

After her phone call, Theresa stood behind the bar as far away from the dead body as possible and waited along with everyone else. Carmen gave Donald's shoulders one last shake and when there was no response, she sat down beside him and held his hand.

Perry appeared in the doorway after hearing Walter scream. His first glance was in Theresa's direction. She was a bit of a mutt. He should have known Carmen was fucking with him. Then he saw Carmen, agitated over by Donald. "What happened to him?"

"He's dead, Perry." Carmen bit her lip. She raised the hand she was holding and let it fall back onto the table. It landed with a dense thud. "Lord knows this was coming."

"What? How?" The police would come now. They would descend on the hotel to investigate and he had a stash of pot in a broken safe in his office.

"I don't know. He was like this when I got back in here. Shit Perry." A sob escaped Carmen's throat.

"The ambulance is on its way," Theresa said. Finally, here was Mr. Storch, younger and more handsome than she imagined. And he wore a suit. He barely glanced at her. His concern was for Carmen.

He pulled Donald's coat off the coat rack and covered his body with it. He didn't cover his face. Somehow it didn't seem right and he wanted to wait for the ambulance to come and make the final decision.

"Come on." He took Carmen's hand and led her away from the table. They both sat opposite Theresa at the bar where she stood dumbly, rooted to the spot. Perry nodded at her but did not speak. He had his arm around Carmen's shoulders. Theresa stared off into the same space as the rest of them.

All the room was quiet. Walter looked over at Ruby to see if she knew what was going on, but she blithely rolled her cigarettes and acted as though nothing had happened. Darren wasn't paying any attention either. Those Indians were smart, Walter thought. Pretend like nothing happened. Outsmart the enemy.

When the ambulance attendants came, Walter ignored them and sipped his coffee, keeping half an eye on Theresa to see who she would bump off next. She seemed to be fixated on Perry which suited Walter just fine. She had made up some business to be here so she could practise her witchcraft.

"He's dead?" Theresa asked. "He's really dead?"

"He's really dead," one of the attendants said. "Probably been really dead for about an hour."

The ambulance attendants had made no attempt to revive him. When they checked him over for some identification they found the notice of eviction folded up in his coat pocket.

"What the heck was he doing with that?" Theresa asked. She sprang from her spot behind the bar. "He had no business having that in his pocket. It's public property."

He had obviously taken the notice down and not said anything about it. Nobody had any idea what the notice was doing in Donald's pocket and now he was dead and being driven to the morgue in an ambulance. He was dead before Theresa walked through the door. As he waited for the perfect moment to execute his grand gesture, his heart sputtered and stopped. And now the rest of them had to figure out what kind of final mischief he had been planning.

The ambulance attendants wheeled him out on a stretcher. They turned the flashing lights off on their truck before they pulled away. Theresa smoothed the notice out as best as she could on the bar counter. If she got nothing else done today, at least the notice would be posted in its proper place. These people deserved that much. Proper and official notification of their fate.

"Listen, you've all had enough for today. I'll just tape this on the door where it's supposed to be and come back tomorrow. So sorry for your loss." Theresa gathered herself together and cast one last glance over the room. They were rooted to their places, quiet and still. A living tableau, she thought. You don't see those much anymore.

Chapter Twelve

Theresa did not go back to the office. After her visit to the hotel, her head was spinning and her legs felt weak. In the taxi on the way back the floodgates opened and the adrenaline spilled forth. Light-headed and dizzy she tapped the driver on the shoulder and asked him to take her home.

The kitchen was empty when she came in the back door and the house silent. Everybody was out. She picked up the phone and called Vera at work.

"You know some old man died right there in his chair. I can't come back to work today."

Vera murmured something soothing into the phone. Theresa carried on. "And you know what else? That guy had the notices in his pocket. He swiped them off the door and was carrying them around with him. What do you think about that? You tell Larry he's got me wading into some demented gene pool."

She hung up the phone and sunk into a kitchen chair. The silence in the house felt strange. These were rare moments when Theresa was in an empty house. It wouldn't last long. She went upstairs and drew a warm bath and poured some lavender bubble bath into the water. She got undressed and left her clothes in a pile beside the tub and lowered herself into the water. The entire scene reeled through her mind without stopping. The worst of it was she still hadn't gotten Mr. Storch to sign the papers and would have to go back yet again to that place where now she had witnessed both insanity and death. More than ever she believed it would be a good thing to tear the whole thing down. She would try to get her nerve up to get down there again this week but the way she felt right now she wanted the rest of the week off. When she got back downstairs she called Vera again and told her she would be back to work on Monday.

"I'm just way too upset about all this. Have you ever seen a dead person?" Her voice cracked and she was afraid she might start to cry. "It was just awful."

She hung up quickly and reached for a Kleenex. The quiet house was now getting to her and she wished somebody would come home. She popped a buttery bag of popcorn into the microwave, poured herself a big glass of iced tea and went to watch television in the living room.

She could not clear her mind, even with *The Price Is Right*. Walter accusing her of murder and Donald dead for hours with those notices in his pocket. She tried to make sense of it all. What was the matter with street people anyway? Always loaded down with bags and bags of the strangest things. This house may not be much, but at least she didn't have to spend her time in a place like the Wiltshire. What could that possibly be like? To get up in the morning and go to a place like that? What was Donald's home like if he preferred to spend his days at the Wiltshire? She had driven along the streets in that part of town. The houses with peeling paint and faded sheets covering the windows from the inside and always a sofa outside on the sagging porch. Who puts a sofa on the porch? And the tiny yards, over grown with weeds and long tufts of coarse grass springing up among rusted car parts and rotted two-by-fours. It astounded her that within those houses living beings dwelled. They slept and ate and lay on their couches watching game shows just as she was now.

The back door opened and shut and Theresa heard with joy the activity of Dustin, Rosa and Antonina getting unbundled and inside.

"Theresa?" Rosa had spotted her boots and coat. "Are you home? What's wrong?"

"I'm in here. Come in and I'll tell you what happened."

Rosa rushed into the living room half expecting to see Theresa in a body cast or with a limb amputated or something. All she saw was a half eaten bowl of popcorn and the lingering smell of bubble bath.

"What are you doing home?" Clearly Theresa wasn't ill.

"Sit, sit. You won't believe this."

She told her story again. Dustin toddled over to her and clamoured onto her lap. She stroked his hair and said, "Do you believe that? He was dead before I even got there and nobody noticed. What a horrible place to die. I'm completely exhausted. I took the rest of the week off to recover. I hope it's enough."

Rosa looked perplexed. People didn't just take time off from work because they were tired. If everyone did that then nothing would ever get done. But, coming from Theresa she wasn't that surprised.

"You can help with supper then, if you have so much time off."

"What? I have been through a trauma today. I can't even think about food."

"I see that." Rosa helped herself to a handful of popcorn. "You didn't go to work?"

"This was work. I had to go to a hotel on Main Street because it's being sold and torn down and I had to go and make sure everyone in there knew about it. Well, it turns out none of them knew anything because this dead man had all the information in his pocket and died before he told anyone. I have to go back there again because the first time the boss wasn't there and today this man died in his chair."

"I thought you were a secretary." Rosa nibbled at the popcorn.

"Geez, I'm not just a secretary. I'm practically a lawyer if you really want to know. I do a lot of legal things."

And that was the truth, Theresa thought. Today she had officially posted the notices on the door and if she hadn't been there it never would have been done. Satisfied, she stood to take the empty bowl to the kitchen. Rosa stayed behind and stretched out on the couch.

* * * * *

Perry sat at the bar and watched Carmen leaf through Donald's collages. "Look at this stuff. This is all that poor guy had going for him. These pictures. Did you know he sold them down at the Forks in the summer?"

"People bought these?" Perry asked as he scanned one that featured wrist watches. "Do you think he was some kind of unsung genius or prodigy or something?"

"Maybe. You never know. I'm going to hang onto these."

"Sure. You do that." He lit a cigarette and handed it to her. "Do you think that lawyer will be back?"

"Oh, probably. She's getting pretty comfortable here and she never had a chance to get to tell you about the hotel. Donald beat her to it."

"She doesn't look anything like Michelle Pfeiffer."

"I never said she did. I said Pamela Anderson and if you believed that then that's your problem. Why would you be so lucky? Besides, I think she's married."

"So? That might be even better. I won't get hurt that way." He laughed at Carmen's scowl.

Ruby and Darren left right after the ambulance was out of sight. Walter had still not uttered a word. Carmen took him a cup of coffee. "You okay there, Walter? Not too spooked I hope."

"She's gonna get someone else. Just wait. You better not let her in here again. That woman is pure evil."

"Not all lawyers are evil, Walter. It could have happened any time. She just happened to be here."

"You'll see," he said and lapsed back into silence.

Outside the light had disappeared and the rush hour traffic lit up the street. Perry came back in his coat and offered Carmen a ride home. In Winnipeg in the dead of winter, one of the most charitable things to do is to offer someone a ride home who would otherwise have to wait for a bus. Carmen readily accepted and the two of them watched Walter make his way upstairs before they left out the back door and locked up.

* * * * *

"What's this? You're making dinner? Didn't you just try to poison us last week?" Theresa rolled her eyes. Anton's attempts at humour were never very funny.

"Well, You didn't seem to have any trouble choking down your food. Right now I'm setting the table and yes, then I'm making dinner. So don't fill up on beer."

"Maybe I better fill up on beer. I don't trust what you might put in there." He already had his head deep in the fridge.

"Don't give me any ideas."

Theresa worked until Paulie came home. The whole time she kept thinking about the hotel and the dead man and then of all the other people there. That handful of people, not even bothering to get out of their seats and watching the stretcher leave the building like they had done it a hundred times. Those were the only people who cared about that man. They stood there like they knew one by one they would all be wheeled out of there dead on a stretcher. Maybe Theresa had actually saved them from that fate. If there was no more hotel then no one else could die in there.

How did it go?" Paulie asked.

"Oh my God," she began. "You wouldn't believe it. This place is cursed. One of the customers died right there at his table. The ambulance guys said he had been dead for an hour. Do you believe that? He's dead for an hour and nobody noticed."

Paulie raised his eyebrows.

"I know," Theresa said. "And you know what else?"

"What?"

"The dead guy had the eviction notice in his coat pocket. Some kind of a prank or something. I taped it back to the door. And that's about all I got done there today. I didn't even get a chance to talk to the manager. There was too much going on with that man dying and all. I have to go back again."

Antonina and Rosa entered the kitchen, having heard the arrival of their beloved men. Antonina crinkled her nose. "I don't smell anything."

"Well, it's not ready yet. You go relax, if you have any idea what that means."

Having their routine interrupted by Theresa's dinner ambition put them in a twitchy mood. They were hesitant to leave the kitchen. It wasn't so unusual for Theresa to help them, but it was unusual for her to shoo them out of the kitchen so they couldn't see what she was doing.

"I was going to make cabbage and ground beef with that," Rosa said.

"Well, there wasn't much else to work with unless you want me to whip up some herring pancakes or something. There's always tomorrow. And the next day. Believe me, you haven't boiled your last cabbage."

Rosa filled her tub with Epsom salts and warm water. She could sit in here while Theresa worked. Theresa stood by the stove and flipped meatballs over in the electric frying pan. Antonina was chattering to Dustin in Portuguese and he was giggling and spitting with delight. They all listened to Theresa's story again and wondered if she ever would tire of telling it.

* * * * *

The table was set and the candles lit. Theresa decided to have supper in the dining room for a change, just to salvage something pleasant after the upsetting day she had. Nobody knew what to make of that but they were hungry enough not to care where they ate. They all sat and Theresa served them each a plate. They rolled the meatballs around on their plates and pecked and sniffed at the sauce.

"What's this?" Antonina asked, not sure she could trust Theresa's cooking after the spicy chicken nearly took out her windpipe.

"Swedish meatballs. Try them. They're delicious."

Antonina speared one onto her fork and licked tentatively at the white sauce. Her face puckered and she smacked her tongue to get rid of the taste. "What's in there?" She asked.

"Nutmeg. Isn't it good?"

"Nutmeg? Nutmeg is sweet."

"Not everything has to be salty to be tasty. You don't like it?"

"I can't eat a sweet meatball. It tastes funny." She licked the meatball and made a face again to make her point.

"Well, fine. Scrape the sauce off. They won't be Swedish then. They'll just be plain."

"Plain is good," said Antonina.

"Swedish is good too," Rosa said and raised her fork to Theresa. "Good supper, my girl."

"Well, thanks. And I think we should all be thankful we can sit here and enjoy supper together and not all alone in some nearly deserted and falling down hotel."

"Sure, sure." Everybody nodded and kept eating. They didn't want to hear the story yet again. They knew what Theresa was getting at. It wasn't often she expressed any gratitude at living with them and they didn't know how to take it when she did.

Paulie and Dustin ate mountains of food. Rosa and Anton tried with the sauce and Antonina had to take hers to the sink to rinse off before she could eat them and even then she shook enough salt on them to take another five years off her life.

"So, Paulie. I've been thinking," Anton said at the table. "We should get back to the basement this weekend. I'll go pick up some more drywall and we'll start over. How about it?"

Before Paulie could reply, Theresa rolled her eyes and let her hand fall onto the table "Here we go again. The insurance money isn't paid yet. You can't possibly be serious. Paulie, we've talked about this. You know how I feel."

Paulie stared at his plate. Theresa slapped her napkin onto the table.

"I am talking to Paulie," Anton said with his mouth full of meatballs. "What do you think?"

"I don't want to talk about it right now." With the back of his fork, Paulie concentrated on flattening the rice on his plate.

"Tell him no, Paulie. Tell him we are moving out soon." Theresa turned to Anton. "We're moving out in the spring, once Paulie gets his job back. As soon as that happens we're going to the bank and they are going to tell us how much of a house we can afford, so don't bother wasting anymore time on the basement. We won't be needing it."

"The basement's gotta be done anyhow. There's money coming for it and that's what we're going to use it for. It will be up to you if you want to stay or go. We can't hold you back."

Rosa and Antonina started removing the dishes to the kitchen. Dustin grunted for more meat, but nobody noticed.

"Well, you're right about that. You can't stop us." In that moment Theresa realized something. The truth in Anton's words. Of course Anton and Rosa couldn't stop anything from happening. It was Paulie then who must be putting on the brakes. Theresa stopped short and turned to him. "What do you think is stopping us, Paulie?" she asked pointedly. "What on earth could it be?"

She didn't bother to let him answer. She plucked Dustin out of his high chair and took him upstairs. Paulie threw his fork onto his plate. Upstairs he heard Theresa giving Dustin a bath. He debated whether or not to go up and help her, but decided the sound of the game in the living room was much safer. Better to wait until things had settled down.

Chapter Thirteen

Perry sat at home watching a classic car auction. There were some beauties up for grabs. A 1957 Mercedes-Benz gullwing, bright orange with the doors that opened upwards and were shaped exactly like seagull wings. That one brought a sweet one hundred grand to some hard working restoration artist. All the bidders were unremarkable, middle-aged men who had scads of cash to spend on these cars. One guy bought four Calloway cars all in a row. Spent nearly seven hundred grand in fifteen minutes.

It was getting on in the day and Perry hadn't accomplished one thing. The entire weekend he had spent on the couch, smoking and watching television. He hadn't even gotten out to the bar. The week had ended on a peculiar note with Donald dying in his chair, that lawyer showing up amidst the confusion, the news of the hotel sale. It all swooped down on them like a flash flood. All those things all at once. Perry was having a tough time sorting it all out. He hoped the lawyer would return right away so he didn't have to smoke pot in the boiler room all week just to keep the office air clean.

That was the closest he had been to a dead body. All he could think to do was cover the guy up so he wouldn't have to feel like Donald was glaring at him from the great beyond. Those eyes bugged out even when he was dead. And Carmen sitting there holding his hand, like he was still dying and might have something to say. His last chance to utter some remarkable gem. Nobody even knew what the guy's last words were. Probably something like, "this soup's not hot." What a downer, Perry thought. Dying in a place like that where nobody even paid any attention to what you said. He died waiting for the moment when he could pull those papers out of his pockets and make everybody sit up and listen. Maybe he croaked at the very moment he was reaching for them, imagining everyone's reaction and his heart couldn't keep up with the anticipation of his great moment and he slumped over in his chair and everyone thought he was napping. It probably was that lawyer that did it. He would have known that that's what she was there for. He wanted to blurt it out before she did and he just ran out of gas. Perry shivered. There was just something so desperate and depressing about the whole thing he didn't want to think about it anymore. He lit up again and once he felt the familiar buzz relax into his brain, he rose from the couch and crawled into bed.

* * * * *

Outside the streets were dark and snow pelted against the window. The pavement below twinkled and reflected the orange glow of the street lights. From his window on the third floor Walter had a view of the back lot and the lane behind the hotel. Every so often a figure would appear and shuffle across the scene. In the distance the sound of traffic, a reminder of a world beyond this view. Walter kept watch at this window most nights until three or four in the morning.

There were two men in the parking lot. They stood just beyond the pool of light under the fire escape. A car idled not far from them. Walter watched for signs of trouble. Deals went down back there all the time and Walter saw everything. He was up high enough not to be able to identify anyone. There had been stabbings that Walter had witnessed, but no one came to question him. When they looked up at the back of the hotel, there was no way of knowing anyone was watching. The door of the car flew open and two of the men had the third one on the ground. They kicked him in the gut and head and left him balled up in the snow. The car fishtailed at the corner and then streaked off into the night. The figure rolled over and crawled a few feet. He threw up in a snow bank, then staggered to his feet and followed the tracks of the car to the corner.

Walter barricaded himself inside by pushing the dresser in front of the door to block it. Recent events paraded across his mind. Donald was dead and they found that notice in his pocket. Under any other circumstances, Walter would have been happy to see Donald go. An overgrown, ugly, long-faced, big-eyed baby. But it was that woman who preoccupied him now. That heifer parading around like a lawyer. He'd never seen any lawyer like that before. Twice now she had come to the hotel and Donald dropped dead while she was there and the hotel was being torn down. Everything was fine before she came along. Walter hoped they had seen the last of her, but those types were hard to get rid of. She'd be back and who knew what else would happen. Walter vowed to be watchful. He didn't want to end up like Donald and he certainly didn't want her face to be the last thing he saw before he flew up to heaven.

* * * * *

Paulie stopped in the bathroom on his way to bed. He could see the light shining under the door to their room. She was waiting for him. The bathroom gave him some time to prepare. Unlike Theresa, who had not really been reading all evening, Paulie had really been watching the game and let himself be lulled into a pleasant beer buzz. The argument at the dinner table now entered his mind with the startling pop of a forgotten balloon. It was going to take some sweet talking to get her back on his side. To be honest, he was in no mood to work on the basement anyway. In his mind, the plan about the car was still the better plan and he wanted to spend his time doing that, rather than making his wife upset with a basement apartment she would hate.

His piss hit the water with satisfying impact. He washed his hands and face with soap. Theresa she loved the smell of ivory soap on him. Hopefully it would remind her of something good about him. Paulie desperately wanted to remember something good about her, too. It was the smell of her hair, at first. It made him think of cold and flowers, like Edelweiss, he imagined. He fell in love with the smell of her hair. It didn't smell the same anymore. Her hair was shorter now and maybe she changed her shampoo. Whatever it was, something had changed. He was also a little miffed about the weight she had put on since Dustin was born. She used to be so slim and sexy.

However, as soon as he saw her in the muted bedroom light, his eyes softened. Dustin was asleep in his crib. Paulie slipped into bed beside Theresa and took her hand.

"Paulie, don't try that on me now. I'm exhausted and we need to talk."

"Aw, come on. You know we don't have the money to move out. If we move now, we'll never get a nice house."

"I don't even care anymore what kind of a house it is, as long as it's ours. I am not living in the basement, Paulie. I will leave you here in this house before I move into the basement."

"Look, I'm working my ass off trying to get us out of here." Paulie flopped the other way.

"How are you working your ass off? You're unemployed, remember? And whatever money comes your way you spend on that stupid car you have that's never even worked. I'm the one working my ass off around here."

"Well, maybe you have more ass to spare than me." Frustration got the better of him and he marched out of the room and down the stairs.

Ass rung in her ears. Theresa got up and covered Dustin with his blanket. The bottle came away from his mouth easily. She set it on the night table and crawled back into bed. Let him try having a baby. Insensitive bastard. Things could not go on like this.

Outside on the back stoop Paulie lit a smoke. The air was cold tonight and it pinched his lungs when he inhaled. He pulled his jacket around him and sat welded to the cold concrete. The sky was clear with thousands of stars. A weak spot in their marriage had worn through, now to be worked at until the raw fibre was exposed.

Paulie moved to the garage and flipped the switch for the light and the heat. He grabbed the corner of the tarp and pulled it back. There she was. It always made him feel better to see it. Last summer he finished work on the axles and shocks before he ran out of money. The interior needed new upholstery, just the seats. Thankfully not the doors. New tires, brakes, the engine was okay, just needed some tuning. He opened the door and slid into the driver's seat. He loved the smell of grease and gasoline. Twenty grand would get them out of the house. Twenty grand would do it nicely. Convinced the car was the answer to all the troubles in his life, Paulie grabbed the bottle of Armor All and a rag and buffed up the dash. The car would be beautiful. Creamy lemon yellow with dark black, brand new rubber tires, blinding chrome hubcaps and deep red vinyl on the inside. Someone would buy it. Someone would know what a dream this car was and have no problem dropping twenty thousand dollars for it.

Paulie worked on it most of the night. His mood improved dramatically and he forgot about his teary-eyed wife. When he finally worked off all his frustrations, he slept in the back seat covered with a wool blanket.

Chapter Fourteen

C armen stepped off the bus into the emerging light of the day. The sky was bright blue for a change and the sun higher than usual. Still, Carmen's steps felt leaden as she trudged around to the back of the building. Donald's death had stamped out all her energy. From the corner of her eye she saw the notices taped to the front door.

She didn't know how to shake this feeling of doom. It was just an old building being torn down, not the end of the world. The metal stairs vibrated under her feet as she dragged the bag with Walter's clothes behind her. She felt dizzy. What would today bring? After last week, anything could happen. First of all, that hoity-toity lawyer would be back. Carmen was beginning to think Walter was right. The woman was bad news. Ever since she came on the scene only bad things had happened. Donald dying right there under their noses, the hotel sold and on the city's demolition list. She had no idea what to expect from Walter today, he got so freaked out by everything he was probably barricaded in his room. There would be a mess to clean up today for sure.

The guy in the Bahamas had threatened to sell the place before and everyone got all worked up and nothing ever happened. It got to the point of real estate agents bringing buyers through and everyone held their breath while they craned their necks to see the details around the moulding and the fine workmanship of the wainscoting. Nobody stayed interested in the place and Carmen had a hard time believing the city would come through either. No matter how many parking lots they needed and how many people in fur coats and white limos they wanted to attract to the ballet's Christmas production of The Nutcracker. The city was forever trying to lure people downtown with their outdoor festivals and free concerts. At the end of the day there was nothing left but plastic beer cups rolling in the wind and dirty Pampers stuffed into public garbage cans. Why couldn't they just let things be? Tearing down the hotel wouldn't make one ounce of difference to the city, but it would make a big mess of things for Walter. And for Carmen too, but she tried not to think about that.

After a while Carmen put it all out of her mind. She padded over to the fridge in her socks and counted the eggs, humming tunelessly. Carmen was blessed with an ability to trust in the rhythms of the universe and simply float atop the waves. She stooped to pull her runners out from under the butcher block. She didn't notice the tack on the floor until it punctured through the sole of her foot. Carmen hopped around on one foot and rubbed the other one. "Shit!" Suddenly, her ankle gave way and she landed with a crash on the mop and pail. Her head barely missed the corner of the butcher block. The pain she now felt was in her wrist and her hand instinctively shot from the foot to her now burning hand.

"Shit, shit shit!" she yelled. The pain seared through her wrist each time she tried to let go to rub her throbbing foot. She sat up against the stainless steel sinks and tried to relax to the rhythmic drumming of pain. Slowly, her breathing evened out and she began to relax.

* * * * *

Theresa pulled into the parking lot behind the hotel and walked up the back steps to the kitchen. Carmen hadn't put the broom in yet so the door was locked shut. Theresa reached up and pushed the buzzer. She could hear the shrill ring inside. She thought she heard something fall. She knocked and shouted through the door, "Hello, is anybody there?"

"I'm coming," Carmen yelled. "Hold your horses."

Carmen struggled to her feet and gingerly stepped towards the back door. Just what she needed. Another visit from that lawyer. And Perry wasn't even in yet.

"Hi, it's me again." Theresa said, before she noticed the pained expression on Carmen's face. "Hey, is everything alright. You look kind of pale."

"I just fell. First I stepped on a tack and then the pain from that made me fall over and now I think I've broken my wrist or some damn thing."

Carmen didn't particularly want Theresa's help, but there was little choice. "Come in, come in. It isn't getting any warmer out there."

"Do you need to go to the hospital? I can drive you there. It's not far." Theresa's eyes darted around the kitchen in search of a chair for Carmen to sit in. "Maybe you should sit down."

"Yeah, I feel a bit woozy."

They headed into the lounge and Carmen sat at Walter's table. Theresa still wasn't sure what to do. "Do you have any ice in there?" She pointed to the kitchen.

"Yeah, some ice would be good. Maybe I better get this checked out. You wouldn't mind?"

"No, no. I don't mind at all. Anything I can do to help. Your wrist looks awful. I'll get some ice and we'll get going. Where are your shoes?"

"Under the table in there." Carmen waved her sore arm and winced. "Ouch."

Theresa retrieved the runners from the kitchen and watched Carmen slide her feet in. "Here, I'll tie them for you." She stooped down in front of Carmen and tied the laces.

"Damn," said Carmen when she saw the time. "Hey, Miss uh…

"Theresa."

"Theresa, I hate to ask you this, but it's getting really late for Walter and the wait at the hospital could be a long one. He'll be starving by the time I get back. Can you go up to his room and get him down here? It'll take five minutes and we'll leave him a sandwich or something."

Theresa stood and straightened her coat. "Walter? The man who lives here?"

"Yeah, he's up on the third floor. Third door on the right. Just tell him he needs to get his butt down here. He'll listen to you if you mention breakfast."

"Well, okay," Theresa said, not sure at all she wanted to go and get this Walter down from his room. "Is there an elevator?"

"Sorry, you'll have to take the stairs. Watch your step, they're a bit wonky in some places."

Theresa headed for the stairs with some trepidation. She stopped at the foot and her eyes travelled upward. From where she stood she could barely make out the top. Her hand gripped the railing as she started up the steps. The railing had a tacky feel but Theresa didn't dare let go even though it was quite loose and wobbled if she put any weight on it. The steps were uneven, as Carmen had said, and Theresa thought it wouldn't be a bad idea to have the elevator fixed. But of course that wouldn't happen now. It was a wonder no one had killed themselves on these stairs. She remembered Donald, the other day, dead in his chair. People didn't need rickety stairs to find themselves dead in this place.

She reached the third floor a little out of breath with a burning sensation in her thighs from the climb. She tugged at the hem of her skirt. How did Walter manage those stairs every day? She found his room and knocked on the door. There was no sound from inside. Theresa tried the door and though it was unlocked, the door banged into something on the other side of the door. "Walter," she called through the crack. "Are you in there, Walter?"

"That depends," Walter's voice chirped from the other side of the door.

"It what?"

"It depends who's out there."

"You met me the other day. Look," Theresa didn't know how to convince him to open the door. Walter was afraid of outsiders. "Carmen, the regular waitress, the one you know, is downstairs. She hurt herself and asked me to come and get you. Do you want your breakfast?"

"Can you bring it here? I can't come down right now."

Theresa stood dumbly behind the door. "Why don't you just open the door and come down as usual? I don't think they have room service here. Besides, there's something blocking the door. How will I get your food in there?"

"Go get my breakfast. I'll have this out of the way when you get back."

Not knowing what else to do, Theresa relented and went back downstairs. Carmen had ice on her wrist. "Where is he?"

"He wants to eat in his room. He had a dresser or something blocking the door. I told him he had to move it or I wouldn't be able to get his breakfast to him."

"Jesus. That little rat. Sorry about all this. Just take him some toast and coffee. My wrist is feeling a bit better. I had some Tylenol in my purse and the ice is helping. I'll wrap it later and if Walter is going to stay in his room all day then I should be able to manage. I'd appreciate it though if you took some food up to him."

"Oh, I don't mind. I have to wait for Mr. Storch anyway. Have you seen him yet?

"No, not yet. He'll be in any minute." Carmen had moved over to the bar.

"Are you doing okay after that man died here the other day?"

"Donald? Yeah. I guess this was the best place for him to die, when you really think about it. At least he was around people who knew him."

"Did he live all alone?"

"Oh, yeah. In a room somewhere around here I expect. I'm not really sure. If he had family he lived with he wouldn't have come here every day, that's for sure. I mean, would you?" She waved her good arm around at the room.

"No, I guess not. I never really thought about it."

She and Carmen went into the kitchen and Theresa watched while Carmen made Walter some toast. He took four sugars and a lot of cream in his coffee and Theresa carried the plate in one hand and the coffee in the other back up the stairs to his room. She hoped he had the door open for her since she didn't have a hand free to open it up.

True to his word, the door was ajar and Theresa nudged it with her foot to get inside. The first thing which struck her was the wall of pungent odour that hit her like a furnace blast. She had never smelled a stench like that in her life and her face reflexively screwed up in an effort not to breathe. Walter sat on the edge of his bed, averting his gaze. He didn't trust Theresa but was in desperate need of that coffee. He had no choice.

"Where should I put your food?" she asked, trying hard to take in the scene without being obvious. How could a person live like this? The room had nothing but a bed, a sink, a lamp and a dresser. Not even a television. There wasn't anyone else on the floor, or in the entire hotel for that matter.

"Over there," he said, pointing at the dresser. "Put it up there."

Theresa placed the plate and cup where he wanted and took a step towards the window. She saw her car out in the parking lot, Dustin's car seat in the back, and she felt a pang of homesickness.

"You can go now." Walter said, getting a bit agitated with Theresa lingering in his room.

"What?"

Walter was staring squint-eyed at her now.

"Okay, I'll go. As long as you're okay up here. Have you lived here a long time?"

"What's a long time?"

"I don't know. Five years maybe?"

Walter didn't answer her. Time meant nothing to him. He wanted Theresa to leave so he could drink his coffee.

When she was at the door she turned once more. "I'm sorry about your friend."

There again was no reply, just a steely gaze.

"I'll bring you some nice food next time I come, okay? What do you like to eat?"

"I like those peppermint patties. Bring me some of those."

"Is that all?" Theresa hovered by the door, not sure why she felt compelled to linger there.

"Hmmph." Walter pointedly looked out the window. It was clearly time for her to go.

"Bye, Walter."

Theresa made her way back down the hall and down the stairs, again hanging onto the sticky railing. She dropped into a chair in the bar and accepted the coffee Carmen offered her.

"How long has he lived up there like that?"

"I have no idea. He was here when I got here. Did he give you a hard time?" Carmen re-adjusted the ice on her wrist and Theresa saw it was swollen and red.

"Oh no. He didn't want me to stay though." Theresa wanted to ask Carmen more about Walter but didn't know what to ask. "I don't know how a person can live like that."

"It's all he knows, old Walter. Some people like to be alone; it feels safer for them." Carmen paused. "What about you? Do you have family here in town?"

Theresa grinned. "Oh God, too many. The house I live in is full to the brim with in-laws."

"Well, it sounds better than living alone."

"Well, I guess," Theresa said uncertainly. "I wouldn't know."

"Be thankful," Carmen said. "Too much solitude isn't so great."

"Yeah, I guess not," Theresa said when she realized they weren't talking about Walter anymore.

They both turned their heads when they heard a bang come from the kitchen. "Must be Perry," Carmen said.

Perry walked through the empty kitchen. He saw Carmen's boots on the mat and the eggs out on the counter. Someone's coat was slung over a chair. He spied Theresa through the round window in the swinging door. Both she and Carmen were looking right at him. He pushed through the door and joined them at the bar.

"Good morning, ladies." His eyes fell on the towel covering Carmen's wrist.

"I stepped on a tack," she said and laughed. "Theresa here was good enough to take Walter his breakfast."

"Great, now he's going to want room service everyday."

"That's what I said, too," Theresa chimed in, even thought it wasn't exactly what she had said. Ever since they had mistaken her as a lawyer she felt a lot smarter. Over the weekend she had gone to Polo Park and picked out a new outfit. She had also gone for a free makeover where the counter girl told her to wear more provocative shades of eye shadow and lipstick. This morning she drew stares from Antonina and Rosa when she appeared in a tight black leather skirt and a blouse with a questionable neckline and a deep, muddy red shade of lipstick.

Empty buses rattled past the hotel down Main Street. A group of natives walked by. One of them spit onto the window, leaving a hefty gob of spit that would freeze there until the spring thaw.

Perry studied Carmen's wrist. "You should get that x-rayed. It could be broken."

"Nah, I doubt it. See, I can move it." Carmen flexed her wrist and winced. "Well, sort of."

"I said I could drive her to the hospital. It won't take too long, I don't think."

"That's a great idea," Perry said. He had decided to pitch his idea to Theresa if she came back today but he wasn't ready. A trip to the hospital would give him enough time to at least open the window in his office and straighten things out a bit and maybe even have time for a quick puff in the boiler room.

"We'll be back in a couple of hours," Theresa said, eager to make a good impression and not all that anxious to get back to the office. Carmen had no say and Perry ushered them out the back door and waved from the steps as they drove off.

"You know, you don't have to do this, You can drop me off and head back and have your meeting with Perry. I know you must be busy, being a lawyer and all."

In the car, Theresa bit her lip. She didn't want it all to end so soon but she couldn't keep the truth from Carmen. She was beginning to like her. "Actually," she began. "I'm not a full lawyer. I'm more like an assistant to a lawyer. They never do any of the dirty work themselves. I mean, I can't imagine Larry in his eight hundred dollar suit taking toast up to Walter."

Theresa laughed and was relieved to see a smile creep across Carmen's lips as well. "Yeah, I guess it does make more sense for you to be here."

The car fell silent and Theresa entered the parkade at the Health Sciences Centre. "I'll come in with you. I'll get us coffee while you're waiting. I'm getting used to carrying coffee around."

"Okay," Carmen said. "I'd appreciate the company. Hospitals give me the creeps."

"Yeah, me too," Theresa said, although she really had no idea if hospitals gave her the creeps or not.

Chapter Fifteen

Perry chuckled to himself. Good for Carmen getting that lawyer to take Walter his breakfast. Give her a chance to see how the other half lives. He turned up the sleeves of his shirts and sat at his desk to roll a thin joint.

He didn't know how long they would be and he wanted to be relaxed when they returned. The office was in pretty good shape. Good enough for him to check her out. See what being a lady lawyer was all about.

He picked up his lighter and his newly rolled reefer and headed down the service stairs to the boiler room. There were ominous looking stains on the floor, none of which had any connection to operating a boiler. He lit his smoke amidst the clang and clatter of the machine. He could not imagine how it was the boiler worked, old cast iron and silver insulation with tufts that frayed at the edges and sounds that must have some bearing on the inner workings. Any minute and the whole thing could blow and leave him scarred with steam burns. Smoking in the boiler room was as dangerous as his job ever got. There was a cloud of smoke above him and he felt the pleasant high take effect. He made his way back upstairs when he heard the buzzer ring from the kitchen. Could they be back already? Carmen must have forgotten her key. Quickly, he ducked into his office and doused himself with cologne to mask the smell of the pot. The buzzer sounded again.

Theresa and Carmen waited on the back steps. Theresa shifted her feet from side to side. "At least it wasn't broken."

"Yeah, and they gave me some pretty wicked pain killers. I feel great!"

Perry opened the door. One look from Carmen told him she knew he was stoned. "Is it broken?"

"No, just a bad sprain. It'll be better in a few days."

Back in the lounge Carmen immediately lit a smoke and poured herself a coffee.

"So," said Perry. "You're the lawyer who is selling this place to the city."

"Well, actually..."

"Yeah," Carmen interrupted, and winked at Theresa. "She's from Lambert and Taylor."

"Which one are you?" Perry asked with what he hoped was a disarming smile.

"What?" Theresa blushed, not sure what Carmen was up to. It must be the pain killers, she thought.

"Are you Lambert or Taylor?" Perry grinned as he stood and pointed to his office.

"Oh," she laughed nervously, flustered at the question.

"We'll be in my office," he said to Carmen.

"Sure, sure. And I'll be in mine. Come back again soon, Theresa."

Still a bit confused, Theresa turned and smiled. "I will. Take care of that wrist."

"Yeah, and thanks again."

* * * * *

Theresa followed Perry down the hall to his office. He opened the door for her and let her in first. He extended his hand. "Perry," he said. "My friends call me Stork."

Theresa shook his hand. Stork? Perry held her hand a moment longer than she was prepared for and she immediately blushed as a result.

"Can I take your coat?" He was thankful he had a smoke before she came. He was relaxed and his mind seemed to be working with amazing precision. Perry assessed Theresa as he shook her hand. She bought clothes a size too small, her make-up was just a shade overdone, and her perfume was a bit too strong. Her calves bulged over the top of her boots. He noticed this before he noticed the dainty gold watch that dug into her wrist. Everything on this woman was just a bit tight. He didn't mind the black leather skirt though. It looked all right on her and made him believe she at least thought about getting laid once in awhile.

The colour she chose for her hair was a bit too orange. This woman overshot the mark every time, he thought. Maybe she was new at her job. She carried with her a slim briefcase from which she pulled a folder containing two sheets of paper.

"Mr. Storch," she began. "I'm sorry about the other day. I didn't think it was the best time to go over things, with that poor man dying in there and all."

"Oh, Donald. Yeah, poor guy."

"Is everyone okay?"

"Seem to be." He tried not to stare too hard at the pendant wedged in her cleavage. As she spoke he had a nagging sense of recognition. He knew this woman from somewhere and hoped he hadn't hit on her in a bar sometime recently.

"Do I look familiar to you?" he asked.

"What?" The question threw her off. She was here strictly for business and was horribly late getting back to the office as it was. She scrutinised his face a moment. "No, I don't think so."

"Oh. People tell me that a lot so I've just started asking them first."

Theresa nodded and laid her hand on the papers on the desk. "I'm here to find out how many people will be directly affected by the sale of the hotel. How many work here and how many, other than Walter, live here."

It was February and she wore boots that went all the way up her calf with a zipper on the inside. The toes were pointy and Perry imagined the shape of her foot when she pulled the boots off. She would have those big toes that drifted towards all the others at acute angles. The kind that would one day need bunion surgery and then would begin her mid-life crisis when the doctor told her she no longer could wear pointy-toed shoes. She would mourn the pizzazz she thought she had lost when there was never any pizzazz there to start with.

He wondered if she was a pot smoker. The car in the back had a baby seat in it and so he guessed not. When people didn't know what he did, he had a hard time knowing what to talk about. He couldn't tell if her clothes were expensive or not. He also wanted very much to fuck her. This feeling came as a surprise to him. The women he went for often surprised him. There was no explaining some urges. Maybe it was that he felt virile in his suit and this was the first person who offered a glimmer of being impressed by that. And, it never hurt to have a lawyer on your side.

"Can I get you a coffee?"

"Oh, I've had tons already. Thanks." There were folders and finance magazines all over his desk. Theresa wondered how busy he could be in this old hotel. She had already decided that she liked him. He had an easy and personable manner and seemed quite intent on being charming.

Perry returned to his chair behind his desk and leaned back. He spied the wedding ring on her finger, tight and constricting, the way they always became over the years. His dick did a little dance. Maybe there was a chance after all. A bored and neglected housewife who probably hadn't had a good fuck in months, maybe years. He stroked his chin thoughtfully. What to do now? She was waiting for him to do something, the way she sat on the edge of her seat and fingered the paper on the desk in front of her. He patted the marble ashtray. "Do you like this? It's an antique."

"It's beautiful. Looks heavy," Theresa said, not sure if she wanted to engage in small talk when there was business at hand. Small talk with this dashing man made her nervous.

"Try picking it up." Perry smiled a smile that made Theresa suppress a giggle.

"Well, all right. Just to see I guess." She got it an inch off the floor and tried not to let it clunk too hard when she lowered it down again. "Wow."

Satisfied, Perry leaned back. "It's a beauty, eh?"

"Yes, it sure is," she said. Perry was paying a lot of attention to her blouse. "Well?"

"Well what?" Okay, so she wasn't a housewife, but there was still a chance she was bored and neglected. He wondered what her husband did. Probably some bloated executive with a dozen hot secretaries to chase around his desk. Perry had a hard time staying focused. The folder for the beach caught his eye. He looked at Theresa and realized for the first time there was someone sitting on the other side of his desk who had no reason to believe he was anything other than what he appeared to be right at this very moment. A grand scheme emerged into the forefront of his slightly stoned brain. A grand beach scheme...

With any luck she had her own money stashed away and wouldn't have to ask her husband. Then again, if she cheated on him, she couldn't very well tell him where all their money went. Besides, he didn't want that much. Just some. For fun, to see if he could get away with it. And fucking her would be the insurance that went with it. A crooked grin slid across his face.

Theresa attempted a stern look. "Mr. Stork, I mean Storch. How many people will be affected by this sale? The eviction notice is for the end of March." For someone about to lose their hotel and their job, the man didn't seem too concerned, Theresa thought. He was more distracted by her blouse than the papers on the desk.

Perry cleared his throat. "Well, there's me and Carmen. She works in the bar and kitchen. Other than Walter, there isn't anyone who lives here."

"I see. And what will happen to Walter?"

"I have no idea. I guess we can help get him into another hotel around here. Unless they're all going down."

"Do you think he can manage in another hotel?" Theresa wished she had brought a pen and paper to take notes. She was having a hard time ignoring Perry's persistent eyes.

"We'll get him packed up and moved over. He'll be fine."

"Doesn't he have any family? Isn't there anyone we should notify?"

I'm not a goddamn social worker, Perry thought. It was Walter. If ever there was a survivor, that guy was it. He wanted to get Theresa's attention back to him.

"I'll take care of everything," Perry said, hoping he sounded genuinely concerned.

"What are you going to do once the hotel is gone?" She leaned forward in her chair, interested to hear what he had to say. She was in no hurry to leave.

Perry suppressed a smile. She had handed him his opening. He took a deep breath and began his pitch.

"What do Winnipeggers love more than anything else?" Perry paused to give Theresa a chance to think about it. He saw her furrow her brow and he grinned. "Come on, you're a smart lady. If you were to invest in a sure thing here in our frosty city, what would it be? Think hot, hot, hot." He stood and popped around the room, arms dancing a jig, still feeling brilliant from the smoke in the boiler room.

"I don't know," Theresa said, grinning right back at him. People usually didn't talk to her like this, like they wanted her attention for something important. "Barbecue sauce?"

Suddenly Perry leaned forward and placed his hands on her shoulders. His face was inches from hers. "I could kiss you. That is a brilliant idea."

Theresa nearly fell backwards out of the chair. She didn't know if she was more shocked at being called brilliant or at being very nearly kissed on the lips by a stranger.

"You, smart lady, have given me a great idea. But, no, it's not barbecue sauce, but that does sound good."

"Well, what is it then?" She giggled again. He was flying around the room abuzz with high voltage frenetic energy. She was flustered and had no idea what exactly he was talking about.

"What do Winnipeggers love most of all?" Perry paused here to execute a dramatic flourish. Theresa stared at him. "Why, the beach. Right? Am I right?"

He didn't wait for an answer. "Of course I am. The city is dead in the summer. Everyone is out at Grand Beach partying their asses off. Have you been to Grand Beach lately? Have you seen the Florida string bikini/beach volleyball meat market? This is the new pick up joint and these people have nowhere to go in the six months we call winter. So what do we give them? An indoor winter beach."

Sweat beaded at his temples. He was having a great time dancing around the room making a big deal about his plans. From what he could tell, the lady lawyer was mesmerised. It was starting to sound to him like a damn fine idea, whether anything came of it or not. His eyes locked onto Theresa's. "What do you think?"

"I don't get it."

"Have you ever been to West Edmonton Mall? They've got something in there like a beach, but it's just a wave machine and it's mostly kids. This is for adults only. There's going to be bars and bands and sand and surf. Sunshine, wind, everything people want when they go to the beach. And thanks to you, barbecues."

"Okay, I get it. How are you going to do that? I mean, it gets really hot at the beach. The sand and everything. It might be a fire hazard." Theresa was getting caught up in the excitement of having a conversation with somebody new. A real conversation about something important.

"Well, I haven't thought of everything. But what do you think? You're the first person I've told about this. In fact," Perry paused as if the idea had just struck him. "You could get in now, before I close the negotiations."

"What? You mean help you with your business?"

"Yeah, kind of." Perry stopped. The brilliance was gone and the paranoia set in. He wondered how smart it was to get a lawyer involved in a scheme like this. He didn't know anything about indoor beaches. Suddenly his idea sounded like the dumbest-ass thing he ever came up with.

"Listen," he said. "You know more about this than me. You're a real estate lawyer right? Let me think about this a bit more so I can impress you. Come back in a few days and I'll do a proper presentation for you. And don't tell anyone about it. I have to figure it all out first. I don't want anyone finding out about this too soon. Because it's going to be huge!" Perry was swinging back to optimism.

"Is that how you are going to pay for this? By asking everyone you know to give you money?"

"That's generally how it works, except you get a cut of all my future profits. When I go to the bank to get a loan, it'll look better if I have some money in the bank. That's where the loans from friends and other interested parties come in. You get your money back plus profit with what I rake in at Grand Beach Uptown. You see, everyone pays a cover charge of six dollars, ten on weekends just to get in. Then there's drinks and food and whatever else I can think to charge them for. It's a licence to print money." He was pretty sure this wasn't at all how it worked, but sometimes he had the problem of not knowing when to shut up. Now he had blurted out all of his ignorance.

"Where is this thing going to be?" Theresa wanted him to keep talking. She was captivated by his voice and his attention and the notion of having some stake in her own business.

Perry couldn't believe she wanted him to continue. No blinks, no head shakes, no concerns. Just genuine interest. Maybe she didn't know what she was doing after all. It wouldn't surprise him one bit to discover there were lawyers out there who didn't have a clue what they were doing. There were people like that everywhere. Then again...

"Well, I figure the best place is an old car dealership. An empty one that's for sale. They have enough space inside and there's parking. If you offer free parking, people will come. I know it."

He was beginning to convince himself once again the idea had merit. Why couldn't it work, an indoor beach? He could even put tanning beds in and for an extra fee people could bronze themselves before they hit the beach.

Theresa looked at her watch. "I really have to get going. I know you're pretty excited by this, but I have to think about it before I give you any money. It sounds kind of crazy. Do you really think people will go to a beach in the winter?"

"They do it all the time, except it costs them a fortune. This will deliver the same thing for nothing compared to what people will spend to get to Jamaica. It can't fail. There's no way."

"Look, I really have to get back to work. Can you have a look at these papers? I'll come back in a couple of days for your presentation and I'll pick them up then."

"Will you think about my idea?" he asked, fingering the papers she slid across the desk.

"Sure, it sounds crazy. But I'll think about it."

Theresa left feeling giddy and a little light-headed. When she got back to the car, she took a deep breath. Now she had a secret. Except she had to tell Vera about it. Somebody had to know. Even if it was supposed to be a secret. Everyone had someone they told secrets too. But not Paulie. If she was going to give this Stork all of her savings, she didn't want Paulie to know about it. It would be a surprise for him later on. His wife would be a partner in a local business. The more she thought about it, the more she imagined herself in cream-coloured suits sitting in a meeting at the bank, or helping herself to free coolers at the beach bar.

* * * * *

Perry sauntered down to the bar. The brilliance and paranoia had now given way to the munchies. Carmen was reading the newspaper.

"Hey, can I get a plate of fries?"

"Donald's obituary is in the paper. Look at this. It's so short." She slid the paper across the bar and pointed at the square that Perry was to read. "The funeral is Monday. I'm thinking of taking Walter."

"Can I get some fries?" he asked again, pretending to read. Thinking about Theresa and wondering if he had gotten himself into big trouble or if things would swing his way. Once the pot wore off there was no way of knowing what really happened in there.

"Yeah, I'll get you some. But you read that or I'll make you drive us."

The brief obituary stated that Donald had been born in Neepawa, Manitoba in 1930. He was predeceased by both his parents. No other family was mentioned. He had worked at the CNR shops. The memorial service was going to be in the church down the street from his boarding house. It was the most depressing thing Perry had ever read.

Carmen turned to Walter. "You going to Donald's funeral, Walter?"

"Hmmph."

"Yeah, that's pretty much what I think. You got a suit to wear?"

"Ha!" Ruby chimed in. "You think you'll ever see him in a suit? I might just show up at that funeral to see that."

Walter banged his cup on the table until Carmen heard and brought him more coffee.

Chapter Sixteen

The snow started mid-afternoon and now lay heavy and packed on the steps. There was a fine layer of ice beneath it. The office management had not yet sprinkled sand and in Theresa's non-grip boots there was zero friction between her and the ground. She clung to the railing on her way down and her feet nearly slipped out from under her three times. Slowly, she inched her way to the car and breathed a sigh of relief once she was inside and sitting down. A thick layer of frost covered the inside and the defrost took a few minutes to make it disappear.

It all sounded convincing to Theresa. On her drive home she imagined the indoor beach. She imagined thin, good looking people walking around in bikinis and drinking fruity red drinks from those big bulbous glasses. Right now, at five p.m. on a Tuesday evening, it was minus twenty-eight and the wind howled from the north and made it feel like the climate on Neptune.

Theresa imagined herself and Stork on the beach, having it all to themselves, like those vacation brochures. She could feel the sand between her toes and the heat from giant heat lamps on her skin and the smell of suntan oil. If it were open right now, she would drive across town and stop at the beach on her way home. The vacation brochures gave her an idea. They could use the same format for their advertising. Have people think it was for a vacation, but then they find out they only have to drive across town. Her heart skipped with anticipation. She couldn't wait to meet with Stork again.

The traffic was heavy and slow. Christmas lights twinkled overhead, no longer very jolly in February. Stork's face bobbed in the sea of Theresa's thoughts. Uneasiness sunk in when she turned the corner to the back lane. She needed to settle into her usual self. If she skipped inside all cheery and grinning everyone would know something was up. She gulped down her excitement and pulled the car into its place beside the garage.

Paulie was out back shovelling the walk while Dustin pulled his toboggan around the yard. Paulie was piling all the snow up in one corner so Dustin would have a hill to slide down. As soon as he saw Theresa, Dustin waved wildly. Theresa picked him up and kissed him on the cheek. "How's mama's big boy?"

He pumped his mittened hand at the back door and grinned.

Inside, the house smelled of baking and on the table sat a plate of burnt and broken cookies. Even though there were tins full of holiday baking left over, the production did not cease. She kicked her boots off at the back door. The table was set for supper and a big pot of mysterious food bubbled on the stove. Everyone was huddled around the five o'clock local news. At five-thirty they would eat. Theresa went into the living room.

"Hi everyone," she said.

Only Rosa looked up. "How was your day?"

"Oh, good. Pretty good. Busy though. This new project is going to take some time."

She carried Dustin up the stairs. They sat on the bed together and Theresa watched *The Young and the Restless*. Victor Newman, in the last minutes of the day, planned some malicious but brilliant take-over to keep Jack Abbott from getting ahead. From the couch, under soft golden light, his latest love watched adoringly as Victor's countenance darkened and he shouted something into the telephone.

Dustin played on the bed with some blocks. Every so often he tried to feed one to Theresa and she pretended to eat it. Then, when he pretended to eat one, she pried it out of his hands and told him 'no'. Soon, he grew bored being upstairs with Theresa and banged on the door to be let out. At a commercial, Theresa pulled herself off the bed and went to the foot of the stairs. "Paulie, come and get Dustin. He wants to come down."

Paulie appeared at the foot of the stairs and waited for Dustin to walk down.

Alone, on the bed, Theresa thought for a moment about the grand scheme of things. Her mother liked to analyze everything by the 'grand scheme of things'. It helped shrink things down to their original size. So, here was the situation as it appeared in the grand scheme of things: a man who was not her husband was paying her some attention. This same man wanted some of her money for a new business venture. If things went well, she could be a rich business woman. The man was handsome and charming and thought Theresa was smart and sexy, from the way his eyes latched onto her cleavage. If she kept things strictly focused on business then she was doing nothing wrong. And if it was Stork and not Paulie that she imagined lying with on the indoor beach, then that had something to do with business too. It was all just good business. In the grand scheme of things, she decided, this was the opportunity she had been waiting for.

*　*　*　*　*

Sunday mornings were for vacuuming and for sex. As Rosa operated the big Hoover downstairs, Paulie reached for Theresa and felt her body give way and move towards him.

195

He wriggled out of his shorts and eased her nightgown over her head. Her body, warm and soft from the night, sighed as he nestled his head between her breasts. She stroked his hair and pulled him on top of her. "Hurry," she whispered. "Before she turns it off."

And hurry he did, because Dustin was now awake and thumping in his crib.

When they were through they lay in bed, both wanting to roll over and go back to sleep. But Dustin was wide awake and the sound of the vacuum had stopped. Now Rosa was cleaning the bathroom across the hall. Theresa said, "I'm running up to Safeway this morning. I need to pick up a few things for one of the men at the hotel. I want to buy him some food."

"Why does he need food if he lives at a hotel?" Paulie sat on the edge of the bed and pulled on his socks.

"He just lost his best friend. I bet he is feeling very sad right now and I want to cheer him up. You can watch Dusty while I'm out."

"Yeah, yeah." Paulie lay back down and watched Theresa get Dustin dressed. She lifted him out of his crib and sat him on their bed. He was almost three years old. He should have his own room by now. He didn't sleep through their love-making anymore and stared at them through the bars of his crib, wide-eyed, sucking on his bottle of apple juice. It wasn't right. It might even be damaging.

"Here, take him. I'm going to have a quick bath." Theresa pulled a terry robe around her and crossed the hallway to the bathroom. For some reason she didn't feel right about pulling on her usual sweats to go to the store. She wanted to be well put together. It was because she had started to imagine all the places she could bump into Stork. It could happen anytime and she wanted to be sure she looked as good as she had the other day. Besides, if she was about to become a local business woman, she better start acting like one.

* * * * *

Once Theresa got home, she laid everything out on the kitchen counter. A bag of peppermint patties, cheese flavoured Ritz crackers, Fudge-O cookies and a frozen chicken. "What's this rubbie going to do with a frozen chicken?" Rosa asked.

"Carmen, the waitress, will cook it for him. He'll have a real meal for a change." Theresa anticipated Walter's bird-like face lighting up when he saw what she brought him on Monday. She would hear what Stork had to say about his beach. If it sounded reasonably safe, then she would consider investing some of her money. Maybe half. He hadn't said how much he needed.

Chapter Seventeen

"She's like a cross between Pamela Anderson and Nicole Kidman," Perry told Tibor and Harv. "Sexy, but smart too."

"Oh yeah?" The guys were hooting and slapping their knees. The three of them hunched around the desk, drinking beer and clinking bottles. Nothing like a hot new woman on the scene to bring on the party.

"And," he paused here for his delicious finale. "She's a lawyer."

Their stunned silence pleased Perry.

"No shit, man. I might start wearing suits myself," said Tibor.

He didn't have to tell them he'd told them so. The man was back on top.

His presentation was ready. On the weekend he sketched out floor plans and had made up some numbers, copying most of them from the hotel records and made them official by printing them up on paper with Grand Beach Downtown, in large font across the top of the page. A bogus Contract of Financial Agreement lay ready in the top drawer. Some of the phrases he copied off some legal papers he found in the bottom of the filing cabinet. No one ever read those things very carefully.

Tibor and Harv pored over the drawings. "This is bullshit," Tibor said. "How are you going to make an indoor beach? There's no way this will work."

"Are you seriously going to open a beach inside?" Harv drawled. "That's wicked. Chicks in bikinis all winter long. Totally wicked."

"Are you going to hire lifeguards? What if someone drowns? There's been all those drownings lately. People will want to see life guards."

"You know, I'm getting sick of everyone I tell about this shooting me down. Seeing nothing but problems. You have a negative vision, which is why you'll never go far."

"I'll go far if it means I can lie on a beach outside."

"Shut up."

"Are you going to wear your suit to the beach?" Harv snickered.

"So, why are you doing this again?" Tibor asked. He fiddled with the joint he was rolling. With his index finger he picked up all the bits of pot that fell onto the desk and ate them. He sold them for five bucks a piece at the junior high school when the kids got out for lunch. It was easy money because most of the kids didn't want to get caught with the stuff at home so they bought it one cigarette at a time.

"I need a business proposal for the lawyer so she will give me some money."

"Does she think this is for real or is she being scammed?"

"Hell, I have no idea. If it works, then it's for real and if not, then she's being scammed."

"And how will you stop her from coming after you. She's a lawyer. She'll have you by the balls so fast your fucking eyes will pop."

"I have a plan," Perry said, a sly grin on his face.

"What, you're going to sleep with her?"

"Of course. It's the best insurance a businessman can have."

"Isn't that blackmail?" Harv reached into the fridge for another beer but Perry stopped him. It was time for them to clear out.

"Only if she calls me on it and she won't. She's married."

"God," Tibor said. "In that case it might work. You're smarter than you look."

"Damn straight." Perry herded them out of his office and told them to stay away the rest of the day. He didn't want the two of them hanging around while he tried to sell his idea to the lawyer.

* * * * *

Theresa packed together her food package for Walter in a cardboard box. "What's that?" Antonina asked.

"I am taking some food to one of the old men at the hotel. That man who died was probably his only friend. He must be feeling terrible right now. I have to go over there again today on business, too."

Antonina went back to the breakfast dishes. "What's he going to do with a chicken? We could use a good chicken here."

"I can't just bring him crackers and candy, can I? He's destitute. He needs something nutritious. Brother."

"Is that another new outfit?" Antonina had noticed the new sweater set Theresa wore this morning.

"As a matter of fact, it is. Do you like it?"

"It must be nice to have so much money."

"If you want to make money, you have to act like you already have some, or else people won't want to work with you. That's the first rule of business."

Watch you don't fall

Theresa didn't have the faintest idea what the rules of business were, but she was about to learn. Antonina didn't know what she was talking about either and chewed on the last of Dustin's toast while Theresa got ready.

Theresa had decided to give Carmen her free day at the spa, the one she won at the Christmas party. It was still stuck to the fridge with a magnet and Theresa thought Carmen needed a day at the spa more than she did.

"I hope the man likes his chicken."

"Oh brother. Enough with the chicken," Theresa huffed. She placed everything by the back door, swung it open with her hip and stepped outside.

* * * * *

Perry paced around the office. The question was whether or not to head for the boiler room for a pre-game smoke. He had no clue how to go about this. He didn't even know exactly where the germ for this idea came. All he knew was that something was propelling him onward.

It was hot in the boiler room and Perry could feel the perspiration ready to spring forth. He took a last toke, convinced he was about to impress the hell out of the lawyer. He brushed his sleeves and gave them a tug. He was ready.

* * * * *

Theresa carried the food box around to the front of the hotel. The bar room had not changed from the last time she was here. Only an absence at the table where Donald had sat at the far side of the room. Otherwise, the same dull light and smoke filtered through the air. Only Ruby was there, watching an exercise program on the television while she rolled cigarettes. Theresa placed the box on a table.

"Do you know if Mr. Storch is here yet?" Ruby was the only one around to ask.

"I don't know," Ruby squinted through the smoke. "You can check his office. Hey, would you mind getting me a coffee? I haven't had any yet. I need my fix."

Theresa looked around. There was no sign of Carmen. Theresa decided it would be better if she brought her coffee than if Ruby got it for herself. The coffee machine was behind the bar.

"Just a minute. I have to find the cups."

"Cups are in the cupboard under the cash register. And bring me some sugar too. It's useless without sugar."

"What's your name?" Ruby asked when Theresa brought the coffee over.

"Theresa."

"I had a sister called Theresa." Ruby kept up her rolling as she spoke.

"Really?" Theresa still wasn't that comfortable talking to these people and was anxious for Walter to arrive so she could get to Stork's office.

"Yeah. She died though. She coughed herself to death." Ruby cleared some of her bags off the chair next to her and Theresa sat down. "The doctors gave her the wrong medicine and she never got better."

"That's horrible."

"Sure it is." Ruby sipped her coffee, indifferent. She grimaced. "Shit, when did you make this? Last night?"

Theresa tasted hers. It was bitter and scalded. "It's awful isn't it?"

"Why don't you make some more? Get us some fresh coffee."

"I'm not sure how to make it."

"You don't know how to make coffee? How did you get this job?"

Just then Walter shuffled into the room in his slippers and layers of sweater. Theresa smiled expectantly at him and waited for his eyes to meet hers. When they did and he recognized her, his face blanched. The reaction startled Theresa and she spilled some coffee down the front of her sweater. "Aww, crap," she said, swiping at the stain. "Look at this! I have an important meeting this morning and now I have coffee down my front."

"I'm not having nothing to do with you, devil woman." Walter turned around and headed back out the door.

"Devil woman," Ruby repeated. She reached over and patted Theresa's arm. "He used to call me that all the time and so I put a curse on him and he's left me alone ever since. Now he's scared of everything."

Theresa brushed at the coffee on her shirt with paper napkins that Ruby handed her out of the dispenser. "Walter, come back. It's okay. I brought you some food. Don't you remember me from the other day? I brought your breakfast to your room? Come here and see what I brought you."

When he heard the part about the food, he wheeled around and made straight for his table. "Coffee," he commanded.

Theresa poured him a cup from behind the bar. "What do you take?"

"Where's the other one?" he grumbled.

"What other one? You mean Carmen?" Theresa couldn't believe he didn't know Carmen's name, after all she did for him. Cautiously, Theresa approached with the coffee.

"Go ahead and put it in front of him." Ruby sat grinning. "He's more afraid of you than you are of him. Like a wild racoon."

Theresa poured cream into his coffee. "Would you like to see what I brought you?"

"Bring it here. But don't stand over me. Bring it here and back away slowly." Avoiding her eyes, Walter flapped his hand at her. "Put it here," he said, motioning towards the table.

"Look, there's a whole chicken." Theresa tried to hurry him along. He stood and rummaged through the box with his crippled hands. He picked up the frozen chicken like a bowling ball and clucked and cooed at it.

"Well, that's a good thing," Ruby said. "Last year someone stole his chicken from the Christmas Cheer Board and he never got over it."

When Theresa took a step closer, Walter hissed at her to get away.

"What's the matter with him?" Theresa backed up.

"He thinks you killed Donald," Ruby said.

"What?"

"The last time you were here, Donald croaked and Walter thinks it has something to do with you. That's why he's all freaked out. He's wondering who you're going to kill today."

"How could he possibly think that? I just gave him some food."

"Who knows with Walter? He can think anything he wants."

Theresa watched Walter lay all the things out on the table in front of him. He tore at the bag of peppermint patties and shook them onto the table. His fingers fumbled with the wrapper but he managed to pop one into his mouth. His face became placid and content as he sucked on his candy, head cocked up towards the ceiling, eyes staring at the world in the stucco. He savoured the first one and then wolfed down five more. The whole time he held the chicken in his arms. He finished his last candy and in a panicky flurry he swept everything back into the box and heaved it off the table and made for the door. The weight of the box nearly toppled him over.

"Where are you going?" Theresa asked. Walter muttered something in reply that Theresa couldn't understand and disappeared out the door.

"He thinks someone is gonna swipe his loot. He's gonna to stash it upstairs." Ruby explained. "Probably won't see him until he's eaten the whole load. Here, use this." Ruby dunked a napkin into her glass of water and held it out to Theresa. Thankfully the stain started to disappear.

"Well he can't eat that chicken. It's frozen solid. It has to be cooked."

"It doesn't look like he's going to eat it. He thinks it's a puppy or something."

Ruby prepared to leave. She pulled her coats on and packed her things into an old flight bag and swished past Theresa. "You have a good day now."

* * * * *

Theresa took a deep breath and knocked on Perry's door. She held her coat tight to her body to conceal the spilled coffee. Perry spun out of his chair and tried to help Theresa with her coat.

"I went and spilled coffee all over myself." Her voice came out high pitched. Her nerves were rattled. "That Walter scared me half to death and made me spill."

Perry thought it was best not to ask. He reached for her coat and their eyes locked, the scent of their perfumes mingled. His eyes dropped downward. A turtleneck sweater. Fuzzy blue, the outline of her bra visible and the stain from the coffee spread across her chest like a map of India.

"What a freak. His Christmas hamper was stolen this year. Did you know that?"

"No, I had no idea. Who would steal a hamper from a poor person?"

Perry stood rooted to the spot, the effects of the pot numbing his tongue. "There are some desperate people around here," he said, hoping it sounded like a reasonable thing to say. Theresa picked at her sweater and didn't seem to hear him.

"I have some plans and numbers for you to go over today." He guided her to the chair opposite his desk. Nothing that came out of his mouth sounded sincere. He couldn't believe she was buying this crap.

Theresa smoothed her sweater over her chest and looked at the floor plan laid out on the desk. It was crudely sketched with a black felt pen. Water, sand, a cabana style bar, washrooms, a cloak room, the kitchen, a stage and a dance floor.

"There's no change rooms," she remarked, wanting to at least contribute something to her future business venture.

"What for?"

"People will need lockers and change rooms if they are coming to the beach in January." Theresa shifted in her chair and again the smell of coffee wafted up under her nose. She waited for Perry to say something.

Shit. Perry rose from his chair and pored over the diagram. "The washrooms. We can expand the washrooms. Good eye," he said, hoping to recover. He rested his hand on her shoulder for good measure. "Here are the projected earnings for the first two years."

Theresa pulled the paper towards her, now fully distracted by the weight of his hand touching her. None of the numbers made any sense, except as the dates extended into the future, the numbers beside them increased. Was that how it was supposed to look? All she could focus on was the smell of coffee lingering on her chest. She crossed her legs. "Hmm, I don't know. How much money do you need from me?"

Perry furrowed his brow. Was she bluffing? "Three thousand would be a great cushion." He regretted immediately using the word cushion. He knew his presentation was bogus. Anyone could see that and yet Theresa didn't seem to find anything wrong with it. She even seemed eager to get things moving. Maybe she was a plant. Sent here to make him screw up.

Three thousand. Theresa quickly calculated in her mind. If everything fell through she would still have a thousand in the bank. And if things went the way Stork had them down on paper then three thousand could turn into thirty thousand over a few short years.

Perry paced around behind her. "You know what?" he ventured. "Let's have dinner. I mean, wouldn't it be better if you had some time to think about it and we ink the deal someplace where we can celebrate? Let me buy you dinner. It's a lot of money you're considering and I need you to be sure."

He didn't want her to feel pressured or rushed and there was still a fair amount of charm and seduction to issue before he could seal the deal. It was making him nervous, her poring over those papers. He should have put more effort into making them authentic.

Theresa's face lit up. She loved the sound of dinner. It had been a long time since she had been to a restaurant. "That sounds great. I mean, I have the money and everything and I love your idea, but I really should think it over. Maybe I'll stop by the library and do some research."

Research? What the hell was she talking about? She was really taking this seriously. He'd have to work fast before she was on to him and asking him all kinds of complicated questions, like the change rooms. God, did she really think people would come to an indoor beach?

"How about Hy's?" he said, and by the way her face lit up, he thought there was still a chance she could be distracted.

Hy's! It was one of the best restaurants in the city. "Sure. When do you think?"

"Thursday. At seven."

Dinner at seven. All Theresa ever wanted was dinner at seven. "All right. That should give me enough time."

Perry sat back down behind the desk and gathered up his papers. "I hope you'll understand that I will have to keep these here. I still don't want word of this getting out. You're going to be the first. Then I'll get to work on some other investors."

"I understand," she told him. "I better get back to the office."

They stood at the door. To her surprise, Perry took her hand and leaned forward and kissed her on the cheek. "I'll call you tomorrow," he said.

Theresa left Perry's office and made her way down the hall to the bar. There had been nothing sexual about it, she told herself. It was a friendly peck on the cheek. And even though her heart thumped in her chest, she convinced herself that everything was normal and even if it was a bit out of the ordinary, at least she had things under control. The fabric of her sweater had turned cold and wet, but it didn't bother her so much. She was on the brink of something big. The tide had finally turned. Here was the chance she had been waiting for to get ahead in life and she wasn't going to mess it up.

Back in the lounge, Carmen had appeared and it gave Theresa a chance to give her the spa gift certificate.

"Here, I brought you something." Theresa handed her the envelope.

"The Lotus?"

"It's a gift certificate for the spa. You can go and have a facial or a massage or your nails done or something. I just thought you might like it. I won it at a Christmas party raffle and I doubt I'll use it."

"Gee, thanks." Carmen doubted she would use it either. She wasn't exactly spa material, but still it was a kind gesture. "Is your business all done now?"

"Almost, we're going to have dinner this week and wrap things up."

Carmen raised her eyebrows. Perry wasn't fooling around with this one. Most of his dates never got anything close to dinner. He obviously was still working on the assumption that Theresa was a lawyer.

* * * * *

"What happened to your sweater?" Vera asked when Theresa returned to the office.

"Oh shoot. I forgot about that. This old man at the hotel freaked out and startled me and made me spill my coffee all over myself. And that was before I even had my meeting." Theresa pulled a cardigan off the back of her chair and wrapped it around her and hugged her arms to her body. Her mind whirred with the thought of being a business woman. She couldn't believe a trip to a rundown old hotel could change her life. Opportunities popped up in the most unusual places.

"Did you finally meet this manager?"

Theresa paused. There was a sinking feeling in her stomach as she realized she forgot to get the papers signed. How could that be explained when she had spent the whole morning at the hotel?

"He didn't have the papers there. I guess he took them home and forgot to bring them back. He's going to call in a couple of days once he remembers to bring them in. He said he'd take me out to dinner." Once the words had been spoken Theresa couldn't hold back. "He kissed me on the cheek," she squealed with delight and spun around in her chair, even though that was the least exciting part, she had to tell Vera something of what happened.

Vera's eyes widened and she instantly rolled her chair over and hung on Theresa's every word. It was this kind of thing that made coming to work worthwhile. "What? Kissed you? What kind of a place is this?"

Theresa laughed and flutter-kicked her feet up and down. "I mean, it was an innocent kiss. I don't want you to get the wrong idea. We talked about other things. The kiss was just something that happened on my way out. I don't actually know why he kissed me. We're going to have dinner later this week to discuss a business matter. I can't talk about it though." The words tumbled out. Theresa took a sip of water to make them stop. She could see Vera's perplexed face and didn't want her to think the worst of her.

Vera chewed her pen. Theresa didn't go around letting men kiss her. She was a married woman with a child. There was a Sears portrait of them all on her desk.

"So, you're going to have dinner with this guy? Why? What kind of business? I thought all you needed was a couple of signatures."

"Why not? It's just a business dinner. He forgot the papers and feels bad and wants to make it up to me."

"More like he wants to make out with you. Open your eyes Theresa. Men never kiss women and make dates for dinner with them unless they want to go all the way. Does he know you're married?"

"I guess so. I mean, I have a ring on my finger. It's right here in plain view." Theresa dangled her hand in front of Vera's face.

"Sometimes that is not a deterrent. Men don't care about that, but you should."

Theresa shrugged. "I'm not having an affair. I can't tell you everything about it, but we might go into business together."

"What kind of business?" Vera was wary whenever it came to men proposing anything to women.

"I can't tell you. It's too early and the idea is too good to let it get into the wrong hands."

"Are you going to tell Paulie?" Vera had to ask.

"Paulie has nothing to do with this right now. This is just for me. I'll tell him once everything is settled. Right now he doesn't need to know. I want something to be just for me for a change. He lies under that car all day long when he should be looking for a job. I will not feel guilty about this. In the end he'll thank me."

Vera was not convinced. "Well you know where to find me. Just be careful before you sign anything. You hardly know this guy."

But, Theresa didn't want to hear it. Stork had been in business a long time and knew what he was doing, she told herself. If he had a gut feeling about her, then she should be flattered and take him seriously. Vera wasn't there. She didn't know how Stork made Theresa feel. She hadn't done anything wrong.

They both swung their chairs back to their desks and worked the rest of the afternoon. Time dragged. The clock on the wall read two-thirty. At four-thirty she would have to go home and act normal. She could not get the image of Stork out of her mind and all she thought about was returning to the hotel to see him again and get going on their idea. It was perfect. He was losing his job at the hotel and so he needed to do something else and his proposition about the beach was as good an idea as any. And he had chosen Theresa to help him with it. A chance like this might never come along again.

* * * * *

For once Theresa didn't tune in to her pre-dinner soap. Instead, she lay on the bed and stared at the ceiling. An indoor beach. There was a lot more she needed to know if she was going to impress Stork on Thursday. The Centennial library wasn't far from the law firm. She would go over on her lunch break and find some information. She wished she could tell Vera about it, but Stork had been firm on keeping things quiet.

The back door slammed and she heard Paulie greet Dustin and then she heard the refrigerator door. Seconds later he was on the stairs, coming up for a shower. He opened the bedroom door, his shirt already off, a beer in his hand. He placed it on the dresser and tugged at his fly.

"Hey," he said, letting his pants drop to the floor. He stood at the foot of the bed in his underwear. Theresa could smell oil on him from across the room. "Not watching your show today?"

"No, just daydreaming for a change. Where were you?"

"In the garage." Paulie came over and gave her a kiss. "Is that a new perfume?"

"No, why?"

"You smell different. Nice. I like it."

"I don't know what you're talking about. But, thanks." It was Stork's cologne and the coffee and her own perfume that Paulie smelled. Theresa's heart pounded. She hadn't changed yet and Paulie saw the coffee stain right away.

"Did Dustin spill something on you?"

"No, I spilled coffee on myself. I guess I should change." She rose and pulled off her sweater. Paulie grabbed her from behind and wrestled her to the bed. He pinned her down and kissed her lightly on the lips and under her breasts. Theresa lay beneath him, distracted and mute. Maybe if she stuck to the truth and acted normal, everything would be okay. She giggled and pushed him away. "I have to make the salad."

"Oh, all right." Paulie said, getting up. He pulled Theresa up with him and gave her another hug and kiss on the neck. "It better be one hell of a salad."

"It will be fabulous."

Paulie wrapped a towel around his middle and went to have a shower.

Chapter Eighteen

The bulb was out in the hallway on Walter's floor. Carmen walked into the darkness towards his door. "Hey, Walter. Time to get up. The funeral's in an hour."

There was no sound from inside. Carmen tried the door. It opened easily and swung directly into the back of Walter's dresser. "Walter, why's the door blocked again? Get up and let me in."

Still nothing from inside. Through one squinted eye Carmen could see through the crack in the door. Walter sat upright on his bed, cradling some pinkish thing. Carmen's first horrified thought was that Walter had found a baby somewhere. "Walter, what is that?"

"What?" he finally chirped. He hoisted the thing up higher into his arms.

Carmen banged the door a few times in frustration. How he got the heavy dresser across the floor with his withered muscles and brittle frame was anyone's guess. "Open the door Walter. Why do you have your self barricaded in there?"

"That devil woman did it to me."

"What? She's not even here. What are you talking about?" She kicked the door hard and hurt her toe. "I'm tired of coming up here every day to batter the door down. Now open up!"

"She brought me this chicken and now I have to take care of it."

Carmen's thought about going back downstairs and coming back later. But there were shuffling feet coming towards her and then Walter was at the door, one beady eye on her through the crack in the door.

"Move the dresser, Walter. Maybe I can help you. Or maybe I should call the police to come and get you out."

He relented and threw his featherweight body against the dresser. Slowly, the heavy oak dresser slid across the floor and the door eased open.

The heat was stifling and a pungent odour overcame Carmen as soon as she entered. Walter's clothes were drenched with perspiration and sweat. The sheets were soaked with piss and all twisted in knots on the floor beside the bed. The radiator hissed and sputtered. A puddle of thin red juice, presumably where the chicken had thawed, pooled beneath it.

"Where the hell did you get that chicken?"

"I told you. That orange haired devil woman brought it. I think it's cursed."

"Theresa? What did she think you would do with a chicken?" Carmen jiggled the window to try to get some air inside. She didn't care anymore what Walter thought. She should have taken care of things herself the other day when she fell and hurt her wrist. Now, along with Theresa's sympathy, Walter had a useless chicken.

"Goddamn it Walter, these windows are swollen shut. I don't know how you stand it in here. Get up now. Let's get you into some dry clothes. You have to have breakfast and then we'll take a cab to the funeral."

"Who died?"

"You'll find out when we get there. Now quit asking stupid questions and get washed."

His bed was littered with cracker crumbs. The Ritz box was wedged between the bed and the wall. Under the bed his jar was overturned and a narrow river of urine snaked its way across the floor and soaked into the bottom of the cardboard box with all the other food.

"That woman is the devil," he said, his eyes spinning. "This is a cursed chicken. She killed Donald and then brought me a cursed chicken."

"Oh Jesus, Walter. All this food is getting soaked. Did she bring you all of this?" She pulled what she could salvage out and put it on his dresser and threw the soggy box into the corridor. "God, most of it is wrecked. It'll have to be thrown out. I don't know what that woman was thinking bringing you all this stuff. How much have you eaten?"

"I saved the chicken," Walter chirped from the floor. He hadn't moved. Peppermint Patty wrappers littered the floor beside him.

"Do you mean you saved it? Like you exorcised it or something? I thought you said it was cursed."

"It is cursed, but now it listens to me."

"Well, that's just great. Does it talk back?"

"What? It's a good chicken now. I saved it."

"It could have been a good chicken. It'd probably kill us now. Full of salmonella. Here, give it to me. I'll throw it out with the rest of this stuff." Carmen reached down but Walter, in a flash, turned his head and bit her hand with sharp, stubby teeth. Luckily she had wrapped her wrist with a tensor bandage.

"What the hell did you do that for?" She shook her hand and stared at him in disbelief. "What's the matter with you?"

"Keep away from my chicken. Nobody touches my chicken but me." He was pale and sweaty and an unhealthy intensity had seized him.

"What is going on Walter? What's happened to you?"

Carmen began to wonder if Theresa did somehow freak him out. If he really did believe she was responsible for what happened to Donald, it wouldn't be a far leap for him to think she would try to get him next. He was shaking and his eyes were darting all over the place. But what was the deal with the chicken?

She walked over to the tiny window and looked outside to the street below. Cars and buses and plumes of exhaust. Tiny people scurrying to get out of the cold, leaving their own trail of exhaled exhaust. Carmen considered Walter, sprawled on the floor, still clutching his chicken, and she wondered for the first time, where he would go. They all had to be out by the end of March.

"Come on, get up and get dressed. Maybe I can cook some soup or something with your chicken."

He growled at her and then squealed when she tried to help him up. There was a candy wrapper stuck to his pyjama bottoms when he stood up and Carmen flicked it onto the floor with the others.

"What the hell are we doing here anyway, Walter? What the hell?" Carmen shook her head at Walter. A crippled up old man, soaked in his own piss and fawning over a chicken.

"I don't want nobody to cook my chicken."

"Fine, you can be buried with that chicken for all I care. Now let's find you something half decent to wear." Carmen rifled through his closet and pulled out some clean pants and a sweater. "Put these on and then come downstairs. And bring that damn chicken with you. Don't leave it up here."

"Of course it's coming with me. I'm not letting it out of my sight."

* * * * *

218

Perry slumped in his chair and stared at the plans for the beach. Change rooms. Any idiot could see this thing wasn't thought through. He hoped Theresa didn't start asking many more questions. But as long as Theresa was showing an interest then he would keep up the act until he had some cash in his pocket. He wondered how quickly he could get the money out of her. Maybe he could suggest she bring it with her on Thursday. He dialed the number at the law firm. Another woman answered the phone.

"Is Theresa there?"

"Is that you Paulie?" the voice asked.

Perry puffed on his cigar. "No. It's not. I'll call back later."

He picked up his cigar and sauntered out to the bar. Paulie did not sound like a rich man's name.

The usual air of languor and idleness hung in the room. The one thing they all had in common was that none of them was ever in a hurry. Ruby gummed half a Denver sandwich. The other half was on a plate in front of Darren. His legs, like fallen timber, crossed and angled across the floor. Nobody sat anywhere near Donald's old table. A flicker of his image still shivered there, visible from the corner of every eye. Walter couldn't even look in that direction without feeling the kiss of death. Above the bar, Carmen had taped the brief obituary that had appeared in the *Winnipeg Free Press*. The noticed taped to the door was his legacy. It hung there and reminded everyone of Donald and then reminded them of the passing days, which no longer passed one after the other in an endless stream, but now marched towards a definite end. Each day a step towards some unknown entity. Something they could only identify as a mild sense of distress, which lodged itself in their minds like a wad of chewed up bubble gum in their cheek.

Carmen stormed in, with Walter not far behind carrying his chicken.

"What the hell is that?" Perry asked. His cigar smouldered on the bar beside a grilled cheese sandwich. He picked up a triangle and dragged it through some ketchup and jammed half of it in his mouth.

"It's a goddamn chicken. From Theresa."

"The lawyer?"

Carmen was too irked to bother explaining. "Yeah, the lawyer. I'm trying to convince Walter to let me cook it but he's grown pretty attached to it."

Walter carried the chicken over to his table and set it in front of him. Overnight it had thawed and now sat in front of him at room temperature, slick with globules of fatty tissue.

"That's disgusting," Perry told Walter, his cigar once again between his teeth. "Chickens aren't allowed in here like that, Walter. They're either cooked or they go. Health regulations. You're going to have to get rid of it or let Carmen cook it for you."

Walter ignored him and kept chirping at his chicken. The chicken sat in a newly formed puddle of ooze. Perry watched the fluid inch towards the edge of the table and then dribble onto the floor. The sleeves of Walter's sweater soaked much of it up. Perry rose and in one swift machete-like sweep, he grabbed the chicken and spiked it into the kitchen garbage before Walter shrieked.

"Scream as much as you like. That chicken is history. And don't give it back to him either," he ordered Carmen.

Outside, the flow of traffic blended into a meaningless blur. Theresa drove up Main Street. The Royal Winnipeg Ballet was performing *Sleeping Beauty* for busloads of school children. In the museum another group of students sat in the teepee and ate pemmican and listened to stories about Nanook of the North and down the street from all of them, a utility grade chicken awaited its fate.

A lazy beam of sun cast its light reluctantly into the room and hit a spot in the middle of the floor where the carpet had snagged and rolled up. Someone had tried to tape it back to the floor with silver duct tape, but that curled up with the carpet and now people less familiar with the place tripped over it with uncanny certainty.

Walter sat in his chair, sunken and morose. Carmen plunked a plate of eggs and cup of coffee down in front of him. He had her in a wild mood already over that damn chicken and she was glad it had been Perry and not her that had the final word.

"Watch your coffee, it's hot."

"It's terrible."

"Well, I made it at nine. How was I supposed to know it would take you all morning to get down here?" She stormed around the room, taking swipes with a wet cloth at random table tops.

"I don't know what's the matter with you these days anyway. You got me in a piss poor mood today, Walter."

"This is terrible," he said and let the coffee dribble down his chin, into his scrawny beard. "What did you do with my chicken?"

"It's in the kitchen at the bottom of a green garbage bag ready and willing to meet its maker."

"I want to see it." Walter's frantic eyes rolled in their sockets.

"What for? It's really gross, Walter. Just forget about it, okay?"

"Bring it here. Bring it here," he yelled and kept yelling.

"Good Lord, Walter. It's a chicken, not a pet. I'll let you see it one more time and then that's it. I've had it with this damn thing already." Her voice got tense and raw.

She brought it out and slapped it down in front of Walter. The wings and drumsticks splayed away from the body. "There. Say good-bye."

Ruby cackled from her table and said, "That your new girl friend? She looks a little beaten up from you slapping her so much."

Walter rolled the chicken around on the table, inspecting it for bruises. He clucked a few times and patted it on the back.

"Are you done, or should I get my camera?"

The chicken lay inert on the table. Walter scooped it towards him and he smothered it with his body. "You're not taking it," he growled. "It's mine."

"Nobody is disputing that. But it's time for your chicken to leave this world, all right?"

"No." He gripped it closer and his body sunk into it. He buried his head in his sleeve and refused to budge.

"Fine. You keep that chicken until it rots. I don't care anymore."

* * * * *

There was no way around it. Carmen and Walter and his chicken, now in a double bag, sat in the back seat of a taxi which drove them to the funeral home. To Carmen's surprise there were three limos and a hearse outside. Though not a man of means, Donald had left specific instructions and enough money for a stately funeral. Inside there were only eight other people. Carmen and Walter sat near the back. Every few minutes Walter peeked into the bag and cooed at his chicken. There was nothing Carmen could do to make him stop. She was thankful there weren't more people there. Up front lay the open casket with Donald in it. Everyone else had already viewed it.

An usher from the funeral home stopped by their pew and asked Carmen and Walter if they would now like to come forward to say good-bye. There was no choice and Carmen shepherded Walter up the aisle. He clutched the bag with his chicken close to his chest. The stood quietly in front of Donald. They had dressed him in a dark suit and had rouged his cheeks and combed his hair. Carmen wasn't sure Walter even recognised him. He swayed on his feet with his eyes closed. "He was a great man," he uttered. "A great man and a great human being. He didn't deserve to die."

Carmen stared at him but said nothing. Walter re-adjusted the chicken in his arms while gazing serenely upon Donald's corpse. Finally Carmen said, "Come on Walter. They want to get started. Those were some nice things you said about Donald."

"Hmmph."

She walked quickly up the aisle with Walter shuffling behind her. He hugged the chicken to him once he sat down again and babbled quietly to it for the duration of the service. They offered Carmen and Walter a ride to the cemetery in a limousine. "Do you want to go to the cemetery, Walter? We get to ride in a limo."

Walter nodded vigorously. They were driven through the city which Walter viewed from the car, a city he rarely saw. The mourners huddled in the brisk wind, shivering while the minister spoke. At the last moment, after the ashes to ashes and dust to dust were spoken, Carmen took a flower and threw it down into the grave. Beside her, Walter shuffled to the edge of the grave and before she realized what was happening, he dropped his chicken onto Donald's coffin. It landed there with an emphatic thunk. Walter stared after it a moment and then bowed his head. "R. I. P.," he said, in a reverent tone.

Horrified, Carmen glared at Walter, but there was nothing to be done. The minister gave her a stormy look. What did it matter if the chicken ended up in the garbage or in the ground next to another dead body, she thought. At least she wouldn't have to hear about it again. And Walter had finally gotten his revenge.

* * * * *

Chapter Nineteen

The bulb was out in the hallway on Walter's floor. Carmen walked into the darkness towards his door. "Hey, Walter. Time to get up. The funeral's in an hour."

There was a message on the answering machine from Vera. Sick today. She coughed half way through the message to make herself sound convincing. To Theresa it was the signal for Vera's mental health day and meant for Theresa to give her a call when she had a chance. Today was a good day for Vera to be off. With the office to herself, Theresa could make a few phone calls without Vera overhearing what she was talking about. Larry and Marshall were in but had meetings all day.

No sooner had Theresa settled herself in her chair than Tibor came tromping through the door. Theresa shuddered as she watched him kick snow off his feet and unzip his jacket. The smell of stale cigarette-drenched clothes hit her from across the room. He had his long hair tied back in a ponytail and it was shiny and slick on top like he hadn't washed it in a week. He wore some kind of a racing jacket with checkered flags on the sleeves. He wiped his mouth with the back of his hand and headed for Larry's office.

"Let me tell him you're here," Theresa said, heading him off and pointing to a chair. "Have a seat. There's no coffee yet."

She made him wait while she poked her head into Larry's office. "Tibor's here for you."

Larry was on the phone and signalled for Theresa to let Tibor in.

"How's your case coming along?" she asked Tibor. The curiosity was overwhelming sometimes. She couldn't figure out what on earth he and Larry talked about in there. She had no idea what it was he needed to see Larry about once a week.

"My case?" he asked, his voice heavy and slow.

"Yeah, whatever it is you need a lawyer for every week." For all he knew she asked everyone these kinds of questions.

"Okay, I guess." His hands twitched nervously. He didn't like waiting in this office environment. A law office no less. If it weren't for the fact that he overcharged Larry by a good fifty dollars each time, he wouldn't provide this kind of service. Usually people came to him. If people had the money though, they could afford the elite service.

"Must be pretty complicated to take this long." She could see he was getting nervous. His eyes darted between a spot on the wall behind her and Larry's door.

"I'm suing somebody." It was all he could think of. His mind didn't do well on the spur of the moment. Anyway, it stopped the questions. Theresa didn't want to associate herself with anyone who might sue her for some dumb reason. It was news to her that Larry dealt with lawsuits.

Larry, not knowing why Tibor hadn't come in to the office came out and got him. He threw a questioning look at Theresa, meaning, why didn't you let him in, and the two of them disappeared into his office.

Alone at last, Theresa flipped to the government blue pages and found a number for small business inquiries. Ten minutes passed before she got someone on the line who told her about business permits and floor plans and square footage and food sales required to have a liquor permit and PST and GST numbers and a thousand other things Stork hadn't even mentioned. Then she called her bank and asked about starting a business and it soon became clear there were other things, like a business plan requiring demographic information and feasibility studies and projected earnings. The woman told her there was a bank seminar on Wednesday at five for free. Theresa signed up. As soon as she hung up with the bank, she dialed the number for the hotel.

Perry answered. "Hi Stork. It's me, Theresa. I was wondering if you wanted to go to a business seminar with me on Wednesday? It's free."

"What?"

Theresa was glad he wasn't there to see her red face. Here she was asking a businessman to attend a beginner's seminar on how to start a business. Of course he didn't want to go. "Oh, never mind. I forgot you have done this before. Well, I'm going to go so I can learn something about all this before we start."

"Start what?" He had just smoked a big fatty and had loaded up his wallet with five hundred in twenties for the casino.

"The beach. Remember. Your brilliant idea. I have been doing some research. We have a lot of work to do. How long do you think it will be before it's up and running?"

"I don't know," he drawled. "Last time I did something like this it took about a year before the money started flowing in my direction."

"Hmm, that's not too bad. A year."

"Look, Theresa, I have to get going. I've got a meeting to get to. Let's get together on Thursday as planned and you can tell me all about your research and we'll get things drafted up. I might need your money then, okay? To get things started."

"Sure, sure. The money's no problem. I'll be ready for our meeting."

"All right. Oh, and don't worry about that seminar. I can fill you in. I have some good magazine articles you can borrow."

"Oh, well. Okay." Her enthusiasm was still fired up after hanging up the phone. She got the impression Stork wanted her involvement and her help and he was willing to help her. She pulled a pad of legal paper out of her drawer and drew up a list of things to learn before their meeting on Thursday. She barely noticed when Tibor left and grunted at her. Three minutes later Larry was in his overcoat at the door, going to his car for a smoke. The office was silent as Theresa worked on her list.

"Theresa," Larry said when he came back inside. "Can you get me all the Wiltshire stuff together. I want to go over it and wrap the thing up."

"I'll have it for you by this afternoon. I need to get those signatures. The last time I went the guy didn't have the papers there. He took them home or something. I'll try to get down there today."

"All right. I'll be in my office." He turned to go and Theresa glanced at his butt out of sheer habit, but it didn't do much for her today. There were more pressing things at hand than fantasizing about the boss. Now Theresa had an excuse to see Stork before Thursday.

* * * * *

The casino on the day the welfare cheques came out was always so delightfully grim. Buses in the parking lot, the Handi-Transit vans, all the desperate people in the city in one place for as long as it took to blow through their money for the month. Perry walked into the blanket of sound and light, an environment so artificial nothing within those walls could be found in the natural world. This was the seduction of the casino. It drew you in like nothing else existed. The soundscape was pure genius. All that could be heard in the din were the sounds of thousands of tokens falling in an endless stream of bells to alert you to someone else's good fortune. It made you quicken your step, every second counted. Every moment not spent dropping tokens into a machine was a lost opportunity. Perry did not fall into this trap. He came here to watch the decline of humanity. To remind himself of all the hopeless people out there. Even Walter and Ruby led lives of grander purpose than the people he observed in this place. Walter and Ruby would not ever spend the last of their government cheques here. He had seen it over and over, people rifling through their wallets and removing the last twenty from the secret compartment, the one they weren't supposed to use because they did not want to spend their last twenty at the slots. And they did it every time. He watched them hesitate and then approach the counter, clutching the empty bucket. This time they would get lucky. This last twenty would pay off. And if it didn't, there was always the ATM and the secret savings account they weren't supposed to touch. Perry delighted in the despair of it all.

He bought a Heineken and lit a cigarette. He circulated with his bucket of tokens and decided what to play. Wild Cherry, Lucky Seven, Betty Boop. There were at least twenty tour buses parked outside and blue hair and bad comb-overs everywhere. They sat with the coil of their debit cards around their neck, plugged into their machines, guard dogs chained to a post. Perry sat down between two such creatures and dropped a token into the slot. He went up five credits. This was his luck. He rarely lost at the slots. Most nights he came out with at least a hundred bucks. If it weren't for the people losing all around him, it would be no fun at all.

The woman beside him was watching. She wanted him to leave so she could take over his machine. It was a jungle and each animal fended for himself. Perry threw one last token in and the machine went berserk. It clinged and clanged for at least a minute. The casino attendant came over and Perry shrugged at the woman sitting next to him. He left her there, more determined than ever and walked out with two thousand dollars and some change. He was a lucky bastard. He went back to the hotel to wait.

In his office, behind a closed door, Perry waited for Tibor and Harv. He realized that after the hotel was torn down, he might have to return to the backdoor drudgery of dealing from home, which was why he wanted to extort some money out of willing young females now. The life of a drug dealer was no sweet feast. The way Perry had it set up now, the only people he had to deal with were Harv and Tibor. There were never any surprises. How those guys decided to peddle their stash was up to them and Perry, though he really had no scruples when it came to the business, didn't really want to know how many twelve year olds the guys recruited to do the dirty work.

Perry knew exactly what he was in for if he started dealing from home again and now that he felt he had taken a step up the ladder he wasn't too keen on tumbling back down. It meant an endless stream of people, any time, on his doorstep. They didn't call first, they just showed up with fat wads of twenties crammed into their pockets. He never knew how much they were going to want, or how many people they would tell about him. Some days his basement apartment had been full for hours, people he had no idea who they were just sitting around, using his toilet and filling his house with smoke waiting to score. People with meagre incomes making him weigh minuscule amount of grass and most of the time he got frustrated and ripped himself off by a bud or two. There was no way he wanted any part of that scene again. He had to think of something else. But the money was too good to get out of it all together and besides, what would he do? He wasn't about to go back to delivering for Chicken Delight. He didn't mind the driving so much, but the smell of that chicken stinking up his car. It was a wonder he ever got a date with his car smelling like a deep fryer all the time.

Tibor and Harv arrived with two for one pizzas and a case of Extra Old Stock. "Party's on," said Harv, stripping off his jacket and tossing it over the back of a chair.

They sparked a joint and passed it around. The pizza didn't stand a chance.

Chapter Twenty

Theresa peeked in the bar. Ruby was there, and Walter. The same old scene. Down the hallway, the door to Stork's office was closed. It sounded like there were people in there. Theresa decided to delay and pushed through the door to the bar. She presented Ruby with three tins of Chef Boyardee and a bag of Gummy Bears. These were inspected with pleasure and the gummy bears were the first to be consumed. Poor people sure liked their sweets, Theresa observed. Ruby sucked on one gummy bear after another as she rolled her cigarettes.

"Do you like them?"

Ruby squished a green bear behind her teeth. "Sure I like 'em. I like these kind a lot."

"Well, that's good, I guess." It interested Theresa that a bag of gummy bears could make a difference in a person's day.

"How did your chicken turn out?" she asked Walter, to remind him that she already brought him something in case he was wondering why Ruby cashed in today.

"His chicken got buried. He threw it in Donald's grave." Ruby laughed. "He's not too upset though. It had a good funeral." Ruby's waited expectantly for Theresa's reaction.

"What? Somebody was supposed to cook it for him."

"He wouldn't let nobody near that chicken. I think you really made his day bringing him that. I know it made mine."

"Why wouldn't somebody eat a perfectly good chicken? How could you just throw it away into a grave?"

But Walter was paying Theresa no attention. He sat hunched over the table and tapped crumbs out of his harmonica. At least he wasn't screaming.

"How's the coffee today, Ruby?" Theresa was behind the bar, helping herself to a cup.

"It's terrible. I could use a refill."

* * * * *

The smell of perfume hit Carmen as soon as she stepped off the bottom step and then she spied the mass of orange hair. Theresa had already helped herself to a coffee and was bringing one over to Ruby. Carmen wondered what brought her back to the hotel again. Ever since she brought that chicken for Walter and all the uproar that followed, Carmen wasn't so sure she wanted to see Theresa again. And what was she supposed to do at a spa for a day? Now the thing was stuck to Carmen's fridge.

"Oh, hi," Theresa said when she turned and saw Carmen. "Do you want a coffee? I was just about to bring one to Walter."

"No more chickens, I hope."

"Oh no. I heard what happened to it though."

"That's Walter. Full of surprises." Carmen changed the TV channel back to the news. The match in her hand burned down to her finger and she shook it out and threw it in an ashtray.

"I kind of thought he would eat it, but if that's what makes him happy. He didn't scream at me today anyway. My blouse is still clean." Theresa said. "I came to see Stork."

Some people were so damn gullible, Carmen thought when she heard Perry had convinced Theresa to call him Stork.

"He might scream yet. You never know with Walter what will set him off."

"So, is Stork around?" Theresa asked.

Carmen laughed. "I wish you would stop calling him that. I can't get used to it. His name is Perry."

"It is? Then why does everyone call him Stork."

"Nobody calls him that. Just you. And maybe those two stooges he has working for him."

"I've got to pick up some papers I left for him." Theresa hovered by the door, wondering if Carmen was going to thank her for the food she brought Walter.

Carmen shrugged and flipped through the channels until she found a talk show. "He's in his office. Go ahead. You know where it is."

Carmen chuckled as she listened to Theresa click down the hall. Perry still thought she was a lawyer and Carmen was not going to be the one to tell him. Let him carry on with his dinners and whatever lies he was feeding her. It wasn't her problem if people lied to each other. Her days of shielding Perry from the world were over. It was time he learned to fend for himself. In a few weeks the hotel would be gone and everybody scattered and one way or another. They were all going to have to make it on their own.

She picked up Walter's plate and cup and carried them into the kitchen. She let them clatter into the sink, not caring if they broke or not. It didn't matter much anymore. Two flies on the windowsill grew more agitated and banged repeatedly into the window. After about six attempts, they fell to the sill and caught their breath before re-launching their attack. Carmen picked up the fly swatter and killed them both, one at a time. "It's either me or the wrecking ball, boys."

Watch you don't fall

*****

Theresa tapped on the office door. Through the frosted glass she could see several people and she could smell pizza. Theresa eased open the door and stuck her head in. "Hi," she said. "Sorry to interrupt, but..."

It was then that Tibor turned around. Theresa's eyes grew wide. It didn't make sense for Tibor to be in Stork's office. There was another guy there with him just as creepy, and Stork, all of them staring at her.

"Umm, hi," she stammered. "My boss needs those papers this afternoon. It can't wait."

"I'll be out in a minute." Perry said, quickly composing himself and trying to make his voice silken. "Give me a second to find them. I'm just in a meeting, but I'll bring them down to the bar if you want to wait there."

On the desk in front of them were two meat lovers pizzas and two six packs of Budweiser. The smell of marijuana hung in the air. Harv took a sip of beer but did not take his eyes off Theresa. Tibor turned back to the table and did nothing to acknowledge her. Perry rose to close the door behind her. "Sorry about this," he whispered. "I'll explain everything in the bar. Go and wait for me there."

"Well, okay." Theresa said. She was stunned at seeing Tibor and allowed herself to be herded from the office. Perry flashed her a smile before she disappeared.

"Shit, shit, shit," Perry said. "You guys have to get out of here. Fuck."

"Was that her?" Harv asked, cramming a slice of pizza into his mouth. "Was that the lawyer?"

"Yeah, that was her." Perry dumped everything out of the top drawer onto the desk and rifled through it to find the papers Theresa wanted. This was the worst possible scenario, her catching him at play with his dealers. The entire scene looked like some scene out of a stoner movie, with the smoke and the pizza and the long haired geeks.

"Not what I expected," Harv said.

"That's because she's not a lawyer," Tibor said. He put a cigarette between his lips and held up his lighter. The flame shot five inches into the air and nearly set his hair on fire. Beside him, Harv was doubled up laughing in his chair. Tibor threw the lighter and hit him square on the ear.

"Shit man, that hurt." Harv grabbed his ear but kept snickering.

"What did you say?" Perry had found the papers. He stopped scribbling his signature on them.

"She's not a lawyer, man. I'm your friend and so it's my duty to tell you. If you're planning on fucking that cushiony piece of ass, then you should know what you're getting into and it ain't no lawyer."

"Getting into. Ha, ha," said Harv and gave Tibor a shot in the arm.

"Well, what is she then? And how the hell do you know anyway? Is she your sister?"

"Naw, she's not my sister. She's the secretary at that lawyer's office I go to. What's she doing coming around here? You got something going down with the legal system?"

Perry finished signing the papers. "A secretary? Are you sure?"

"Course I am. She glares at me every time I'm in there. Gives me a hard time. How much money you getting out of her?"

"Wait a minute. She knows you? She pops her head in here and sees you sitting at my desk and she knows you sell drugs to her boss? This sucks." Perry twirled a pencil on his thumb. It spun to the floor and rolled under the radiator.

"She has no idea what I'm doing there. This morning I had to tell her I was suing someone. She was asking a lot of questions."

"What? Are you shitting me?" Perry grimaced. It made too much sense now. Of course she wasn't a lawyer. Lawyers never did any of the dirty work themselves. They sat in their sleek offices and splattered ink from their Mont Blanc pens onto their daytimers. All the pretty colours of the rainbow. But why did she want him to think she was? Was she that eager to impress him? It must have been the beach idea. She was really into it and wanted to make sure Perry took her seriously. That was it. "That's fucking unbelievable."

The guys snickered and Perry snickered right along with them. She had no idea what was about to hit her.

"So, she doesn't know you sell drugs?"

"Nope." Tibor said. His eyebrows had been grazed by the lighter and flicked bits of singed hair onto the floor.

"Good," Perry pulled his suit jacket on and strode to the door. "I have an idea. I'll be right back."

He found Theresa waiting at the bar, in her coat and clutching her bag. But when Perry flew through the door with the papers, he was all smiles. He reached out to shake her hand. "Theresa, I'm sorry. Let me explain that scene. I don't usually party on the job but those guys are two potential investors. They've got a lot of cash and are interested in the beach. So I wined and dined them a little. The same way I was planning on wining and dining you tomorrow night. Except it won't be pizza and beer, of course. We're still on right?"

"Those guys are rich?" Theresa tried to read Perry's face but he gave nothing away. She decided it was best not to let on she knew Tibor.

"You never know what a millionaire is going to look like. At least that's what I've found in my years doing business."

Bettina von Kampen

Tibor was a millionaire? Theresa couldn't believe it. No wonder he was so secretive about coming around the firm. People with money didn't always want everyone knowing their business. She couldn't wait to get back to the office and tell Vera.

"Well, I better go. Good luck with the millionaires. I hope my measly contribution counts for something still."

"Trust me," Perry said. "Every little bit helps. In business you never turn down an investor. So, tomorrow's good?"

"Yeah, sure. I'll be there. Seven o'clock. I'll bring my check book and we'll make it official. Thanks for the papers." Theresa patted her briefcase.

Perry put his hand on her shoulder and let it rest there. No more kisses. That first one had been a slip. He'd get to kissing her again soon enough. "I'll be there too," he said.

Theresa swallowed the butterflies that erupted in her stomach. Everything was still on track. She decided to tell Stork at dinner she wasn't a lawyer and get things started on the right foot. There was no use having any deception between them.

* * * * *

The party was still on in Perry's office and the mood was high. But, at five-thirty they were getting hungry and they discussed where to go and eat. Harv wanted to go somewhere where they could see strippers and Tibor wanted to watch the Leafs game and Perry was too giddy to care. He had a fine catch. Tomorrow he would reel her in and finish her off. Carmen stopped by and said she was leaving.

"Hey, Carmen. Come on in here. Listen to this." He handed her a beer that she took, for once. "Would you have any interest in investing in an indoor beach?"

"You're kidding right?"

"Just hypothetically, if someone was to open a place like that, with sand and water and sunlamps and a bar. Do you think that would be something that would give you a return on your investment?"

"No bloody way! What a stupid idea. Who would go to an indoor beach? Women don't want to shave their legs in the winter. Forget it."

"That's what I thought."

"Why, did that lawyer proposition you with that idea? I'd steer clear."

"No, not the lawyer, but I heard about it and I wanted to know if you thought it might be something people would go to."

"Uh,uh. I doubt it. Save your money."

Just as Perry suspected. It was a stupid idea. But why was Theresa so into it? Where was the catch? Could it be that she really was bored out of her head and had some flighty fantasy about making it big with a minuscule investment of three grand? If that was the case, then he would have her eating right out of his hand. He didn't have a clearly formulated plan, just a situation with lots of potential. It would come to him when the time was right. And the time would be tomorrow night. All he wanted was a bit of amusement. And Theresa was turning out to be highly entertaining.

Chapter Twenty-One

Theresa got to work before anyone else. The night before she hardly slept. All night she thought about Tibor and the beach and Stork and worried how everything was going to turn out. She desperately wanted to talk to Vera. She was near to bursting when Vera finally trudged up the steps and entered the office.

"What do you know about Tibor?" Theresa asked anxiously.

"Tibor? You mean Larry's guy?" Vera booted up her computer and viewed the files which had piled up on her desk from one day off.

"Yeah. What's his story? What's this lawsuit about?"

"Lawsuit? What lawsuit?"

"The one he's in here every week to discuss with Larry."

Vera smiled. "Do you mean it?"

"Mean what?"

"He said he was suing someone?"

"That's exactly what he said. And then yesterday I saw him sitting in that hotel manager's office eating pizza and smoking what smelled like drugs, and Stork told me he was a millionaire and that he was going to ask him to invest in his business. The same one he's asking me to invest in. I mean, it makes no sense. How can that smelly, unwashed man be a millionaire?"

"Whoa, slow down Terri. I can't make any sense of what you're saying."

"Well, neither can I. That's what I'm talking about."

"You think he's a millionaire?"

"I don't know. He might be."

Vera squealed. "That's too much!" She paused and slipped on her office shoes. She wasn't sure just how to break the news to Theresa. She thought it was clear what Tibor was doing there every week. Something that needed no explanation and wasn't really supposed to be mentioned. But Theresa didn't know and now Vera had to tell her that Larry was a pot fiend.

"Theresa, do you really think Tibor is really one of Larry's clients?"

"Well, what else would he be? Most millionaires have accountants, not lawyers, unless he gets rich by suing people." Theresa furrowed her brow.

Vera took a deep breath, glanced around. All the office doors were shut. She decided to be blunt. "Listen, Tibor sells drugs to Larry. Every time Larry goes out to his car for a smoke, he's smoking a joint. I don't know how else to tell you. I just thought you knew like everyone else."

Theresa bottom lip trembled. She felt stupid and betrayed. How could everyone know something this big and not tell her? "Well, how the heck was I supposed to know something like that? I don't have any idea of what a drug dealer might look like."

Vera wondered whether to continue or to let the rest unfold on its own. After a moment Theresa asked, "You don't think Stork smokes drugs too, do you? I mean, there was a lot of smoke in there. It would have been all of them smoking the stuff."

Vera shrugged. "It's possible."

The news unsettled Theresa. All her life she thought the only kind of people who smoked drugs were the ones that hung out behind the school gym and never took their jackets off. People like Tibor. It didn't surprise her at all that he smoked drugs. Even she could have guessed that. But Larry? And Stork? These were professionals. They had responsibilities and authority over people. She decided to do a test.

"Vera," she said, not sure if she wanted to know the answer. "Do you ever... you know. Smoke?"

Vera pulled the earpiece from her ear. "Drugs, you mean? Yeah, once in awhile. You know Theresa, it's not that bad. It takes the edge off."

"What edge? It's illegal. How's that for an edge?" If Vera smoked and Larry and maybe Stork, then Theresa had no idea how she was supposed to tell. For all she knew Antonina snuck out to the garage every afternoon to light up.

"All I can say is that it's not as bad as you think and all people who smoke aren't losers." Vera turned back to her work and left Theresa to stew.

Theresa finally decided it didn't matter that much if Stork's friends smoked drugs. At least Stork had the decency to try to protect her from it.

* * * * *

Larry came back inside and slipped his overshoes off at the door. Theresa sniffed the air when he walked by, but all she could smell was his peppery cologne. Nothing that smelled like drugs. He went into his office and closed the door. Ever since she met Stork her torch for Larry dimmed, and now that she knew about the drugs, that was fine with her.

At four-thirty Vera straightened up her desk and pulled her coat on. "Well, I'm getting out of here, see how my cats are doing. Are you still meeting your man for dinner?"

Theresa nodded her head. "I'm meeting him at seven."

"What are you doing until then?" Vera kicked her shoes under her desk and put on her Sorels. She pulled on a wool toque.

"I think I'll stay here and work. The restaurant isn't far from here."

Vera squeezed her hand. "Are you sure you know what you're getting into? Good looks and charm can be a horrible combination."

Theresa grinned. "I'll be fine. I've done my research. It's exciting to do something new. Once it's final I'll tell you all about it."

"Well, okay. I promise not to call in sick tomorrow."

They hugged and Vera left. Theresa carried on with her work until at five-thirty Larry came out of his office, dressed for the outdoors.

"You still here, Terri?" He checked his watch. "It's time to get going. That can wait until tomorrow."

"Oh, I'm just going to finish this and then I'll be out of here." She couldn't bring herself to look at him. He reached over and dug his hand into the box of vanilla wafers and scooped out a handful.

"Whatever that is, you can do that tomorrow. It's not urgent."

"Well, I feel like this hotel sale is taking up a lot of my time and I need to catch up. I'll only be another hour or so."

"Terri, I never meant for that hotel to overwhelm you. It's all standard paperwork. It should have been taken care of in one afternoon." He munched hungrily on the cookies.

"I'll have it finished off tomorrow. I have an appointment in a while and it's not worth it for me to go home first. I'll just have to turn around and come all the way back."

"You don't have a key. I'll get you the spare and you can lock up, all right? But don't leave the door open while you're alone in here."

Bettina von Kampen

* * * * *

Alone in the office, Theresa sat waiting at her desk. She was anxious to see Stork and get things rolling. She wanted to know everything was still fine. It had to be. The backs of her legs were sore from sitting all afternoon. What was she going to do for the next hour? She focused on the hum of silence. Larry had not closed his office door.

His chair was one of those with a high back, cushioned in quilted leather and worn where he sat. She opened the top drawer. A pack of gum, a plastic container of TicTacs, paperclips, pens, white out, the same kind of stuff she had in her desk. The marijuana was in a plastic baggie, clumped together in greenish brown buds. There was a pack of Zig Zag rolling papers in there, the same kind Ruby used at the hotel to roll her cigarettes. Theresa opened the bag and sniffed. It smelled like moss, mouldy moss. Not the nice fresh moss that feels like carpet on bare feet. There was half a joint in the bag too. Theresa picked it up and held it to her lips. She inhaled. The taste of stale ash filled her mouth and she threw it back into the drawer, disappointed that her discovery hadn't been more spectacular.

Theresa went to the bathroom and checked her make-up. If she left now she would be early, but better that than late. She got her coat and locked the door behind her.

The roads were slippery with ice hardened from weeks of temperatures in the minus thirties. A fresh layer of snow blanketed everything. Before Christmas such a sight put everyone in a festive mood. But now, four months into winter, it was just another layer that had to melt before the grass could grow again. The wheels of her car glided in the deep grooves rutted in the road. At each stop sign was a sprinkling of sand. Salt was useless in these temperatures and a bit of sand was supposed to prevent cars from sliding into one another. It didn't make much difference. Cars slid into each other all the time.

* * * * *

The parking lot behind the hotel was lit with a single light that hung above the kitchen door. Perry stepped outside and pulled his collar up over his ears. His lungs clenched when the cold air hit and made him cough. He had promised Carmen a ride home before he made his way to the restaurant to meet Theresa.

He had decided Theresa's little deception had been more to impress him than to deceive him. Something he found hilarious, though not unexpected. It happened to him all the time; women falling for him. It amazed him sometimes what he could get away with. Being a jerk had become a fine tuned act. He didn't really know much else. It was animal instinct and he based his behaviour on the knowledge that most women were attracted to jerks.

The light that shone from the back of the building did little to illuminate the parking lot and the car was covered in snow. Perry slipped on his gloves. The lock was frozen shut and he chipped away at it with his key. The cold was freezing the tip of his nose and his lips felt numb. The key wouldn't go into the lock and so he walked around to try the other side. Something caught his eye, lurking in the shadow. He glanced at the door but Carmen was still inside. Probably just some rubbie trying to find a warm air vent.

The passenger door opened without much coaxing. The vinyl seats were cold and unwelcoming and gave him a chill through the thin material of his pants as he crawled over to open the driver's side.

The car started on the fourth try. Perry cranked the heat and grabbed the brush and got out to clean off the windshield. The shadow suddenly sprung to life and Perry was thrust back into the car by a man with vile breath who wielded a long knife at Perry's face.

"Ah, fuck. You've got to be kidding me." Perry sat back down sideways in the driver's seat, his feet in the snow. He had never seen the guy before, half crazed, his boozy breath hanging in the cold air.

"Leave the keys in and get out of the car or I'll cut you." He jabbed the knife at Perry's face again. People got knifed in this neighbourhood all the time. Carmen and Perry often saw the evidence of fights from the night before pooled on the pavement in the mornings when they got to work. Sticky patches of brown that stained the cement.

"You're not taking my fucking car," Perry said and kicked his foot out at the guy. It caught him in the knee, but he didn't stagger.

"Give me the keys." The man flicked the knife at Perry's jacket and cut a slit in the fabric.

"Shit, you asshole. Get away from me." Perry's options were limited. He was stuck in his car with the thief blocking his exit. The blood-stained parking lot got that way because people like him didn't hand over whatever people like the guy with the knife wanted. He either gave the guy the car or risked ending up dead.

Walter sat up in his room with the lights out, watching. He saw the glint of the knife before Perry did, but what was he supposed to do? If he ratted the guy out who would be here to protect him? So, Walter sat and watched Perry's car get stolen. He guessed Perry wouldn't put up much of a fight. The guy had no muscles. The new suit wasn't exactly a suit of armour and Walter let out a low whistle when he saw the guy flashing his knife around and Perry yelling and not getting out of the car. "He's asking for it."

Suddenly Perry lunged forward and pushed the thief to the ground, but in his shiny shoes, he didn't have good footing and he slipped, landing face first in the snow. The thief got up, kicked Perry once in the ribs and once in the head before jumping into the car. All Perry saw when he opened his eyes was the one functioning tail light of his vehicle disappearing into the night. He let his head fall back into the snow. His cheek throbbed and the snow felt cool and soothing.

Faintly, in the background Perry heard the kitchen door swing open. Carmen's body cast a long shadow over the white ground.

"Perry?" She couldn't see him at first in the dark. "Where are you?"

"Over here." His raspy voice rose from the snow. The cold air made him cough, shallow, gasping coughs.

"Oh God, what happened?" She leapt off the steps and hurried to Perry's side. She didn't notice the car was gone. There was no blood in the snow. "What happened?"

"Some guy pulled a knife on me and stole my fucking car. The car is gone."

"What? Which way did he go?" She ran to the lane and looked up and down the alley. There was no sign of any thief or car. She rushed back to Perry's side. "Are you hurt?"

"Yeah, a bit." The pain was settling.

"Can you get up? Let's go in and call the police."

The police. Perry was never keen on involving the police in anything. He had two pounds of pot stashed in the safe and nearly four thousand dollars. The car wasn't worth it. "Let's just call a cab and get out of here. The fucker can have the car."

"You can't just let someone steal your car and do nothing about it."

"I'm not calling the police in here, okay? I might as well jump off a bridge."

"Well then, get up and come inside. I'll get you a drink."

She helped him to his feet. His legs were a shaky and his head throbbed once he stood up, but he managed to stagger back into the bar. He took the brandy and cigarette Carmen offered and slumped into a chair. The place was empty except one old guy at a far table, finishing his last beer before they kicked him out. On the television two hot chicks and a chubby, sweaty guy were taking turns eating live slugs off a glass table. The camera angled under the table and shot up at them, in case one of them puked. What a great shot that would be. It would look like they were puking right into the camera.

The man at the far table sat and stared at the television. Carmen glanced at Perry's pale face and decided this was not the show for him right now. "You watching this?" Carmen asked.

The man slowly turned his head.

"Are you watching this?" Carmen asked again. "Or can I change it?"

"Yeah, I'm watching. The guy isn't going to make it. Guys are more squeamish when it comes to putting things in their mouths. Chicks are built tough that way."

Just then the camera caught the guy gagging and it was over. They got the under the table shot of the slugs spraying out of his mouth and onto the table. The girls were jumping up and down and hugging each other and squealing.

"Chalk another one up for the ladies," the man said.

The phone rang and Carmen answered. "Perry, Theresa is on the phone for you. Says you two had a meeting tonight." Carmen delivered the news just as the guy on television puked up the slugs. "I told her you had been in an accident but she wants to talk to you anyway."

Perry got to his feet. He gasped for air when he straightened up. If he played his cards right, things could still work out for him.

"Hey, Carmen, I'll see if she can pick us up and drive us home, okay?"

"I think you should get her to take you to the hospital."

"I'll get her to give me some attention at home," he said and Carmen rolled her eyes.

"I don't know what these women see in you." Carmen was getting hot in her coat and boots. "I must be the only woman in town who doesn't want to sleep with you."

"Hey, that's your problem."

Perry's choice in women baffled Carmen, especially this one. She didn't know what he had told Theresa to make her believe he was interested in her. Maybe that stupid idea about the beach had something to do with it. She wondered if maybe she should have stepped in and said something. It was too late now. People had to learn to fend for themselves.

Perry moved slowly towards his office and eased into his chair. Line one blinked on the telephone.

"Hey Terri, sorry about tonight. You wouldn't believe what happened." He swung back in his chair and tried to get his feet up on his desk but his ribs screamed.

Theresa was indignant. "Why aren't you here? I've been here half an hour sitting by myself like some idiot watching everyone else eat. Our meeting was for tonight wasn't it?"

"Terri," he said, making his voice weak. "I need your help tonight. Could you come over here and take me home? Some guy nearly killed me trying to steal my car. Well, he did get the car but not me."

There was silence on the other end of the phone.

"Terri," he whispered. "Are you there?"

"Are you hurt? I'm so sorry. We can do this another time."

"Nothing serious. I took a boot to the ribs, that's all. And my head, but I'm not hideously misshapen or anything. Look, if you could come by here and give Carmen a lift, then you and I can go back to my place and drink some wine. We can go over some things there, if you want."

"All right," she said. "I'll be there in twenty minutes." She expected everything to happen tonight and if there was still a chance, then Theresa wanted to do it tonight. The sooner she had her life on a new track, the better.

"Thanks Terri. You're the best. We'll be waiting out front."

When he hung up the phone, Perry chuckled. Even if he didn't get laid, this chick was a blast. Anyway, he felt he was pretty much guaranteed a blow job tonight and it wouldn't cost him a cent. Losing his car might just turn out to work in his favour.

"You know," Carmen said. "I'm going to call a cab. I don't feel like getting a ride home in a car with two horny people. It doesn't sound safe."

"She said she'd give you a ride." Perry stirred the ice around his drink with a straw.

"No thanks. I'll see you in the morning."

"Yeah, yeah." He lit a smoke and watched Carmen. "Sorry about all this. I know I said I'd give you a ride."

"You can give me twenty bucks for my cab, rich boy."

He reached into his jacket pocket and pulled out his wallet. "I guess you deserve at least that."

The man watching television finally left and Perry locked the door behind him. He could see the street from where he sat and watched and waited for Theresa. The building was silent all around him. Only Walter upstairs somewhere. Perry didn't even know for sure which room was his. The liquor was warming and relaxing. All things considered, Perry felt pretty good. He forgot his bruised and aching ribs and considered his car gone for good. It allowed him to think of his next car while he waited for Theresa. Maybe he could convince her to stay here. He had never had a woman in the hotel and didn't want to miss his chance.

Chapter Twenty-Two

T heresa left the restaurant and hurried to her car.
There was not much time left before she should be
home. Already it was eight o'clock. If she was home
much past ten, she wasn't sure she could account for that.
As she neared the hotel, the streets became empty. On a
cold night like tonight most people were at home. A few
taxis waited outside the concert hall and empty buses
rattled along without making a stop. Stork waved from the
doorway to the hotel, but didn't get in the car when she
stopped. He motioned for her to come inside. She turned off
the car and joined him.

* * * * *

At home the family sat down to supper. Theresa had told
them she would be late but there was a place set for her,
just in case she made it home after all. Antonina cut two
hefty slabs of blood sausage onto her plate and asked if
anyone else would like some. She took the opportunity of
Theresa not being home to let Dustin try some of the dark
red, fat-flecked meat. Much to her delight he gobbled it
down and grunted for more. She popped a piece into his
mouth and one into hers. He giggled when she chewed
noisily, pretending to be a pig and oinking while she ate. He
oinked back and they grunted and oinked at each other

until it was no longer very amusing to anyone but the two of them. Suddenly, Antonina tried to oink and no sound came out. Her hands flew to her throat as her face turned red.

"What's the matter. You choking?" Rosa asked. "Anton, hit her on the back."

Anton, who was closest to the old woman, gave her a hard slap on the back. A strangled sound came from her throat and Dustin laughed heartily at the entire scene, clapping his hands and spitting, finding it hilarious that Anton was now pounding Antonina's back and she was flailing around the kitchen like a crippled bat. She leaned over the sink and made a horrible sound as she tried to cough or throw up. Her face turned deep red and then purple and it suddenly occurred to everyone that she was choking for real and they had no idea what to do.

"She's choking to death. Jesus help us." Anton roared as Antonina lost her grip on the counter and crashed to the floor. On the way down, her head hit the bucket of potatoes she had spent the morning peeling and water and cubes of raw potato swamped the kitchen.

* * * * *

"Are you badly hurt?" Theresa asked Stork, who walked with one arm splinting his ribs. For someone who had just been robbed of his car and assaulted by some low life criminal, he was holding up pretty well.

"No, I'll be fine. Let's get a drink." He opened the door for her and followed her musky scent inside. His cigar smouldered in an ashtray on the bar. Stork took a seat on the stool and asked Theresa to fix them a drink. He liked watching her behind the bar.

"What'll it be, stranger?" she leaned up on the bar. Stork looked so handsome and helpless. The hint of his beard shadowed his face, his tie loosened and askew, his eyes sinking into Theresa's every time her glance met his. She tried to ignore what she thought those looks meant. They moved to a table with their vodka and sodas and sat side by side.

"Should we go to your office?" she asked as she sipped her drink through a straw. The wine she drank at the restaurant had made her a bit tipsy and she didn't want to drink too much more before they signed the papers. Her chequebook was in her purse.

"Sure, that might be a good idea. I have the papers ready."

They walked side by side. Theresa helped Perry along even though he didn't really need it.

In his office, Perry pulled the financial agreement from a drawer and laid it on the table in front of Theresa. "Read this over before you sign it," he said. It didn't matter if she signed it or not. Once he had the cheque, she'd be screwed. He watched her read it over, frowning once in awhile. He held his breath to see if she would notice that it was all meaningless.

"I guess everything looks okay. I trust you."

Perry smiled and took a drink. "Wait, let me get a bottle of champagne."

Theresa waited for him and read over the agreement again. None of it made any sense, but she figured Stork knew what he was doing. When he came back with a bottle of beer, he said, "Who am I kidding? There's no champagne here. I'm sorry we can't do this properly, but at least the beer is bubbly."

"That's okay," Theresa said. She had already retrieved her chequebook from her purse, something Perry noticed right away and so he was quick to get on with things.

"Okay, so you write me a cheque, we sign the papers and then we have a special toast."

* * * * *

They were all screaming now and even Dustin's giggles had turned to frantic wailing but nobody had time to pick up a baby. Paulie lifted Antonina's body up enough for him to get behind her on the floor and try the Heimlich manoeuvre. His hands reached under her massive arms and around her mountainous bosom. He gripped either side of her ribcage with his knees and squeezed. But, no amount of squeezing the old woman's body would dislodge the blood sausage that was killing her. He tugged and pulled and heaved at her leaden body until his arms could do no more. He gave up and the old woman's body slumped against his.

"Check her pulse," he said. Rosa scurried over and fell to her knees. Her shaking hand reached for Antonina's throat. Her fingers pressed into the soft, doughy flesh.

"Nothing. I feel nothing."

"Put her on the floor." Anton reached for Antonina's thick wrist and pulled with all his might to get onto the floor. He rolled her onto her back and pounded on her chest with both fists. "Come on, mama. Spit that sausage out. You hear me?"

He pounded as Antonina's body flopped and shuddered with each blow. Paulie pulled him off and for a few minutes the three of them panted in the silence. Antonina's body lay inert on the floor and finally at rest.

"Where the hell is the ambulance?" Anton shouted.

"No one called an ambulance." Rosa replied. She leaned over Antonina's body and folded her arms across her chest.

* * * * *

With a satisfied smirk that he could not help, Perry sat back and waved Theresa's cheque. "This is a beautiful thing," he said. "I'm going to put it in a safe place." He got up slowly, his ribs raw and throbbing, and put the cheque in the safe. He pretended to twirl the dial and then sat back down behind the desk, pleased with his performance.

Theresa drank the last of her drink. "Do you want to go over anything else tonight or should I drive you home? It's getting kind of late." She suppressed a giggle. "I'm anxious to get started. You know, find a location, get things fixed up and then advertise. Oooh, don't you think people will be thrilled when they find out there's a beach they can go to that's inside? They'll see it in the paper and won't believe their eyes. Oh, I'm sorry. It's too much for tonight. I'm just so excited."

"You're right. They won't believe their eyes." He paused. Theresa sat across from him, eagerly waiting for him to tell her what the next step was.

But Perry was looking at her with an odd expression. His face seemed different, harder somehow. Before he said anything, she felt a sinking feeling in her bowels.

"Theresa, there's not going to be a beach."

She smiled at first, the way people do when they think somebody is joking with them because what they are hearing is too awful to be true. And Perry smiled back at her, but it was a mocking smile.

"What do you mean?" she stammered.

"What I mean is, I can't believe you were so stupid that you just gave me a cheque without scoping things out. How desperate are you?"

Theresa's hands clenched the armrests of her chair. "I can put a stop payment on that cheque. It won't be cashed."

"I guess it'll be a race to the bank then. I have connections you know. There are places that will cash cheques in the middle of the night. I doubt there are any banks that will stop payment in the middle of the night. Or are there?" He made an innocent face.

"You're awful. What do you want with me anyway?" She was too embarrassed to scream and didn't want to cry in front of him. She couldn't believe she had fallen for a con artist that easily. "Why are you doing this? You don't need the money, do you? I know exactly what Tibor was doing in your office. He's no investor. He's a drug dealer and you are probably in on it too. I could go to the police."

"No, I don't need the money. And yeah, I have some connections in the drug world. As a matter of fact, I know a little something about you too."

"Like what?"

"Like you're not a lawyer, are you? That's why it was so easy to fool you. Almost too easy. Fun though, but pretty damn easy." He laughed quietly as her face turned a deeper shade of red. He was waiting for tears to stream down her face but they never came.

"I never said I was a lawyer. You assumed I was. You never bothered to ask so I never bothered to tell you. What does that have to do with all of this anyway?"

Perry ran a hand over his chin. "Say, I wonder what your husband would do if I told him what you've done with the family nest egg. I bet he'd be pretty upset."

Theresa's stomach tightened. Never had she felt so furious with another human being. Perry sat back in his chair and winced. He wasn't a very big man, Theresa thought. And he was hurt. She rose from her chair, fists clenched beside her. "You are not going to get away with this."

"Aw, don't get so upset. There is a way you can get it back."

"What? How?" She had no idea what he could be talking about. She stood in front of him now and he smirked at her from his chair. Her mind was racing with details of when the bank opened and if she could leave a message there tonight and leave instructions.

"We're already at a hotel. There's plenty of available rooms."

"What are you talking about... you must be joking! I'm not having sex with you." She took one step forward and thrust her arms out with all her might and gave Perry a heavy shove. The chair tipped backwards and sprung upright again with enough force to make Perry cry out in pain. Theresa looked around for something to hit him with. Suddenly she wanted to pummel this creep for making her feel so stupid and ashamed. She wanted tear him limb from limb. She eyed the ashtray and remembered her first attempt to lift it. Perry wasn't defending himself and found it hilarious that Theresa would even fight like this.

"Come on, Theresa. What are you going to do?"

That was all it took. She braced herself and lifted the ashtray off the floor. She swung it like a baseball bat and connected with the arm of the chair. The chair splintered and the marble base broke off the ashtray and clattered to the floor.

"Jesus, what the...You can't be serious." The smirk had disappeared and Perry realized his ribs hurt way too much to fend off another attack. If she managed to connect with his head, he'd be dead. She swung the ashtray again and he managed to block it with his arm, but it knocked him to the floor. The chair tipped right over and crashed with him against the radiator. His head cracked against the hot metal and he let out a low wail.

"Give me back my money you asshole!" she yelled, as she swung once right over his head and cracked the radiator behind him so hard it dented the silver stand. The impact gave her a sudden surge of power and she swung the ashtray back and forth over his head. All Perry could do was cower under the chair.

"Wait, Theresa. Calm down. Just give me a second. You can have the cheque. I don't know what I was thinking. I'll give it back. Just put that thing down for a minute, okay."

"No way," she lunged at him, wielding the ashtray like a sword and jabbed it at his face. "You stay right there and tell me how to get into that safe."

He did a quick inventory in his head. There was half a pound of weed and about four thousand dollars plus her cheque. He had no way of knowing what she would do with it all. But she hovered over him like some banshee and odds were she would hit him hard on the head next.

"Go ahead and help yourself. The safe is broken. You can open it with your little finger."

Theresa paused and wondered if he was trying to trick her again. She backed away from his sprawled body, still half in the chair. When he tried to shift his body weight so that the arm of the chair wasn't digging into his ribs, she tapped his knee cap with her weapon as a warning. "Don't move. I mean it. I'll bust your head right open. Just lie there and shut up." The words tumbled out now, no problem.

The safe swung open easily. Theresa retrieved her cheque and ripped it up, letting the tiny pieces fall to the floor. She saw the cash and the drugs. She held the baggie up to her nose and immediately recognized the smell from Larry's desk drawer. And all that money. It could only mean that Perry was a drug dealer. Theresa took in the scene. *The Godfather* poster was leaning up against the wall on the floor. Was that what he was up to? Pretending to be some mobster? She hung onto the broken ashtray and Perry still lay on the floor watching her every move.

"You're sick," she told him. "Doing this to innocent people for your amusement. You don't need the money. You've got gobs of it in here. Some of us struggle to make an honest living and you sit behind that big desk pretending to be something you're not and sell illegal drugs and make more money than you ever will need. You're despicable. Surrounded every day by poverty and you don't do anything to try to help. What does this all mean to you?"

She didn't really want any answers. She just wanted to leave. His money and his drugs were safe. Theresa didn't want any part of them. She threw the ashtray at him and forced him to contort his body into a painful arc to stop it hitting him. It smashed into the wall behind him. "I'll see myself out."

The first thing Perry did when the sound of Theresa's footsteps disappeared was to wriggle out of the chair and roll himself a joint. His head was still in one piece and his stash and his money were safe. Another gamble and another win. Or, to give her some credit, he would call it a draw. He blew smoke up into the unmoving ceiling fan. Once he had reached a comfortable state, where his ribs didn't hurt and his mind was clear of bad thoughts, he took a hundred dollars from the safe, called a cab and went home.

* * * * *

In his room, Walter prepared to leave. He struggled into his boots and found his enormous winter parka at the back of the closet. The weight of it nearly knocked him over but he sat back on his bed and managed to get each arm into a sleeve and when he stood it felt as though he were carrying a dead body on his shoulders. All the money he had in the world was crudely sewn into the lining of his coat. He had no idea how much he had but knew he had not yet run out.

His harmonica and moccasins he left behind. They had been acquired along the way by chance and he knew from experience that other things would appear to replace them. There was no time or need for sentiment. He could not afford to waste time being sentimental. There was no last glance around the room he had lived in for the past twenty odd years, no last glimpse of the view out the window. Right now he wanted to leave the hotel before the devil woman murderer discovered he was a witness. It wasn't the first time he heard things crashing to the floor and breaking glass, loud voices, but it was going to be the last. He skulked down the hallway as silently as he could in his heavy coat and boots. The arctic air hit his face with a familiar blast and he turned and walked with the wind. It was a silent night, the snow crunched underfoot as he walked. Soon, the hotel was out of sight, but he did not turn around to see.

* * * * *

The ambulance attendants did not try to revive Antonina. They checked her pulse and shone a light in her eyes and shook their heads. "Sorry," they said and then began asking questions about what had happened and in what order. Questions nobody could rightly answer. Rosa and Anton sat at the kitchen table. All the while, from the corner of their vision they watched the attendants struggle to lift Antonina's body onto the stretcher. Paulie called Theresa at work to come home but got no answer. Maybe she was already on her way.

Curious neighbours gathered outside on the boulevard. Their eyes did a quick head count as they deduced who was under the sheet on the stretcher, and clearly no longer living. Nobody came forward to console them. They just stared and shook their heads mournfully at the sight of Dustin in his grandfather's arms. Everybody waited until the ambulance pulled away and then, as though someone reversed the film, they all went back into their houses and the street once again was quiet and dark.

An oppressive silence befell the house once Antonina's body was wheeled away. It was not even the silence but the sudden absence of activity in the house which was noticeable. The women were always in a constant state of animation and now with the absence of Antonina, the house seemed uncomfortably still. Even Dustin sat unmoving on Paulie's knee.

"Where's Theresa?" Rosa said, for lack of anything else to say.

"She's on her way home." Paulie said as he patted distractedly at Dustin's hair.

"It's taking her a long time to get home."

They sat and thought about that for awhile until finally Paulie began to quietly cry. He rested his chin on Dustin's head and let the tears stream down his cheeks. Rosa mopped up the water and potatoes from the floor and then, searching for something else to do, she went to strip Antonina's bed. Having just lost his mother, so suddenly and unexpectedly did not affect Anton in the profound way he thought it would. His body sensed the loss in a vague sense of space being freed up somewhere, but his mind wandered and he craved a cold beer the way he did most of the time with the usual mounting urgency once the thought took hold. He got up and wandered to the kitchen and returned with a bottle for Paulie too. The next thought to enter his mind was to see what was on television.

"Paulie, put the TV on."

"No, that's not right." Dustin banged the beer caps together on the coffee table.

"Well, then put Dustin to bed. It's late."

It was late. Paulie worried where Theresa might be. He tried the office once more, thinking maybe last time she was in the washroom. It rang ten times and then he hung up.

Chapter Twenty-Three

Theresa drove home through the empty streets. Her whole body shook. The heat blasted into the car but she could not get warm. She drove slowly behind a snowplow, wanting to get home but needing to process all the events of the evening. The wind howled outside the car, the kind of wind that crystallised the lining of your lungs. The snow solidified into drifts at the sides of the road. It was nearing ten o'clock. She had no idea what to expect when she got home but hoped she could slip upstairs and crawl into bed without too much fuss.

The ashtray had been heavy and she had wrenched her shoulder. It now throbbed from her shoulder blade and up the back of her neck. The muscles twitched and spasmed. The violent energy was still inside of her. She wished she had hit him harder. She could have killed him there in his office. Her body possessed the strength, of that she was sure. What a mess that would have been, but only part of her regretted not having really hurt him somehow. Her imagination reeled through the scene and each time she got to the part about the ashtray cracking over his head she embellished it to reveal splinters of skull and sprouts of brain and lots and lots of blood and no sign of any crooked grin or smirk at all on Perry's face. Her grip on the steering wheel tightened and Theresa knew these images would stay with her for a long time.

She turned up the back lane and into the carport. All the lights were on in the house. This was unusual, especially for this time of the night. There had been no time to formulate any kind of reasonable explanation for being this late other than work. Theresa had been in such a hurry to flee the hotel once she ripped up the cheque she didn't even think of what to do once she got home. She wasn't able to tell anyone anything and really, since she had the money back and Paulie didn't know about it anyway, nothing much had changed.

Theresa paused and steadied her breath. All she had to say was that Larry instructed her not to answer the phone when she was there late. That was all. They would believe that. When she walked into the kitchen it was empty and she heard nothing in the rest of the house. The aroma of dinner lingered in the air though she could not make out what she smelled.

Anton sat alone in the living room. As soon as Theresa saw the television off, her heart jumped.

"Hi," she said weakly. "Where is everybody?"

Ignoring her question he said, "You're late."

"Yeah, I know." Guilt joined all the other emotions welling up inside of her. Why? There was nothing to feel guilty about and Theresa squelched the feeling. All the rest was overwhelming enough. She joined Anton in the living room, awash with relief at being home finally and in a comfortable space. "I'm bushed. There was so much to catch up on today. Larry wants everything ready for the accountant next week. It's tax time again."

Anton tipped the bottle of beer to his lips and the light caught the tears glinting at the corner of his eye. It caught Theresa off guard. "Is something wrong? I won't have to work late again for awhile. It was a one time thing, really."

"Theresa," Anton said, weary at her fumbling chatter. "Sit down. Something happened tonight. Something terrible."

Theresa caught on that she had nothing to do with whatever was going on here. Anton never spoke to her in such a subdued tone, with no cutting remark ready to escape his mouth. If he was mad at her, he would have insulted her by now and he did not appear to be in the mood to amuse himself. She sat on the sofa and watched him drain his beer. He sagged in the chair, his corset gaping. She was mortified to see him slump forward and begin to weep. Why was Anton sobbing? Clearly this had nothing to do with Theresa and how she spent her evening. And where was everybody? Why was the television off?

"Anton, what is it?" Instinctively she rose and perched on the arm of his chair and put her hand on his back.

"Oh God. Oh my dear, sweet God. He's taken her to heaven."

"What happened? Is it Antonina? Where is she?" Theresa felt frantic. This could not be happening. Not tonight.

Rosa paused by the doorway. "They came and took her over two hours ago. To the funeral home." Rosa clucked sympathetically at Theresa's stunned face. "We didn't know where you were."

Theresa followed Rosa into the kitchen. Where was Paulie? And Dustin? Were they all right? It felt like anything could happen this night.

Paulie came in and sat down beside her. He held her hand, seemingly oblivious as to how late she was. It no longer mattered where she had been. It only mattered that now she was home. Nobody was angry with her. Nobody accused or belittled her. They were complete now that she was here. The house was calm for the first time in years and even with her tumultuous evening behind her, Theresa felt the change immediately. The attention was off her.

"She died right there," Paulie said, pointing to the floor by the stove. "She choked on some sausage and we couldn't save her. Dustin laughed his head off."

Theresa looked at the floor where Paulie pointed. A cube of raw potato lay under the stove.

"Where were you tonight?" he asked with a distracted voice.

"I was at work. I just didn't answer the phone, that's all." Theresa became aware of the ache in her shoulder and a headache which pounded at her temples. The horror of what happened to Antonina was her fault, in some remote way. She never should have even thought she could venture out and do something on her own. There could have been a whole lot of trouble at the Wiltshire tonight. Theresa had put herself in a terrible position and through brute strength and a little luck she managed to escape with most everything intact. The whole night could have turned into an even bigger mess than it already was. She should have been at home tonight. Perhaps she could even in some way have prevented Antonina from choking to death.

Theresa began to cry. She felt Paulie's arm around her and leaned heavily against his shoulder and inhaled the comfort of his scent.

Paulie, as he stroked Theresa's tangled hair, felt oddly content. Her body, limp in his arms, his strong arms, gave him what he had longed for since the beginning. A reason to be in her life, as she too had searched for a reason to be in his. It was what they both wanted and never could find before tonight. In their sad embrace, they found it and felt no desire, for the first time in ages, to let go. Each time Theresa tried to stop her sobbing, she thought of Stork behind his desk, grinning that evil grin and waving the cheque she had so innocently handed over and then felt Paulie beside her and the tears sprang forth anew.

Their bodies rested against each other and this was how Rosa found them when she came into the kitchen with Antonina's sheets bundled in her arms to be taken to the basement and laundered.

They stayed up most of the night. Paulie and Theresa on the couch, she comforting him, and Rosa and Anton on the other sofa. Each of them comforting their men. Dustin slept soundly upstairs. The energy in the house had balanced. Sometimes the loss of a powerful force can leave behind surprising resolve to those that remain.

Chapter Twenty-Four

January, February, March, the three-headed monster to conquer before the redemption of spring. The snow outside was dirty and grey. The ice harder than marble, layered in strata to define the aeons of winter on the prairies. Carmen got off the bus. Nobody was in the bus shelter. The hotel's front door was locked, the eviction notice tattered and curled at the edges. Only two more days and then the Wiltshire would be closed forever. Salvagers had already been through the building to see what they could make use of.

It was getting harder for Carmen to deny what was happening and so today she was going to take Walter down to the Victory Hotel and get him set up there in a room. What else could she do? For herself, she had not yet made any plans other than to place a call to the unemployment office to determine how many weeks she had before she had to do something.

Carmen put the coffee on and lit a cigarette. After today she wouldn't be back. Once Walter was moved, there would be no reason to. She would tell Ruby and Darren today. They had other places to go.

In the refrigerator was enough for Walter's breakfast. She had stopped ordering food last week. She got the eggs and bread out and set them on the counter and went upstairs to let Walter know the day's plan.

Watch you don't fall

The door to Walter's room was open. She stepped gingerly towards the shaft of light coming from the open door. She gave it a push with one finger. The door swung open with a low moan. The room was empty. The bed rumpled with twisted sheets. There was no way to tell if it had been slept in or not. Silently, she took it in. He was gone. In the closet hung one of his sweaters. The moccasins lay under the bed like long forgotten kill. His harmonica lay among the sheets. There were stacks of newspaper stashed into each drawer of the dresser along with Walter's scratchy wool socks and dingy underwear. Her heartbeat quickened. The panic was slow to rise. Carmen stripped the sheets from the bed and then, not knowing what to do with them, bundled them into a tight ball and threw them onto the floor in the corner, where they would remain to be hauled away with the rest of the rubble.

She should have known. She should have taken care of this a long time ago. Now it was too late. Outside, the wind howled. It was a bright day, the sky so blue it hurt the eyes. Carmen scanned the street as far as she could see from the window but it was useless. He probably left in the night. But where? How far could he get in those heavy boots? She sat on the bed. The springs dug into the backs of her legs through the thin mattress. The building was silent except for the anxious sigh of the wind through the cracks in the window.

Carmen pulled herself off the bed. She shut the door to Walter's room and went downstairs. Her first instinct was to call Perry. The office was freezing cold with the window broken and the cold air rushing in.

"What the hell?" Carmen felt panicky. Someone must have broken in, she thought. Come in through the window. She spied the broken ashtray and noticed the chair was bent and misshapen. Assault? The only person Perry was expecting here last night was Theresa and so it was either her or Walter or some other intruder. The guy who stole

Perry's car? Carmen crunched over the shards of glass to get to the phone. She scanned the floor for signs of blood. When she didn't see any it didn't offer much relief.

The phone rang eight times before Perry's groggy voice answered.

"What happened in here last night? Are you all right? Walter's gone. Do you know anything about that?" Carmen picked at the layers of a Moosehead coaster.

"What?" Nothing Carmen said was sinking in. Perry's ribs ached and his head pounded.

"I'm sitting in your office and the window's been bashed in, there's glass all over the floor, your chair is broken and the ashtray too. What the hell happened in here? And where did Walter go? Did you see him leave?"

"What do you mean he's gone? He'll be back in time for breakfast. Walter isn't stupid. Once he gets hungry he'll come back for his egg."

"What happened last night?"

"Ah, I'm okay. Just a little skirmish. A minor disagreement I had with Theresa."

"Let me guess. She didn't want to fuck you. How did the office get turned upside down?" Carmen knew there must be some connection between Theresa and the mess the office was in and Walter but Perry wasn't admitting anything. "Wait, you didn't assault her or anything? What the hell did you do, Perry?"

"Nothing. She came after me, okay? Luckily she didn't kill me."

"Yeah, I bet you were completely innocent. You should know better than try to get it on with a lawyer."

"She's not a lawyer. She's a secretary. And we didn't get it on so everything's square."

"Except that Walter is gone. What do you know about that?" Carmen didn't much care anymore what Theresa was or wasn't. The joke was over.

"This is the first I heard about it." Perry's head throbbed and he wished he knew a way he could make Walter walk through his office door at this very instant because it would throw Carmen off this rant and running to the kitchen to make him breakfast.

"Yeah, well, if he's not here in a hour, I'm blaming you and that broad you were dumb enough to try to tangle with." Carmen slammed the phone down and hoped he popped an eardrum. Why should he care? She went to the kitchen to start Walter's breakfast. Perry was probably right. He would be back to eat. And he wasn't stupid. There were places open all night where he could have sat and he was more than likely on his way back right now. The gas hissed and she lit the element and Carmen cracked two eggs into the pan and made four slices of toast. She went to check the front door to make sure it was unlocked. Nobody was on the street. A bus zoomed past filled with people all going somewhere else. It was already March but spring seemed as far away as Neptune. Eventually it would come, but it was too early to hope.

Carmen carried Walter's breakfast to his table and poured him a coffee. There. It was all ready for him. She lit herself a smoke and leaned against the bar and waited. After and hour when the eggs were hard and cold, she took them back to the kitchen and scraped them into the garbage. She could always make him more later. If she went to look for him, then she wouldn't be here when he returned. But if he was out there somewhere, lost, then how would he find his way back? She didn't think he even knew the name of the hotel. Calling the police would be pointless. There was nothing else to do but wait.

* * * * *

Perry's ears rung after Carmen slammed the phone down on him. What was she doing snooping around his office anyway. Some chicks just didn't know to leave well enough alone. Now she thought it was his fault that Walter took off. Anyone could have told her the guy would disappear before they shut the place up. He wasn't stupid, just nuts. But, Perry pulled on some jeans and a t-shirt and called Tibor to see if he could borrow his car.

He pulled up behind the hotel a half hour later. Perry found Carmen seated at the bar, a cigarette burning in an ashtray beside her, a cup of coffee and a plate of French fries all in a row.

"What? No suit?" Her eyes burned.

"Come on, I've got Tibor's car. Let's see if we can find him."

"It's useless, Perry. He's long gone."

"He's not long gone. He's probably down the street getting some other broad to serve him eggs. We'll find him."

Carmen glared at him.

"Okay, woman. Some other woman is bringing him eggs."

He sat down beside her and helped himself to a fry. She wouldn't look at him and stared off out the window. "I wish it was spring."

"Why? What's so different about spring?"

"If it was spring this would all be over and I would know how everything turns out."

A figure wrapped in winter garb waddled past and peered in the window. Carmen bolted to the door let in an icy blast, but the man moved on.

"It wasn't him," she said needlessly.

There was a hum in the air, the usual smell of cigarettes, coffee and fries. Perry didn't know how to console her. This was the last day they would spend here and no customers came. All the years behind them, a blur of days and weeks, all the same, like watching from a rolling bus an endless stream of meaningless scenery.

Neither of them wanted to leave. It was a big step from where they sat to the world outside. "Funny, that we're the last to leave," Perry said.

"You going to watch them tear it down?"

"No, I doubt I'll remember. I'm going to buy a new car and start over. Delivery service."

"Sounds good. I'm going on pogey as long as I can and then I'll probably head back up this way. Don't know much else."

"Hey, I just remembered something. Come here. I need your help." Perry pulled her off her chair and down the hall to his office. Carmen helped him pack up his magazines and the bottles in the fridge. They took the posters off the wall and piled everything at the door.

"I guess we don't have to bother with the mess. It's all going to end up like this," Perry said sweeping the glass into a small piled with the side of his foot.

"I guess not," Carmen said. "You want a hand getting this out to your car?"

"Sure, but there's one more thing." He stepped over to the safe and took everything out. The pot he stuffed into his jacket pocket. The roll of bills he handed to Carmen. "Your severance pay."

"How much is it?" she asked as she weighed the bills cupped in her hand.

"I don't know. Two grand maybe. Take it. You deserve it."

Wordlessly, she jammed the money into her pocket. They carried his things out to the car. "You want a lift?"

"No, I think I'll stay a while longer, just in case."

"He's okay, you know. Where-ever he is." Perry said, already seated in the car, key in the ignition. "Just like we don't know where he was before he came here, he's moved on to another place. Walter's a survivor. He won't let things get too uncomfortable. He knows when it's time to move on and that time came last night and he was right. Don't hang out here too long."

"Yeah, I know." Carmen hugged her arms to herself in the brisk wind. She held the heavy kitchen door open with her foot. "So, I guess I'll see you then."

"So long, Carmen." The Reliant backed up into the back lane and drove off. In the rear-view mirror, Perry and Carmen exchanged a wave and a smile.

Carmen sat down at Walter's table and gazed around the room. Everybody but her knew when to say good-bye. Everybody else took it upon themselves to choose their time and not be dictated by the notice on the door. What did she expect? Walter would have left anyway. He knew what was happening. His entire life was spent moving from place to place as circumstances required. Perry was right. Just because he was old and lame didn't make this any different from all the other times he had to move on. She had underestimated him and soon, as her thoughts envisioned his deranged antics and queer mind, it dawned on her that he had toyed with her. He had taken advantage of her good nature and compassion and had ridden the wave probably as he had done many times before and probably as he was doing right now to someone else.

Carmen stubbed out her cigarette, turned off the radio, the coffee machine, the lights. On her way out she tore down the eviction notice and the notice of demolition and stuffed them into her pockets. From her bus stop across the street she took in the building one last time. In the sharp light of late winter, when the snow banks were covered in grit and dirt, the sidewalks rutted and treacherous, the sky a mismatched bright blue, there stood the Wiltshire Hotel. A sagging monument to better times.

Watch you don't fall

Her bus pulled up and Carmen stepped on. It drove away, down Main Street, past all the other old hotels, each once unique and now unremarkably drab and hollow. An unknown population inside their walls, stirring idly, waiting for a breeze to turn the page.

Chapter Twenty-Five

T he days before the funeral Theresa spent in bed, mulling over that night and trying to get a grip on it. Guilt lodged deep inside her like an inoperable bullet. Guilt about nearly letting some sweet-talking scam artist get away with all her money, shame that she was so naïve to think he was serious about her as a business partner, more guilt that Antonina had died while Theresa was blindly chasing after some idiotic idea she thought would change her life. But then, she could have done nothing at all. Or worse, she could have slept with him. The very thought made her queasy. Instead she fought back and got her money back and left Perry lying on the ground afraid she would hit him again and there wasn't a damn thing he could do now to get her. There were all those drugs in his safe and if he tried to get near her all she had to do was let the police know he was a drug dealer and they would take care of him. She wished there was some way of making sure Perry was trapped inside the hotel when it was torn down, but just getting rid of that awful building would be enough. In all those thoughts and the reruns in her mind of her actions was a glimmer of pride.

That soap opera life was only meant for those who had it, and Theresa did not have it. It was not as easy as slipping into a smart suit and closing your eyes. She had something else, another kind of existence. Not a bad one, just a different one. And it was hers to discover. After resisting for so long, she was now open to experiencing life under this roof. She had three thousand dollars in the bank and that meant she was on the right track. It would just take awhile longer.

* * * * *

Things started happening after Antonina was gone. Rosa and Anton decided to take the room downstairs and let Paulie and Theresa move into their room and take over the upstairs and let Dustin have his own room. They cleared things out of Antonina's closet and filled green garbage bags with her old clothes and sent them off to the Good Will. Theresa felt hopeful that the new plan would work out.

Theresa went with Paulie to the paint store to choose paint for the walls. They bought new bed sheets and some art prints for the walls. Even though the mood was sombre, everyone seemed to be filled with energy and industriousness with changing things around. Even Theresa, whose usual response would have been to dig in her heels and complain, found herself enjoying the transformation going on in the house. In a way, nearly losing the money and then saving it again made her feel like she had new found riches. She bought Rosa a new sweater set and some bath salts. For Anton she found a navy blue robe and matching slippers. It was her way of letting them know she had given up the fight and had resolved to get along in the house until she and Paulie could get out on their own.

* * * * *

By mid-April, spring was quickly transforming the city. Hard, tiny buds appeared one by one on trees and shrubs, still weeks away from blossoming, but still a welcome sight, a sure sign that the worst was over. Piles of sand lay where the snow and ice had melted away. Street cleaners roared up and down the city streets, creating clouds of thick dust in the effort of clearing away the grit and debris from a long winter. The sun, high in the blue sky and finally some warmth emanated from it onto upturned faces everywhere. Bicycles, motorcycles, inflatable pools, children in strollers, all the signs of summer began to emerge. There were people outside, populating the parks and sidewalks, determined to make the most of the warm weather after a long and harsh winter. It was hard not to think how long the winter had been and how soon it would be here again. Summer on the prairies was a brief and fleeting experience and everyone got into their shorts and outside as soon as possible so as not to miss a moment of the thrilling sensation of a warm breeze on bare skin.

The hot dog vendors were back. Vera and Theresa sat out on the ledge feeling the warmth of the sun and eating their lunch. There were people everywhere, out for a noon hour stroll or just getting some fresh air. The buds on the trees cast a green hue over everything.

"Hey," Vera said. "I guess that place is finally coming down this week."

"What place?"

"The hotel. The one you spent so much time at this winter and nearly got bamboozled by that jerk. I drove past this morning and saw the crane setting up in the back."

"Oh yeah, that," Theresa said, as though straining to remember what hotel Vera was talking about.

"Do you want to go and watch?"

Theresa thought about it a moment. "Nah, I don't think so. Just let me know when it's gone."

* * * * *

In the end it was just Carmen who came and stood on the sidewalk across the street the day they swung the wrecking ball. It was by accident she found herself there on that day. Her unemployment was about to run out and so she returned to the old neighbourhood to knock on some doors to find work. Out of sheer habit, she rung the bell to get off at the Wiltshire. The bus stop and shelter had not been moved. A plyboard wall had been erected around the building. Indecipherable graffiti scrawled snakelike all over the walls. The windows were boarded up and in the parking lot behind, a crane sat, its motor roaring and the wrecking ball dangling precipitously. Men in hard hats all around prepared and conversed. Carmen walked around and got someone's attention.

"When are you starting?"

"Any minute now. You'll get the best view from across the street. You can't stand here."

Carmen crossed over and sat on a bench in front of the Chinese restaurant. With half an eye she watched for anyone familiar. They wouldn't be far, but they would be hard to find. Other than the boards surrounding the Wiltshire, the street was unchanged. Gritty underfoot and dust through the nostrils. The same smells of exhaust and urine and rank garbage. Traffic whizzed past without a thought or glance. Nothing worth stopping for along this stretch.

It didn't fall without a fight. Nearly the whole morning passed before daylight could be seen through the craggy walls of the hotel. It astonished her how quickly her memory faded and was replaced with the gap which now appeared before her. In half a day, the building was struck down.

Down the street, just beyond the old Savoy Hotel, Carmen spotted Ruby, trekking along, her orange Edmonton Oilers toque bobbing along like a guide buoy. Carmen walked towards it, her heart singing at the sight of something familiar. "Ruby," she shouted as she drew nearer. "Ruby, wait up."

The tiny figure did not stop, but turned into a hotel entrance. Carmen followed her inside and was greeted by the smell of oxidising liquor and ammonia. Ruby had her stubs dumped onto the table and was sorting through them. Carmen pushed through the door. Still, Ruby did not notice her.

"Ruby, what's up? You hanging around here now?"

Ruby gave her a puzzled look and went back to her task.

"Don't you remember me, Ruby?" Carmen's heart sank as Ruby ignored her. "Well, shit."

Finally, when Ruby had her tasks sorted on the table, she grinned at her and said, "How about a coffee, doll?"

Carmen looked around the room. There didn't seem to be anyone around. The coffee was behind the counter, fresh pot. She slipped behind the counter and poured Ruby a cup and on second thought poured herself one as well. They sat together at the table and Ruby twirled her cigarettes while Carmen turned the pages of the newspaper.

"Want one?"

"Sure. Same price?"

"Same price."

Carmen slid fifty cents across the table and Ruby flicked her a cigarette. "Enjoy," she said. "While the pleasure lasts."

"Hey Ruby, you want to sit outside awhile? They're tearing down the old hotel."

"What old hotel."

"The Wiltshire. Where you used to go and I poured your coffee. You remember Walter and that chicken?"

Ruby's face brightened. "Yeah, I remember. Crazy old Walter."

"Do you ever see him around here?"

"Walter?" Ruby asked. "Never saw him again. He's probably gone on the bus back to Regina."

"How do you know that?"

"Because that's where everyone goes when they're not here no more. Regina. Everyone knows that."

"Well, I don't know that. Do you think he's okay?"

"Walter? Course he's okay. Why wouldn't he be?"

"I don't know," said Carmen.

When she left later in the afternoon, fresh new boards surrounded the remains of the Wiltshire with vivid colour photos of the parkade which would soon stand on the site. Carmen admired the expanse that now was visible beyond the old Wiltshire site. It wouldn't be missed. Where the building once stood, now powerful shafts of light beamed across a clear blue sky.

Chapter Twenty-Six

T he car was finished. Paulie was close to tears as he ran the soft buffing cloth over the hood one more time. It was beautiful and now it was time to drive it one last time. The guy on the phone said he would be by at around two. Paulie went indoors to get Theresa.

New blades of green grass sprouted everywhere in the back yard since the last of the snow had melted. A few tulips had started to push through the dark earth along the sunny edge of the house. Dustin's swing set and sandbox were cleaned up and he had been able to play outside almost everyday since the beginning of April. Now it was nearly May and summer would be upon them. Last weekend they had pulled the barbecue from the garage and fired it up to grill some sausages. The lawn chairs were folded up and resting on the side of the house. The laundry fluttered outside on the clothesline. Things had settled to a peaceful existence ever since the night Antonina died. For one less person, the house felt a lot more spacious. Dustin had his own room, Theresa and Paulie, too. Rosa and Anton were happy to be on the main floor. Paulie had been promoted to sales and now wore dress pants and golf shirts to work and carried a briefcase and cell phone, details that pleased Theresa no end.

"Terri, come here. I have to show you the car."

Watch you don't fall

When Theresa appeared he made her put on her shoes and a sweater and took her by the hand. They walked to the garage. Theresa was truly awe-struck by what she saw. The last time she had seen the car it had been nothing but rust and bolts and ripped upholstery. Now it stood gleaming before her, creamy lemon custard on the outside and dark red on the inside. The chrome finish was blinding.

"Oh my god, Paulie. It's amazing. You did all this?"

She couldn't believe all the time he spent in here he was actually doing something. She thought he only came out to the garage to get away from the house. She imagined him sitting in the car smoking and reading race car magazines.

"You really did this?"

"I did. Now, let's go for a spin. There's a guy coming to look at it in a couple of hours."

They drove slowly down the backlane and stuck to the sidestreets. Paulie didn't want to risk getting it scratched before he sold it. People stopped and stared when they drove by. Men, women, children. They all stopped and gawked. It was undeniable. This was a special car. A smile crept across Theresa's lips. People were looking at her and her husband in their amazing, exclusive, and very expensive car.

"Keep driving. Let's go down Notre Dame."

"Too much traffic. We're sticking with the quiet streets. I can't risk an accident. Let the guy who buys it get the first scratch on it." Just saying it made Paulie sweat and he aimed the car towards home.

"I'm going to back it in for the guy," he said after some thought.

It was a bit tight but he eased the car in, inch by inch while Theresa leaned out the passenger window and said in a steady voice, "Good...good... you're good."

She reached for the latch once they were at a stop and Paulie had turned off the engine.

"Watch the door doesn't hit the wall. Maybe I should have left it outside."

"I'll be careful." Theresa slipped out of the car and shut the door. There was not much room for her between the car and the wall. She made her way along the passenger side towards the lane. Her hand got stuck between her hip and the car. The three carat diamond ring jammed a faint streak into the pale paint job when Theresa tried to pull her hand free. Paulie was already in the back yard, having seen the potential buyer enter the yard. Theresa was seized by a wave of panic. The scratch was not obvious. The longer she stared at it the more menacing it became. It was about an inch long and a bit below the door handle. She spit on her fingers and rubbed at the spot. There were voices at the door. Theresa disappeared into the back lane and used the back gate to get into the yard.

* * * * *

Perry had no trouble finding the house. In fact, he was sure he had been down the street before. Maybe a party some years back. He couldn't remember exactly. Even the house looked a bit familiar. He rang the doorbell. Somewhere inside, a child wailed. The door was opened by an old man in an undershirt and girdle.

"I'm here about the car." Perry said. The man checked out Perry's silk tie and tailored charcoal suit and tried to see behind his sunglasses.

"He's in the back. The gate's on the left."

Perry walked around the house just as Paulie stepped out of the garage. "Hey, you here about the car?" This was the kind of man who could afford his car. He thanked the good Lord he hadn't dropped the price to fifteen.

"Stork," Perry said and held out his hand.

Paulie extended his hand. "Paulie."

They walked to the garage. Perry and Theresa's eyes connected from where she stood at the back gate and he at the garage door. Paulie held the door open. He followed Perry's gaze and saw Theresa there.

"My wife," he said. And then, "The car's in here."

Perry looked away and stepped into the garage with Paulie after him. Paulie grinned at Theresa and crossed his fingers so only she could see. He disappeared into the garage after Perry, leaving Theresa leaning against the chain link fence, her palms sweaty. In a few minutes the bastard would be gone. She wasn't even sure he had recognized her.

Perry's heart leapt when he saw the car. It was even more beautiful than he imagined. He let out a low whistle and forgot about driving a hard bargain. Paulie started the engine and raised the hood. Perry thought he would pass out. He didn't even want to drive it first, didn't have to. He wanted this car. Twenty grand was a steal for this baby.

"You want twenty-three for it?"

"Yeah, it's what I'm asking."

"Why aren't you keeping it? It's gorgeous."

"Yeah, I know. My wife loves it too. We need the money though, to be honest."

His wife, Perry thought. Theresa, the woman he had nearly bamboozled out of her life savings. He wondered if she had ever told her husband. Probably not, given the look on her face just now. Sure, he recognized her. How could he not? That bright orange hair was unmistakable. Now he was about to buy a car from her husband for a whole wad of cash. It didn't matter. He wanted the car and he had the cash. Past was past. Perry had decided just to stick with dealing drugs. The episode with Theresa was a near miss. He didn't want to tangle with a woman like that again. There was no need to.

Perry reached into his pocket. "Would you take twenty? I've got it in cash."

Paulie stared in disbelief at the twenty bills this man had conjured up and was now waving at him. He plucked one out of his hand and studied it. There really were twenty thousand dollars right there in front of him. At that moment his only thought was of Theresa and marching up the stairs and presenting her with the money. Slowly, he nodded his head.

"Twenty thousand dollars it is."

Perry handed him the money.

"Don't you want to drive it first?"

"Nope," Perry said, walking around the car again and running his hand lovingly across the hood. "I want to know this is my car when I pull her out of here."

"Allow me" Paulie opened the door for him and Perry got inside. The seat sighed as he lowered himself in. He pulled the car into gear and felt the wheels gently roll beneath him. He watched Paulie's furrowed brow and made the car jump into the back lane.

"Hey," Paulie yelled. "Watch out."

Perry slammed on the brakes, laughing, just before the bumper hit the fence. He took a deep breath. Paulie leaned into the car. "That would have been tragic."

"She's my girl now. Don't worry." He patted the side of the car. "I'll take good care of her."

There was no sound but the wheels on the gravel. He waved once at Paulie and was gone.

* * * * *

Paulie had a huge smile across his face. "Wait till you see this. That was the guy I was waiting for." He flapped the twenty bills in the air. "Here, hold it. Twenty thousand dollars. Count it if you want. Man, did you see that guy's suit? Like some gangster, he floats in here with twenty grand cash. I can't believe it." Paulie was giddy with excitement.

Theresa took the money and let it drop it into her lap. She stared at it. The gasoline fumes from the Barracuda faded. Paulie waited expectantly at the foot of the chair. "Well, what do you think? It's great isn't it?"

She lifted her head finally and managed a shaky smile. There were too many thoughts and images flooding her head. "I'm sorry I'm not more excited. I think I'm in shock."

"Well, that's exactly what I wanted." Paulie leaned over and kissed her. His fingers grazed the bills once more. "You hang onto those as long as you want."

Dustin played in the sandbox where Paulie joined him. The screen door swung open and shut, supper sizzled in the kitchen. The air was filled with the warm spring smell of new grass and mud. Dustin hit his head and came over to Theresa, squalling and clamouring to get into her lap. Theresa plucked the crisp bills from where they lay. She regarded them, each in turn as she absent-mindedly stroked Dustin's hair. He had told Paulie his name was Stork. That suit he had on was the same one from the night at the hotel. There was nothing different about him at all. He had barely glanced at her when he saw her, as though he were struggling to figure out where he knew her from.

Suddenly, Theresa was struck by the image of the scratch her ring had left on the car. The one she was so worried about Paulie seeing and now she hoped it leapt out at Stork and struck him like a wound.

Theresa lay back and let out a long deep breath. She stared up at the moving clouds, with her son in her lap and twenty thousand dollars in her hand. With each breath, Dustin bobbed up and down on her stomach and giggled. Theresa closed her eyes. The sweet smell of lilacs blooming in the yard surrounded her and somewhere out in the folds of the universe there issued a resounding snap.